When you don't know how the story will end . . .

After years of hard work honing his craft, Blake Morgan is now an international bestselling author. But one thing he never imagined was that his fictional world would become all too real. When a stalker turns Blake's latest book tour into a treacherous and nearly deadly trap, it's time for Blake to hire protection. But the body assigned to keep an eye on him is someone he never wants out of his sight . . .

As a bodyguard for Vigilance, the private security agency in Blake's hometown of Arrowhead Bay, Samantha Quenel has found the perfect outlet for her military experience. But her latest client is also a former high school flame, which might explain her willingness to protect Blake at all costs—even if that means staying in the same room with him, on the same bed, under the same torrid sheets . . .

Visit us at www.kensingtonbooks.com

Books by Desiree Holt

Finding Julia

Game On
Forward Pass
Line of Scrimmage
Pass Interference
Fourth Down

Vigilance
Hide and Seek
Without Warning

Published by Kensington Publishing Corporation

Without Warning

Vigilance

Desiree Holt

LYRICAL PRESS
Kensington Publishing Corp.
www.kensingtonbooks.com

Lyrical Press books are published by
Kensington Publishing Corp. 119 West 40th Street New York, NY 10018

First Electronic Edition: March 2018
eISBN-13: 978-1-5161-0368-3
eISBN-10: 1-5161-0368-8

First Print Edition: March 2018
ISBN-13: 978-1-5161-0371-3
ISBN-10: 1-5161-0371-8

Printed in the United States of America

To Joseph Patrick Trainor, who helps me make it all real

Author's Foreword

People ask me all the time if I always wanted to be a writer. I don't know if "always" is the word but certainly for all the years I can remember. I was a voracious reader, as were my mother and sister, and books held a royal place in our home. The funny thing is I always thought I would write mysteries because that's what we all read. I didn't read my first romance until 2004, when I was sitting with the same three chapters of a mystery on my computer that had been there for three months. But then my eyes were opened and they never closed.

Writing a book is a solitary experience but it never comes to the bookshelves, virtual or other, alone. For me it starts with my treasured friend and beta reader extraordinaire, Margie Hager, who has the best eagle eye in the world. Thank you, Margie my love, for all the hours you put in to help me bring my stories to life. And for your friendship, which is a highlight of my life.

And to Janet Rodman and Brenna Zinn, whose support has been and continues to be so very valuable and important.

Thanks to Joseph P. Trainor for letting me pester him with a million questions and for keeping me honest and providing me with invaluable information on all things law enforcement and military elite.

To my family, who believed in me from the beginning, and are my biggest promoters: my daughters Amy and Suzanne, my son, Steven, and my granddaughter, Kayla.

Last but very far from least are all of you, my wonderful readers, who send me such great emails and posts and are so faithful, who buy and read my books. My success is due to you. I love you all so much. There are a lot more stories to come. Please stay tuned.

Prologue

He sat in the semi-dark, the only light coming from his little desk lamp and his computer. Gently, he pressed his hand to the screen, his fingers stroking her smiling face. He pretended he could actually feel the silky skin, trace the line of the arched eyebrows, caress the delicate bones.

And the eyes. Lord, he loved looking at those eyes, a bright emerald green that flashed with fire and humor and complemented the rich auburn of her hair. He wanted to sift his fingers through that hair, rub it against his own cheek, smell the flowery shampoo she used.

And that body. Damn! His palms itched to touch her curves, evident in the soft blouse and shorts she was wearing. He could practically feel the curve of her butt in his hand, the swell of her breasts, the hard points of her nipples. He'd never have the chance now to touch her, kiss her, hold her against him.

He'd waited so many years for her to realize how he felt about her and turn to him. He had held back his feelings all that time, waiting for the right moment. When it finally happened, he'd barely been able to contain his excitement. At last! He could be her champion, right a wrong, and confess his love for her.

Then a cruel twist of fate had robbed them of any future together. A rainy night, a slippery highway, and a vibrant life snuffed out. His grief had been overwhelming. For days, he'd walked around in a trance, trying to understand and accept what happened. Just when his dreams were about to be fulfilled, it was all taken away.

But he could keep her memory alive. He could—

Yes! He could champion her cause. He could right a terrible wrong and get her the recognition she so deserved. He had all the copies she had sent him. The evidence was very clear. He knew what he had to do. The man who stole what was hers would be destroyed.

Energized, he clicked the computer keys as he searched for information he needed to put his plan in motion. By this time next week, the first message would be received. He opened a new blank document and typed in one line:

I know what you did.

Chapter 1

I know what you did.

Blake Morgan stared at the piece of paper in his hand, pulse accelerating, a tiny finger of ice slithering down his spine. Again. Someone had left it again. A message with the same words.

Goddamnit!

He looked around to see if he could spot whoever this was, the familiar fear gripping him, his stomach knotting. But he knew he'd see nothing. He never did. Whoever this was moved like a ghost, silent and unseen, leaving his taunting messages. If he wanted to keep Blake on edge, he was doing a damn good job of it. In a fit of anger, Blake crumpled the paper and stuck it in the drink holder of the car. He wasn't going to let some unknown asshole frighten him. He'd faced worse than this.

He'd found the damn stupid note stuck under his windshield wiper when he went to get his car from the hotel parking garage. Anyone could have done it. Who paid attention to cars in a parking garage, anyway? And why would they? But Jesus. How the hell had someone known which car was his? It was a rental, for crap's sake.

Wait! Were those footsteps? Was someone running toward him? Away from him? A car door slammed somewhere and an engine turned over. He looked around, wondering if he'd see someone hiding in the shadows, every nerve on high alert.

Okay, get your shit together. You aren't a character in one of your books.

Anyway, whoever was doing this wouldn't be quite so obvious. He—or she—would be careful and silent. He closed his eyes, drew in a deep breath and let it out slowly. Calm, he told himself. People were waiting for him. His readers. He couldn't freak out on them.

Crap. Double crap.

Who in the fucking hell was doing this? Who could he have pissed off so much they'd do something like this? A reader he'd offended? Reviewer? Blogger? Not anyone he'd been dating, for sure. He was so busy these days that dates weren't even on the horizon.

So really. These messages. What the fuck?

He'd blown off the first note as a prank, a harmless joke, although he didn't think it was very funny. Or maybe even a case of mistaken identity.

Just the one sentence on a plain sheet of paper, typed on someone's computer.

I know what you did.

He had no idea who it was from. There was no signature, no return address. The postmark was Boston, but he was pretty sure none of the people he knew in that city would be sending him a message like this. He had a lot of readers from that area, but he never gave out his address or phone number. And nothing had been coming in to his public email.

So how the fuck did whoever this was know where he was staying?

Maybe they'd followed him to the hotel, a thought that brought another attack of the creeping chills.

I know what you did.

His agent had made light of it. "The price of fame," Henry had joked. "It brings the weirdos out of the woodwork. This is your third best seller so you've got a lot more eyes focused on you. You've had nutty stuff like this happen before. Okay, maybe not quite like this. But eventually, when you don't make a big deal about it in the media, they give up and move on to someone else. Whoever this is will get tired of the game and disappear."

But that hadn't happened. The notes kept coming, showing up in different cities wherever he was signing. Different hotels and venues. Someone was tracking his tour. Not just the cities but also the facilities—bookstores, event centers, wherever.

The police weren't much help. They were courteous, but the events all happened in different cities, so nobody really had jurisdiction. And, as one overly polite detective told him, he didn't think this was a case for the FBI.

I know what you did.

Five words that plagued him.

In the past three weeks, the frequency increased. He found notes left everyplace for him. When he checked in at his hotels there was one waiting for him at the front desk in an envelope. No, no one could remember who left it. In a restaurant, he went to the restroom and when he came back a note sat at his place setting. And of course no one had noticed anyone leaving it. None of the notes were handwritten. They were either printed with marking pen or typed on a computer like this one had been.

Then came two emails, but when he tried to reply to them they bounced back.

Twice.

And phone calls, four of them now, at the hotels where he stayed.

"I know what you did."

Just a whisper, but unnerving in its very anonymity.

He rubbed his forehead, willing away the headache blooming just beneath the surface.

Just last week both his agent and publisher told him to toss his existing cell and get two new ones—one for business and one for personal. But then, this week, something new was added—text messages on his cell. His damn personal one. How the hell had anyone gotten that number? When he tried to reply, his message came back undeliverable.

Today was his last stop before a one-week break. He just needed to get through this afternoon and then he could regroup.

He pulled out of the garage on to the street, heading for Slater's Books, where today's signing was scheduled. He had less than an hour to get there, get set up and make sure to thank the people hosting it. The manager had called an hour earlier to let him know the store was already full and a line was forming. He really wanted to enjoy his success. Bask in it a little, after the hard climb to get to this point, one book at a time. Having some asshole tarnish it and throw him off his game really pissed him off.

He sure couldn't let all that show. He needed to get his shit together before he faced everyone.

Other authors had told him horror stories about fans who stalked them, or people who were jealous of them and tried to make trouble. He considered himself both blessed and lucky. After slogging in the trenches with his first three books, at thirty-five years old he'd finally hit the best-seller lists with number four and number five. His current release, *Deep Cover,* had been in the top ten for five straight weeks.

Now it seemed in his celebrity he'd acquired a stalker. Apparently someone was determined not to let him enjoy his success.

He wasn't a man easily frightened, but so many incidents in such a short time could sure make a person uneasy. If he could just figure out who the hell was doing this to him and why.

And then, of course, he had to deal with Annemarie leaving, with almost no notice. She would have known what to do about this. She knew what to do about everything. She'd been the personal assistant from heaven for four years, efficient, not rattled about anything, able to juggle multiple chores and situations and relieve him of any stress. All he had to do was write, go over research with her, and show up wherever she told him to. She'd handled his social media, kept his schedule, assisted him with his research, kept his notes organized. And on the weeks he didn't need her, he'd arranged for her to have paid time off. In all that time, they'd hardly had a disagreement.

He still hadn't figured out why she'd had to leave. And those were the exact words she'd used.

"I have to leave," was all she said. "I'm sorry, Blake. I have some personal things I really have to deal with."

He had no idea what those things were, because she never discussed her personal life with him. He'd asked her if it was family and she said no, she had no family, a situation he found sad in and of itself. She'd never mentioned any socializing she did on her days off, and he wondered now if he should have queried her more. He just hated to invade her space. Everything with her was always about him and the writing and the books. She was as excited about each success as if it was her own. And, in a way it was. He never could have done this without her, and he made sure she knew that.

He had noticed a slight edginess to her in the days leading up to her departure, as if something was bothering her. They were hip deep into the research for his next two books and going crazy. He didn't think the stress had been any greater than usual. But every time he asked her about it she just pressed her lips together, shook her head, and repeated she just had to leave.

So what the hell had upset her life so much that she had to leave? He really needed to take some time and hunt her down. Find out what was going on. He'd do it just as soon as he got past today's book signing and could take advantage of the upcoming break in the tour.

A horn blared, startling him, and he realized he was still sitting at a light that had turned green. Oh, great. If his stalker wanted to find him, all he had to do was look for the stupid driver at the green light.

Finally he pulled into the parking area behind the bookstore. As he climbed out of his car and locked the door, he couldn't help looking all around, searching for…what? Did he really think whoever this was would be lying in wait here, to strike without warning?

Maybe.

Holy shit, Blake. He wrote mysteries for a living. He knew so much of this stuff was made up. Things were different in real life.

Except this wasn't fiction and someone kept doing things and leaving him these notes.

I know what you did.

Sticking his professional smile on his face and hefting his messenger bag, he pulled open the back door to the bookstore and was immediately assaulted by a raucous din of voices. A tall brunette with a big smile spotted him and came forward to greet him.

"Welcome, Mr. Morgan. I'm Jocelyn Ayres. We're so glad to have you with us today." She waved a hand in the general direction of the noise. "We're packed to the walls here and I wanted to make sure I got you safely to your table."

He shook hands with her, thinking, holy cow! With the huge success of *Deep Cover,* his agent had told him to be prepared for an overwhelming response. He guessed his spot on one of the local television shows that morning had also contributed in part to this.

"Thanks for having me."

"Are you kidding?" She flashed her grin again. "Everyone's so excited about this. I hope the store employees don't mug you in their eagerness to meet you. Come on."

She led him down the short hallway into the main portion of the bookstore and Blake had to blink his eyes. The entire store was wall-to-wall people. They were jammed into the open areas and between the shelved displays of books. Off to his right against a wall a table had been set up with a stack of his books, water, and pens. Ropes and stanchions partitioned it off from the crowd so he'd have a little breathing space.

As he reached his station another woman came forward, hand extended.

"Margaret Breakstone. I'm the manager and have to tell you how delighted we are to have you. I hope you don't get writer's cramp, because when you're done we have a ton of presolds for you to sign."

"Great. My publisher will be pleased."

She laughed. "Oh, I'd say they're already pretty happy with you."

He placed his messenger bag against the wall behind him, pulled out the chair, and sat down. When he took another look around he thought it was a good thing he didn't get claustrophobia. People were jammed together so tightly they were a solid wall behind the ropes and stanchions.

"This is…amazing." He looked back at Margaret. "They don't bite, do they?"

She laughed. "We haven't had that happen yet, although I suppose there's always a first time. Your publisher was quick to let us know you still hadn't gotten used to your celebrity. It's nice to meet someone who isn't way over the top."

"Thank you. I think."

She waved a hand at the table. "The confirming email told us to be sure and have bottled water for you, and a supply of the pens you like to use. Jocelyn will be your guardian. If you need anything else, just let her know."

"Thank you again."

He picked up a pen and got ready to greet the first person in line. After that there was no time for conversation except with the people waiting so patiently. He lost track of time, as the readers kept on coming. Each one had a smile and a compliment and he tried to think of something special to say to each of them. And then, finally, he was done. He looked around and saw most of the crowd had cleared out. A few souls were still browsing but the mob had dispersed.

"You're a hardy soul, Mr. Morgan." Jocelyn smiled at him. "Thank you again for this."

"No, thank *you*. For having me." He leaned back in his chair, wound his fingers together and cracked his knuckles.

"You have to stop doing that, Blake. It drives people crazy."

He could hear Annemarie's chiding voice in his ear. In the past few weeks he'd come to realize exactly how much of his life she was involved in, and how much he'd come to depend on her. Another item high on his list during the break was finding her replacement. He hoped to hell there was someone out there as good as she was.

"Mr. Morgan?" Margaret Breakstone interrupted his mental wanderings.

"Yes." He dug out his professional smile. "Presolds, right?"

"Before that a reporter is here and would like an interview for the newspaper. He said his photographer got some great shots with you and the crowd."

"Oh, sure. Of course."

"We have a conversation area set aside for it," Margaret told him. "Come on."

He rose from the chair, turned to pick up the messenger bag…and froze. On the flap of the bag someone had affixed a sticky note.

I know what you did.

What the hell?

Blake closed his fist around the note, the little icy finger stroking his spine again. He looked around, but all he saw was the end of the crowd still wandering around the store. Did he expect whoever this was to be standing there waiting to be recognized? He wanted to ask if someone had seen anything, but he was pretty sure it was hopeless. With people jammed against the velvet ropes and everyone focused on him, placing the note had to be easy.

He hated the fact that his pulse ratcheted up and his nerves were getting the best of him. Someone was playing a joke, was all. And not a very funny one. If he caught them—*when* he caught them—he'd find out what the fuck was going on. Then he'd beat the shit out of them.

"Mr. Morgan? Blake? Is everything alright?"

He turned to see Jocelyn standing by the table.

"Yes. Sorry." He dredged up a smile. "Just lost in thought for a moment. Reporter's waiting, right?"

"Yes. If you don't mind."

"Not at all." He'd labored for too long in anonymity to blow off publicity. "Let's do it."

By the time he finished with the interview, signing the presolds, and autographing special books for the store employees, the afternoon was long gone. He shook hands with everyone again and headed outside right into the dark. He gave thanks for the lights in the parking lot. He tossed his messenger bag in the car, climbed in, and started to back out of the parking space when he realized the car was bumping along.

Sighing, he put it in park and climbed out. He'd missed the flat tire because he'd only seen one side of the car when he came out of the store.

Fuck.

He turned off the engine, tossed his sport jacket in the back seat of the car and rolled up his shirt sleeves. He thought about calling road service, but he could easily change the tire in the time it would take for someone to show up. Swallowing a sigh, he opened the trunk to pull out the jack and the spare.

And froze.

Neatly stuck to the spare was yet another note.

> *I'm watching you. I know what you did.*
> *I know what you did and I'm going to make you pay.*

Okay, now his nerves kicked in full force. Blake had heard of the little electronic gizmos you could buy cheap online that opened any car lock. He just never thought it would play into his life. Enough was enough. He didn't rattle easily but if some maniac was stalking him, even going so far as to use electronic devices to access his vehicle, how much longer would

Desiree Holt

it be before there was a physical attack?

He looked around the parking lot, trying to spot someone, even as he realized how stupid that was. What did he expect? A man popping up wearing a T-shirt that said *Hey! I'm your stalker*? Whoever left it was probably long gone. Or not. He wanted to scream or throw something but that wouldn't be very productive. He had to figure out what was going on here.

He crumpled the note and stuck it in his pocket. He'd finally stopped throwing them away and now he had quite a collection, if he ever found the fucker doing this. Then he sighed and went to work changing the tire. Thank the Lord he was turning the rental in tomorrow at the airport.

Goddamnit.

No one left the store through the back entrance the entire time it took him to change the tire. By the time he finished a light rain was falling, the dampness and chill in the air only adding to his foul mood. He tossed the jack in the trunk and wiped his hands on his handkerchief, then slammed the trunk closed.

As he reached to open the car door, the light in the parking lot made it possible for him to see himself reflected in the window. His thick dark hair was disheveled where he'd run his fingers through it staring at the flat. He had a smidge of dirt on one cheek and the late day scruff of beard was beginning to show. His beard was so dark he probably should have shaved again early afternoon before leaving for the signing. Hardly the image of a polished, successful author.

Right now, all he wanted was a hot shower and a stiff drink. And food. He'd eaten very little for lunch and he was suddenly hungry. Room service sounded very good to him.

He tried to watch the traffic around him as he drove back to the hotel. Then realized how stupid that was. He had no idea how he'd spot someone following him. He could write about it with no problem but doing it in real life was a whole lot different. Maybe he could write his next book about this when it was all over. Whatever *it* was.

He was damn glad to get back to the hotel. He found a parking spot in the garage close to the elevator and he hurried to it. A nervous ninny, for God's sake.

He had just returned to his room when his cell rang. He looked at the readout.

His agent.

"Yeah, Henry." He closed the door, put his messenger bag down and dropped into a chair.

"So how did it go?"

"Great. It was great. Big crowd, lots of enthusiasm." He chuckled. "Lots of pictures for Facebook. You should like that."

"Social media works," Henry agreed. "So, anything else happen?"

"If you want to know about any more notes, then yes, something else happened. Two somethings."

He related the details, biting down on the anger at the unknown stalker.

Henry was silent for a moment.

"Listen, I know you aren't going to like this, but I think we need to get you a bodyguard."

"Are you kidding me?" Blake bit off the words. "Because some joker is sending me some notes?"

"This joker," Henry pointed out, "is persistent. He may be no more harmless than leaving these notes for you. Maybe he gets his jollies thinking he's frightening you. But then again, maybe he's not. And you're too valuable a commodity to ignore this."

"Fuck."

Even as he said the word, Blake saw the wisdom of Henry's position. Attacks on celebrities in all venues were far from uncommon. Having his trunk broken into wasn't all that unusual, either. Obsessed fans did a lot of crazy things.

"Let me make a couple of calls," Henry told him. "Some of my other clients have needed bodyguards, and either agency they used will work just fine. Depends on who has someone free right now."

But the word *bodyguard* pinged something in Blake's brain.

"Never mind. I've got an agency I can call."

"Blake, you can't just hire anyone off the street," Henry protested.

"Depends on the street. You familiar with Vigilance?"

"Are you shitting me? Of course I am. I've tried to hire them a couple of times but they're very selective about the contracts they take. And while I love you, buddy, you aren't quite up there in the Vigilance stratosphere yet."

Blake snorted a laugh. "Shows you what you know. Do you happen to remember where they're located?"

"Well, they were in New York, but I heard they relocated."

"Uh-huh. To Arrowhead Bay, Florida. The place where I grew up."

"Huh. Well, then, I'd say it might just be time for you to go home for a visit."

Blake nodded, even though Henry couldn't see him. "My thoughts exactly."

Chapter 2

Blake was glad he hadn't driven his car to the airport at the beginning of the tour, making it one less place the stalker could leave his nasty little notes. Instead he'd used Uber. Still, when he got home he carefully searched the area around the entrance to his condo. Even checked his car in the residential parking garage, sighing in relief when he didn't find anything.

He'd only been living in the condo for about six months. Before that he was living in New York, renting a townhouse. Then when his first best seller hit, he decided to move back to Florida. Tampa had as much big city as he wanted; he had a lot of friends there, including several from his home town of Arrowhead Bay, which was only a two-hour trip away. One of those friends introduced him to a real estate agent who was addicted to his books. Two weeks after his search began he was the owner of a three-bedroom condo on Tampa's Harbor Island, overlooking the water.

Too bad he was in no mood to enjoy it.

I know what you did.

It played in a loop in his mind. What the hell had he done? No matter how many times he went over things in his mind, even going back to the release of his first book, nothing stood out that would generate something like this.

He slept uneasily, and in the morning checked again for notes of any kind. As he made his way through downtown Tampa, he found himself constantly checking in his rearview and side mirrors. Did the car behind him look familiar? Was the one driving beside him familiar?

He had specifically told his agent and publisher he didn't want anyone to know where he was going on this short break. Better for the public—and whoever was after him—to believe he was staying in Tampa as he usually did. Still, he continued to check any traffic around him. Just in case, he told himself. Even when he finally hit the Interstate he remained alert, although he had to admit to himself how farfetched it sounded to think someone would actually be following him.

His call to Vigilance had gone better than he'd hoped. He had never met Avery March, but he knew about the agency. Everyone in the small, southern town of Arrowhead Bay knew about them. But the agency had taken up residence long after he moved away. Avery's sister, Sheridan March, was the Arrowhead Bay chief of police. When Avery had been looking to relocate the agency to a smaller environment than New York, she'd come down for a visit and fallen in love with the town.

They'd made themselves a low-key part of the community, guarding their privacy. What he did know about them was that they were a high-risk security agency and bodyguard work was one of their specialties, with some hostage rescue thrown in now and then. Rumor was they did black work for the government, too. Their clients ranged from international corporations to political figures and rock stars.

He hated that having a bodyguard would mean an invasion of his privacy, but as his agent said, "Better than being dead."

He didn't want to broadcast the fact that someone was after his ass, but he wanted to make sure Vigilance was what he wanted and needed. He'd hoped Avery had at least heard of him and his books, so he could get a foot in the door. He'd smiled at her response when he asked her.

"Damn straight I've heard of you," were her exact words. "As a matter of fact, I have every one of your books."

"That's great, because I think I need your help."

When he explained his situation, she set an appointment for the next morning.

"Come on down. I can't let anything happen to one of my favorite authors. Right?"

"Thank you. See you tomorrow around eleven."

"She reads your books?" Henry was astounded when Blake called to tell him the meeting was set up. "How lucky can you get? Okay, then. Call me afterward and give me the details. I'm sure she'll want to get all the information about your tour and I want to be comfortable with the arrangements."

Fueled by a go cup of coffee, he tried to sort out in his head what he wanted to say to Avery. He'd given her a brief overview, but he knew she would probe for as many details as he could remember. He had saved all the rest of the notes in a large envelope along with a list of where and when he'd received them. Henry had advised him to save the texts, which he had, but he had nothing on the phone calls, only a list of where and when. He hoped that at least gave Vigilance something to start with.

When he left the Interstate to follow the two-lane highway into Arrowhead Bay, he rolled down the driver's side window in his car and inhaled the air. Fresh and clean, a little windswept and tinged with salt from the bay, it was headier than any other scent. Maybe the memories it brought helped a little, too. Growing up in the small town had been great. In fact, he had used Arrowhead Bay and its lifestyle as a model for the town in his fourth book.

The minute he hit the town limits and headed down Main Street, the past came flooding back. Grabbing rides on anyone's boat at the marina and begging fishing time. High school football games, especially the one after the homecoming parade. Serial dating, because at that age he wasn't interested in anything that lasted longer than six hours. Being part of the crowd that everyone envied. The jocks and cheerleaders and leaders of the class. Looking back on it, he realized how shallow it all was, but when you were a teenager those things were important.

There was one memory, however, that had taken root in his mind and intensified over the years. Whoever said teenage love disappears had never met Samantha Quenel. Two years younger than he was, she'd drawn him to her the first time he got a really good look at her. Tall, slender and graceful, with her long blond hair that swayed when she walked, she'd captured both his heart and his cock at first sight. Every time he saw her he felt as if a fist had struck him. And her smile was pure sunshine.

He'd found himself looking for opportunities to bump into her. Maybe chat with her. Every time he looked into her eyes he got lost in them. One time he found himself in line with her at Fresh from the Oven, where he'd gone to get their special chocolate chunk muffins for his mother. He'd coaxed her into letting him buy her an iced tea and his fifteen-minute run to the bakery turned into one of the most memorable two hours of his life. He was so affected by it, he invited her to the upcoming Valentine's dance.

Talk about a night to remember. He still felt the imprint of her body against his as they danced close together, her breasts soft against his chest and the faint perfume she wore tantalizing his senses. When he kissed her goodnight, one kiss wasn't close to enough. She tasted like seven kinds of sin, her mouth soft and pliant. He still remembered every detail of that night, the sweet heat of her kisses when he took her home and the feel of her lips against his.

He'd gotten hard as steel thinking about those sweet lips wrapped around his cock. Horny teenager that he was, he'd wanted to take her someplace private, strip off all her clothes and make love to her all night. Only his respect for her kept him in check, and his message to himself that you didn't grope girls like Samantha on the first date.

The last thing he said was, "I'll call you about this weekend. Can we do something together?"

She'd smiled and nodded.

And then he'd made one of the worst mistakes in his life. One of the drawbacks of being part of the so-called in crowd was they dictated what you did and who you did it with. And Samantha Quenel was not part of their closed circle. Too bad his friends had acted like assholes, but shame on him for being swayed by them. After that he went out of his way to avoid her, even ignoring her or walking away when she tried to talk to him. Then he got caught up in graduation, the parties with his friends, plans for his last summer before college, and she just never appeared on his horizon.

His first few trips home after he started college he'd tried to look her up, but she gave him a shoulder colder than ice. Who could blame her? He'd been a total ass. To this day he regretted the way he'd handled the whole thing. He hadn't met a woman since then that he enjoyed as much or wanted as badly. How was it that after just one date she was so firmly implanted in his brain? That all these years he'd measured every woman who came into his life against her?

Because it was more than one date, jerkoff.

It was the girl herself, a very special girl he'd treated shabbily. Even after he left Arrowhead Bay to pursue his writing career, an image of her would float in his brain when he least expected it. He'd remember the feel of her slender body in his arms, the silken brush of her hair against his cheek, and the tantalizing flowery scent of her shampoo that had ignited every single teenage hormone in his body. Sometimes he thought if he could just see her one more time he could get her out of his system, but the older he grew the more he realized he might never get her out of his system at all.

Could the chemistry between two people linger for so many years, so strong that you never found it with another woman? Was that even possible?

Yes. You idiot.

Idiot was right. Not to mention being a classic asshole. Could being an asshole haunt you for the rest of your life?

Yes to that, too.

Well, one thing at a time. He had to take care of his immediate problem. But that didn't mean while he was here he couldn't try to find out where Samantha Quenel was now. Did she still live here? Would it be that easy?

When he found her, he planned to make the biggest apology of his life. Then he'd see if there was something there between them or it was all in his overactive writer's imagination.

The sidewalks were crowded today with the first early rush of snowbirds. As usual there was a line out the door at Fresh from the Oven. Blake's mouth watered as he thought of the incredible muffins they sold.

Note to self: get muffins right after meeting with Avery March. And French press coffee from Fresh Roasted.

People stood on the sidewalks in small groups, chatting or looking in the colorful windows. Kids still rode their bicycles through town going to the beach or the community pool. A wave of nostalgia and homesickness hit him with the punch of a fist. He didn't spend enough time here, now that he was such a so-called big shot. Time with his parents and any of his friends still here. He made a mental note to check with his agent and publisher about doing a signing at Read the Book here in town.

Then he was through the downtown area and following the GPS directions to Vigilance. The long narrow road he turned on to wound through a heavily treed area, finally emerging into a clearing. Exactly in the center sat a house built in the distinctive Key West style with a gabled roof and a wide front porch. Off to the side was a long two-story building that looked new, and he wondered idly what it housed.

The house had stood empty for quite a while after the owners died. Apparently not too many people wanted to live in the woods, but he figured for Vigilance the isolation was a good thing.

There were windows across the front of the house but they were opaque glass. Blake would have bet his next royalty check someone was watching from inside, probably through cleverly concealed cameras.

Blake climbed the stairs to the porch and pressed a button set into the framing.

"Yes?"

The voice came from a speaker embedded somewhere so cleverly he couldn't even find it.

"Blake Morgan. I have an appointment with Avery March."

"Can I see some identification, please? Just hold it up to the coach light next to the door."

Blake would have laughed if he didn't know how seriously agencies like Vigilance took their security. Hell, he wrote about them, didn't he? Maybe when this was over they'd help him with further research. Meanwhile he took out his driver's license and held it up to what he figured was a concealed camera.

"Okay. You're cleared."

"Thanks."

The door opened and a man in jeans and a Vigilance T-shirt looked him up and down. Then stepped back to let him in.

"Sorry. Security's our middle name here."

"And I'm sure your clients are grateful you translate it to them."

The man nodded, then closed the door and punched some buttons in a keypad next to it. "This way."

Blake was familiar with the layout of Key West houses and it was obvious a lot of renovation had been done in this one. The living room and dining room were now enclosed rooms separated by a narrow hallway. He had no idea what went on in them because the doors were closed and his guide wasn't very forthcoming. He just led Blake to the end of the hallway and knocked twice on a door.

"Your appointment is here."

"Well, bring him in."

Blake stepped into an office that was not at all what he expected to find for the head honcho of a high-profile security agency. A woven area rug covered a good part of the hardwood flooring and the furniture, rather than being utilitarian, had a Spanish flavor to it. Colorful prints brightened the walls, and a tall leafy plant stood in one corner.

Avery March impressed him right from the start. It wasn't just her looks, although she presented a totally businesslike appearance, in her tailored blouse and slacks, reddish-brown hair held back in a clip. But beyond that, and more important, she exuded a quiet confidence that made him think at once, *Oh, yeah. I'll bet she can handle any problem at all.*

She rose from behind her desk and held out her hand. "Nice to meet you, Blake. I have to say my sister and I are big fans of yours."

He made a mental note to send signed copies of his books to both sisters. "Thank you. Maybe when my, uh, problem gets resolved you can help me with some basic information for my research."

"I'd be glad to." She grinned. "As long as it doesn't touch on sensitive areas. Sit down. Please." She looked at the guy who had ushered him in. "Thanks, Tom. You can go back to your toys."

The man gave a half-grin, nodded and backed out, closing the door behind him.

"I appreciate you thinking of Vigilance," Avery told him.

"I've heard you're the best and that's what I need. And lucky for me you're even in my home town." He took a business card from his wallet and handed it to her. "My agent. He asked that you give him a call after our meeting."

"Of course. I'll need to coordinate with him to make sure we're prepared for anything."

He sat in one of the client chairs, pulled a large manila envelope out of the slim briefcase he carried and handed it across the desk.

"I saved all of these except for the first two," he told her. "By the time the third one showed up, my agent decided I should hang on to them, just in case we were dealing with some crazed fan. Oh, and I don't think there's much use checking for fingerprints since I wasn't too careful about handling them. Unfortunately."

"You'd be surprised. We'll take yours so we can eliminate them and go from there. People aren't always as meticulous as they think."

"Whatever you say. You're the expert. I made a list of the places where the notes were left. That's in there, too."

Avery shook the contents of the envelope onto her desk and separated them, using the end of a pen. Then she sat studying them for a few moments. "Someone obviously has a serious issue with you."

"No kidding. And I haven't got the faintest clue who it could be." He leaned forward. "Avery, this whole thing came at me without warning and is just blowing my mind."

"You said you received some texts, also?"

He nodded, and reached into his briefcase again for the cell phone.

"This is my personal one. I don't know how whoever this is got the number."

Avery gave a dry chuckle. "In this era of sophisticated electronics, absolutely anything is possible. All it takes is someone who has half a brain and a minor understanding of the stuff. It could even be as simple as someone sitting near you in a restaurant and cloning your phone."

Blake grimaced and handed over his cell. "I'd have a hard time believing this stuff if I didn't write about it."

"I hope you bought another phone."

Blake nodded. "The same day. I try to be cautious about who I give that number to. Almost everyone has my business number. The unlisted one I only give to my agent, my editor, my parents, a couple of other people." He held up a hand. "I know, I know. Widening the circle, but trust me, Avery. You can thoroughly vet these people."

"And trust *me*." She smiled at him. "I will."

He rubbed his jaw. "It's just been the damnedest thing. "These messages or whatever they are started showing up out of nowhere. I blew off the first couple because I always have a weirdo or two doing stuff like that. After their first episode or two, they usually disappear and go after someone else. But look." He waved his hand at the notes spread out on the desk. "Whoever this is just won't let go."

Avery picked up her desk phone and punched a button. "Mark, can you come into the office for a moment? Thanks."

In seconds, there was a tap at the door, then it opened and a thin man about thirty, with hair almost to his shoulders, poked his head in.

"You need me, boss?"

Avery nodded and waved her fingers over the notes on her desk. "These have to be tested for prints, but we need to eliminate Mr. Morgan's. Blake, have you ever been fingerprinted?"

He nodded. "I actually went through the entire application process for a Concealed Carry license because I was using it in one of my earlier books."

"Good. Then we can pull yours up out of the system."

He raised his eyebrows. "You can access them?" Then he shook his head and grinned. "Of course you can. You can access anything anywhere, right?"

Avery chuckled. "You might say that." She looked at Mark. "Get your goodies and take these notes with you. Let's eliminate Mr. Morgan's prints first."

"Back in a sec."

He returned carrying a wooden box and a pair of tweezers. Blake watched, fascinated, as the man carefully lifted each note and placed it in the box.

"I figured we've got enough prints on these already." He looked at Avery, one corner of his mouth twitching with a grin. "I assume you want these yesterday?"

"Absolutely. So get going on them." When Mark left she turned back to Blake. "The first thing I want to tell you is I agree with your publisher and your agent. You need a bodyguard to travel with you."

Blake shifted uncomfortably in his chair. "I know you're right, but the idea makes me uncomfortable. I'm not used to traveling with someone being with me so much."

"But I understand you travelled with an assistant, didn't you? Or rather she travelled with you."

He nodded. Avery had done her homework. "But that was different. Personal assistants are common in the industry."

Avery grinned. "Then we'll just get you someone who can handle both jobs. I actually have one of my agents in mind, but let's go over everything first. I want to backtrack a little and see if you can pinpoint something that might have triggered this. The note says he—or she—knows what you've done. Do you have any idea what this person is referring to?"

Blake ground his teeth. "I wish I did. It would be a lot easier to handle. But honest to God, Avery. I've tried to recreate everything from the time I signed my first contract and nothing jumps out at me."

She wrinkled her forehead in a slight frown. "Forgive me for being blunt about this, but everyone has something they wish they hadn't done. Including me."

"Oh, well." He crossed his legs, resting one ankle on the opposite knee. "Do I regret a lot of things? Sure. Like you said, everyone has something. I'm sure I probably pissed off a fan at some time, or got a little testy with someone criticizing one of my books. Or got some woman angry with me because she wanted more than I planned to give her. But do any of those sound like something that would trigger this kind of campaign?"

"No, I have to agree with you there. Still, you never know what sets someone off. So, that said, tell me every single thing you can remember about when the first one appeared and when you found it."

With the deft touch of an expert, she pulled everything out of him he had to give. Anyone he'd ever had a run-in with. Someone he might have pissed off. Women who thought he'd dumped them without reason. Women who'd expected to marry him. Authors who thought his celebrity was not earned. And on and on and on. Nothing, she told him, was too insignificant.

Blake gave her as much detail as he could. By the time they were finished he felt as if he'd been run through a wringer, and Avery had pages of notes.

"Are you really going to check into every single one of those?"

"It's what we do," she told him. "The person you dismiss out of hand could be the one in the end doing it all. Let me ask you again. Did anything special happen around the time you received the first note? Anything out of the ordinary?"

"My practically indispensable assistant left without any notice. One minute she was into details of the next signing and any promo she'd set up. The next she was throwing stuff into her suitcases and flying out of there. She said she had to take care of personal business, but—"

"But she gave you no notice? No indication of why she had to leave in such a hurry?"

"Nada. I was upset, her just walking out that way, but she seemed on edge, which was unusual for her. All she kept saying was she couldn't take it anymore. I asked her if it had to do with us and she just shook her head and kept telling me not to push her. That's all I can tell you."

Avery looked at her notes. "That's Annemarie Schaefer."

"Yes. But, she was with me for four years and I know she felt bad about leaving. It can't be her."

"I'm keeping that in mind, but no one gets a pass on this. I'm still going to check her out."

He shook his head. "This is not who Annemarie is. You can say it's possible as many times as you want, and I'll still disagree with you. You can't work that closely with someone for four years and not get a sense of them. Of who they are."

Avery made more notes, then looked over at him. "Blake, I wouldn't be doing my job if I didn't take her life apart to see if you're right and I'm wrong. We have to look at everyone. And maybe what we find out will give you some peace as far as she's concerned. So I'm including her on the list."

"Yeah, I can see that you have to." But he hoped she didn't waste too much time barking up the wrong tree.

"Just out of curiosity, what have you been doing for an assistant since she left?"

"Making do." He laughed. "Remember, I didn't have an Annemarie in the beginning. My agent has had someone pick up the slack for now answering emails and keeping up with social media. My publisher is handling the media. All I've had to do, really, is get myself to the signings, smile at people, and sign my name."

"But now you have a little break on this tour, right?"

He nodded, giving silent thanks for that. "A week, then five more signings. We end with a big deal in Tampa at a small event hall. After that I'm done for a while."

Thank God, and did I ever think I'd say that?

"Good. This gives us time to go over everything and anything you can think of and get this all set up. Maybe we'll get lucky and figure this all out before you have to take off again. If not, we'll get you fixed up with a bodyguard who can double as your assistant."

"I hope so." He raked his fingers through his hair. "I'm worried this will start to spill over where my fans are concerned. I mean, what if whoever this is decides he hasn't harassed me enough and zeroes in on my readers? I mean, this person obviously shows up at my signings. What if he decides to follow someone, and—"

Avery held up a hand. "Stop. We aren't there yet. Let's concentrate on finding this person and protecting you before it gets to that."

For the next hour Avery took him back over everything yet again, until he wanted to scream and bang his head. Had he forgotten any names? Any events? Any little thing?

"You never know what the trigger could be," she explained, when she saw him grinding his teeth. "I know this is tedious but trust me, Blake, sometimes it's the tiniest detail that gives us the clue."

He wanted to tell her the CIA could probably use her as an interrogator. At one point, unable to sit still any longer, he jumped up and began pacing. The reality of someone stalking him made him nuts. Why him? The question plagued him nearly every minute of every day. What had he ever done that drew this kind of nut into his orbit? He turned to Avery and asked her the question.

"There could be a million answers." She shrugged. "And, in cases like this, there's often no sane answer. You may not have done a thing. It's what the stalker perceives and you can't control that. Unfortunately, yours isn't an isolated case. After your call yesterday, I did some research. You're lucky your stalker isn't sneaking into your hotel room or breaking into your car. Or any of a million other things they could do to grab your attention. Because trust me, this is what they want. Your attention. All of it, so they can tell you just how you made them do this."

"Don't forget. This person did break into the trunk," he reminded her.

"Yeah." She snorted. "But at least whoever this is didn't lie in wait in your car and bash you over the head."

"Sometimes I wish whoever this is would do that." He held up a hand. "Not bash me over the head but jump into my car with me. At least then I'd know who it is."

"Yes, but you could also end up dead."

"Dead?" Now that was a chilling thought.

"It's a possibility. That's why you're hiring us," she reminded him. "So that doesn't happen."

It was a little scary, when he looked at it like that, to realize how dangerous fans could be. What an ironic twist of fate it was that when he'd been merely a midlist author hardly anyone ever bothered him with crazy stuff. He guessed fame brought out all the crazies.

"Okay, I think that's it." Avery pushed her little Bluetooth keyboard aside and sat back in her chair. "I think we've got enough to start with. We're going to take care of this," she reminded him. "That's why you're here. I've been pulling all of this out of you so I can have a complete picture and the agent I assign to you can be prepared for anything."

He sat, reluctantly, but he was close to the end of his patience. He still couldn't find anything in his life to incite something like this.

"As I said before, the agent I assign to you can do double duty as your personal assistant without drawing a lot of questions."

"I guess that's the best cover. A lot of authors have male assistants." He swallowed a smile as he visualized some well-muscled guy with a shaved head and tattoos passing out flyers and telling a bookstore manager what kind of pens he liked.

"That smile you're trying to hide tells me what kind of image you have of the person I've tagged for this."

"He just needs to blend in," Blake told her. "Look the part."

"*She* is not a male, but I believe she's the perfect person for you. Acting as your PA allows her to be with you at all times. After your call, I reached out to her. She lives in Tampa but drove down here for the day to meet you and go over all the details with you. I didn't tell her who you were, just in case after we chatted I didn't think she'd fit the bill. But she will. Perfectly."

"She?" He raised his eyebrows. "I thought we were talking about a male bodyguard."

Avery laughed. "Don't tell me you're prejudiced about women taking traditional male jobs."

He shook his head. "No. It's just…well…I guess I expected you to assign a man to me." He chuckled. "All the women I know would chop off my head if they could hear me. Or some other part of my anatomy. Anyway, I'm sure you know what you're doing, Avery, but this person also has to have some public relations and organizational skills."

"How about someone who has a degree in business from Florida State, served in the military, is overqualified in marksmanship and hand-to-hand combat, and looks like a model for a fashion magazine? Would that do?"

Blake grinned. "I'd say that's about damn near perfect."

"Okay, then. Get ready to meet your new personal assistant." She pressed a button on her intercom. "Hey, guys. Is Sam in there?"

"I sure am," came the answer.

"Great. Can you come to my office right now? The client is here. Thanks."

Blake got a strange feeling in his gut when he heard the name. No, he was imagining things. It just couldn't be. Hadn't he just been thinking how determined he was to find out where she was? That would be the mother of all coincidences. A knock sounded on the door, and every muscle in his body tightened with anticipation.

"Come on in," Avery called out.

"Hey, Avery. You wanted to see me?"

Blake's brain did a hula twist at the sound of her voice.

Holy shit! Was this really possible? Had fate decided to answer his prayers and drop his second chance right into his lap?

"Yes. I've got a new assignment for you, at least for the next month. Meet your new client, Blake Morgan. Blake, meet Samantha Quenel."

He froze in place, staring at her, and did his best not to swallow his tongue. Little Samantha Quenel was way more than the hot teenage girl he took to that dance and then dumped. The girl whose memory he'd carried all these years, who filled his dreams with erotic fantasies and made other women seem dull and uninteresting. Again he cursed himself for being so easily influenced by his so-called friends.

The memories that had roared to life on the drive from Tampa were now out in the open, sharp and vivid. But the image of the younger Samantha faded in the presence of the woman who stood in the office. She was nothing less than a knockout, tall and slender, with curves that made a man itch to run his hands over them and an air of unconscious sensuality about her. Her blond hair was still long but worn now in a utilitarian braid that somehow still seemed to look sexy. Jeans and a T-shirt outlined a body that was as tempting as it was toned. He tried not to stare at the way the soft material of her shirt displayed her nicely rounded breasts, or the way the jeans clung to hips he wanted to touch and long legs he wanted to feel wrapped around him.

God, he hoped his cock would behave and not try to poke out of his pants at her. He was here on business, not pleasure, especially since it appeared she was going to be part of that business.

But fate had given him an opportunity that he had no intention of wasting. Here was the chance he'd wanted all these years and he was going to take full advantage of it.

The look on Sam's face told him she was as stunned as he was. Blue eyes were opened wide in surprise and her mouth, looking sexier than he remembered, formed a perfect O.

Wishing he had a bucket of ice to shove down his pants, he pulled himself together, rose, and turned toward the doorway.

"Hey, Sam." He smiled at her. "Long time, no see."

Chapter 3

Oh, no. No, no, no.

Blake Morgan here? The man who still haunted her dreams no matter how she tried to replace him? Who had dumped her like day-old coffee after a night filled with promise? *That* Blake Morgan? The unexpected punch of lust froze her for a moment.

As long as she hadn't seen him all these years, she could bury the hurt feelings and the anger at what he'd done, right along with her unfulfilled yearning. Unfortunately, those feelings consumed her too damn often and had lasted too damn long. Who could be so stupid they still longed for a man they'd barely had a relationship with?

Her, apparently, no matter how much she tried to make it go away all these years.

"This isn't going to work."

The words were out of Sam's mouth before she could stop them. She probably should have found a more professional way to say them. Better yet, she should have asked her the client's name before agreeing to do this.

Avery stared at her. "Excuse me?"

Sam cleared her throat. "I'm sorry. I should have put that in a more businesslike fashion. I think it would be in everyone's best interest if you assigned another agent to Mr. Morgan."

Blake just stared, her words obviously a shock to him. Then his lips curled in that very sexy grin that she'd never been quite able to forget. Along with the press of his body against hers on the dance floor, or the warmth of his hand when he held hers. The touch of his mouth and the heat of his kiss. His brown eyes, so dark they seemed almost black, with little gold flecks that caught the light, were focused on her now so intently the nerves on the surface of her skin tingled. The air between them shimmered with suppressed sexual tension and Sam needed every bit of her learned discipline to maintain control.

Fifteen years, she thought. Fifteen years since she had last seen Blake Morgan and still every pulse point throbbed with jubilation at the sight of him. Why couldn't he have gotten fat and sloppy, or lost his hair, or any of the things that would have made him unattractive to her? But no, he had to turn into sex-on-a-stick, and a very successful stick at that. He had been very appealing then, but now maturity had given a richness to his look. He was still lean but his body was now corded with muscle, something she found strange. She knew he was a writer. Everyone in Arrowhead Bay knew of his success. But she'd figured he spent his days in front of a computer. His face still had that carved-out-of-granite look and sported a closely trimmed beard that she found incredibly sexy. Age had made him even more ruggedly masculine.

How was it possible the stupid teenage crush she'd had on him all those years ago had never gone away? And that's all it was, she repeated over and over in her head. Nothing more than a teenage crush, based on one night. Just one night.

At that time she'd been so thrilled that hot, hot Blake Morgan had taken her to a dance. If she'd gone out with him again, she probably would have ended up hating him, something she'd never stopped telling herself. Actually, it was more like trying to convince herself, if she was completely honest. But she'd been lying to herself then and she was lying to herself now. Especially when she could never seem to erase the memory of his kisses.

She needed to forget about the feel of his hard body pressed against hers, the surge of teenage hormones that made her want him with an inappropriate desperation. Instead she should remember how quickly he'd dropped her after that. Well, now she had a chance to return the favor.

Damn it! Stop this, Sam. That was all years ago and you were sixteen, for God's sake. You're an adult, supposedly a disciplined one. You're past the age of romantic daydreams. Where's your discipline? Get your shit together, so you don't embarrass yourself or Vigilance.

But lord, it didn't help that he was the best thing she'd looked at in a long time.

Avery glanced from one to the other. "I take it you two know each other?"

"We dated in high school," Blake told her, a smile still teasing his lips.

"Dated?" Sam made an effort to even out her tone of voice. "Uh, not exactly. One date. One dance. That was it. Just the one night."

She hoped she sounded calm and collected. No way did she want anyone to see the shock she felt at facing Blake Morgan again after all these years.

Avery looked from one to the other. "So you two know each other. That might make this easier."

Sam felt her control slipping.

"Yes, we went to high school together. Sort of. But we didn't exactly part friends, so this might not work out. Sorry, Avery. It's probably better if you assign someone else to this case."

"But you don't even know what kind of case it is," Blake pointed out to her.

She ignored him and focused on Avery. "I'm assuming it's a security job, since that's a good part of what we do."

"It is." Avery nodded. "But there are some specific requirements of the person assigned to it."

She frowned. "Like what?"

"Blake needs someone to travel with him who can also function as his personal assistant. It makes for a very good cover and will allow you access to all facets of his routine without looking out of place and generating questions from people. Marcy and Lora are both on assignment and neither of the guys I have available could pass muster on that."

Shit!

Shit! Shit! Shit!

Now what? Could she carry it off? She certainly had the background for it in spades, but could she be aloof and professional? Be around him and not want to constantly kick his ass for the way he'd treated her all those years ago?

Get over it, Samantha. We were teenagers, for God's sake. All that is in the past, anyway, so put it there where it belongs.

"I'd consider it a personal favor." Blake's voice, still as smooth as melted chocolate, interrupted her thoughts. "Avery read me your background information and you're almost overqualified. It would really ease my mind a lot to have you on my team."

"I'm not..." She stopped and wet her lips.

Avery motioned to her. "Why don't you come in and sit down. Let me fill you in on what's needed. I'm sure the two of you can get past whatever history you had in high school. You're both adults. And I think you'll find this interesting, Sam."

Translation: quit acting like an ass and embarrassing me or I'll assign you to guard a scientist in Antarctica.

"Of course." Putting on her best impersonal demeanor, she took the chair next to Blake. Maybe this was her chance, after all these years, to show him he meant nothing to her. That right now he was just a Vigilance client. Period. "And Avery, I apologize for the knee-jerk reaction."

Avery gave her what the other Vigilance agents called "The Look."

Sam knew she'd hear about this later. A relaxed environment was only good to a point. There were specific rules about behavior in front of clients. Or anyone else, for that matter.

"I apologize, Blake." Avery slid a glance at Sam that felt like the edge of a knife scraping over her.

Sam cleared her throat. "I apologize, too. And of course I'm happy to take the assignment." She stole a look at Blake. "Whatever you need, Vigilance can provide it better than anyone else."

Avery gave an unladylike snort then looked at her notes. "Let me fill you in on everything."

Half an hour later, Sam had been thoroughly briefed on everything. Despite whatever resentment she harbored toward Blake Morgan, she was well aware how serious something like this was and how much worse it could become.

"I'm sorry this is happening to you, Blake." She wet her lips. "I'll make sure you're well protected. I'm really very good at my job."

One corner of his mouth twitched in a half-grin. "So I understand."

"Where are you staying while you're in town?" Avery asked. "With your folks or at the B and B?"

"They're out of town on a cruise. I've got a key and the run of the house. Much preferred to the B and B, as lovely as it is."

"Alrighty, then." She pulled a folder from a drawer. "I have some paperwork here for you. Then I suggest the two of you go someplace for a late lunch and, Blake, you can fill Sam in on what kind of schedule you have and what a PA does for you. If people see the two of you together, you can just be two old acquaintances catching up with each other."

Sam didn't dare tell her boss that anyone who might remember all those years ago would know they were anything but acquaintances. But fifteen years had passed, so it was old news by now. And she was dreaming to think anyone would remember or even care that Blake Morgan had taken Samantha Quenel to a Valentine's dance, dumped her and continued to ignore her after that.

"Sounds good to me." He flashed that smile again.

Sam went to fetch her purse while Blake signed his contract and gave Avery what she knew was a big fat check for a retainer. For this to work she'd have to set some definite boundaries. For herself as well as for Blake.

When he came out of the office she pasted on what she hoped was her most professional smile.

"Do you have any preference as to where you'd like to go?" She looked at her watch. "The lunch crowd should be thinning out so we can probably catch a table almost anyplace."

"I always try to hit the Driftwood."

Sam nodded. "They still have the best seafood in town. Of course, you're probably used to eating at all the best places with the rest of the elite crowd."

His smile dimmed. "You've got it all wrong."

She cocked an eyebrow. "I do? In what way?"

The look in his eyes was intense. "I'm still Blake Morgan from Arrowhead Bay. My father still sells insurance, my mother still works a couple of days a week as a home health care nurse. I write books that suddenly a lot of people are buying and for that I'm very grateful. But I don't consider myself any kind of elite."

Sam bit her lip. She had to stop her mouth from running away on its own. "Sorry. That was uncalled for. I don't usually mouth off to Vigilance clients. Avery would hand me my ass in two pieces."

He smiled again, the same smile that had melted her when she was a teenager only now it was more mature and a whole lot sexier. And, despite her resolve, it still had the same effect on her. How the hell was she supposed to handle this?

Because you're a mature adult, former military, and a highly trained bodyguard.

Oh, yeah, bodyguard. I'll be guarding his body.

"Sam?"

With a start, she realized he was talking to her, a quizzical look on his face, and she had no idea what he'd been saying.

"Uh, the Driftwood would be great for lunch."

"I'll drive." He opened the door. "Ladies first."

Sam stole a look at him as he buckled himself in and started the car. The man he'd grown to be had a richness about him, a strength that the younger Blake had been missing. It hadn't taken anything more than seeing and listening to him to tell her that.

It wasn't just the sexual attraction, although God knew it was there in spades. Her entire body thrummed with need for him. This was the kind of man you could settle into life with, and it stunned her to realize that after not seeing him for more than fifteen years, her mind and her body had a sudden need and craving for him.

How on earth was she going to handle this assignment? She didn't want to say or do the wrong thing. She certainly didn't want Avery to know that the minute she'd laid eyes on Blake that the feelings she'd been hiding all these years popped out like a jack-in-the-box. Very bad form.

She couldn't help wondering what he was thinking. Feeling. They were silent on the short drive. She had expected a barrage of questions that didn't come. She wondered if he was as busy with his thoughts as she was with hers. What an unlikely twist of fate this was.

Well, if she'd learned anything in the military it was discipline, something she needed right now. Something that would help her deal with that same sizzle from all those years ago that now snapped and crackled its way through her body and made her pulse leap into overdrive. They'd have to talk about this. No way they could go on ignoring what was sure to be the elephant in the room. She swallowed a sigh as they turned into the parking lot.

The Driftwood was a mainstay in Arrowhead Bay. Owned by the same people as Bayside Marina, it drew a steady business from both locals as well as people docking at the marina, whether for a day or a week or even longer. A place where people also went to celebrate special occasions, the dress was everything from casual to cocktail.

The ambience was what drew people first. Made of wood weathered to look like real driftwood, it boasted a high-ceilinged dining room with both booths and tables, and a long bar with high-back stools. A long porch framed two sides and in good weather those seats were prime territory. Diners could look out at the boats on the water, at the fishermen celebrating their catch of the day, at people zooming by on water skis.

But the real attraction was the food, which was always mouthwatering. People docked at Bayside Marina from all up and down the west coast of Florida just for a meal at the Driftwood.

As Sam had predicted, the weekday lunch crowd had diminished by the time they arrived, allowing them to snag a table out on the covered porch overlooking Bayside Marina. Funny, she hadn't eaten here all that much when she'd lived here, but now whenever she was in town it was one of her favorite places.

He looked at her with those whiskey eyes that she was sure could see deep inside her. She used a trick she'd learned in the military, thinking of a black curtain wrapped around her so no one could see what she was thinking or feeling. She certainly needed it now. Letting him know he could still get to her after all these years made her too vulnerable.

"Well." The corners of his mouth tipped up in a grin. "This is weird, right? You and me, sitting here, after all this time? You being my bodyguard and all. Who'd a thunk it."

"We need to remember that's all this is," she told him in what she hoped was a matter-of-fact voice. "You're a client; I'm your security detail." Better to lay it all out on the table before this went any further.

"Care for a drink before lunch?" he asked. "Maybe a glass of wine?"

She shook her head. "Thanks, but I never drink when I'm working."

"You don't mind if I do?"

"No. Please. You probably need one after that story you told."

When the waitress came she ordered ice water and he ordered a glass of the house white wine. He took a sip, set the glass down and looked across the table at her. Could he feel the sizzle in the air between them, or was it all her imagination?

"I'll tell you the truth, Sam, I'm nervous as hell being with you."

Well, that wasn't what she'd expected. "What?"

"You heard me. Confession time, here." He paused as if searching for the right words. "Not a day has gone by in all these years that I haven't thought about you. It still bothers me the way I treated you." He sighed and rubbed his cheek. "I was a jerk and an ass, and I don't even have an excuse for it. If I could go back and do it all over again, I would."

Her eyes widened. "You would?"

"I would, and that's not a lie." His eyes darkened with something that hinted at desire. "I don't know what would have happened if I hadn't been such a self-involved ass. I'm still ashamed of the way I treated you. It's bothered me all these years. You have every right to turn down this job and I wouldn't blame you. Although I hope you don't, because I'm thinking maybe fate is giving us another chance."

The waitress arrived with menus, recited the specials, and told them she'd be back to get their orders.

"Please just let me say this." Blake rested his elbows on the table and leaned forward. "I asked you to the Valentine's Dance because I was very attracted to you and I wanted to go out with you, not to humiliate you. In my immature teenage stupidity, I didn't stop to think that my equally immature friends would behave the way they did. I've waited a long time to say this to you. I'm sorry, Sam. More than you'll ever know."

Sam felt her mouth hanging open. Not on any day in all this time had she ever thought she'd hear those words. Maybe she'd hoped for a very curt *Yeah, well, it's water over the dam. History. Let's move on.* But a full-out apology? Never. Not ever.

"Sam?"

She blinked, realizing that for the second time she'd spaced out on him. She wet her lips and drew in a deep, settling breath.

"Tell me this isn't just some line you're feeding me so we can work together, because you don't have to do that. I'm a professional, regardless of what my initial reaction was."

He shook his head. "No line, Sam. And that's God's truth."

"Your friends back then made it very clear it was bad form to take someone to the dance who wasn't part of your crowd." She gave an unladylike snort. "Your rather obnoxious crowd, I might add."

His face reddened.

"I can only plead adolescent stupidity." He reached across the table, took her hand in his and wrapped his fingers around it. "I was ignorant, childish, and rude. If I had it to do all over again, I'd just tell them to go to hell and ask you out again. I am more sorry about what I did afterward than I can tell you."

She looked down at her hand in his. "Okay. So I may have blown it out of proportion in my mind, too." *Not.*

He brushed his thumb back and forth across her knuckles. Just that simple touch made her nipples tingle and the pulse between her thighs set up a percussive rhythm. When he gave her hand a gentle squeeze, the warmth of his palm sent heat spiraling through her.

Control, she kept repeating in her head.

"I've spent way too much time regretting it." His husky voice played havoc with her nerves. "When you walked into the office I thought, *I have a chance to make this right.* But—"

"But?" she urged.

"Okay, if I'm way off base, just tell me and we will pretend we never had this conversation." He took another swallow of wine. "I can apologize all day, but here's the deal. I'm still attracted to you. Big time. The chemistry that nearly blew up that night is still there."

"You—"

He held up his free hand when she started to say something. "Not yet. Let me finish." His thumb continued its soft stroking rhythm and every pulse-point in her body pounded in reaction. "I'd really like it if we could make a fresh start. Pretend none of that self-involved shit I did everyhappened. Like I said, we have chemistry, Sam. Don't you want to find out if it takes us somewhere?"

For a very long moment her breath was trapped in her throat and Sam thought her heart had stopped beating. Start again?

"I don't know. That was so long ago, and we're different people now. Besides, the situation has changed, Blake." She looked down at her hands for a long moment before lifting her gaze to him again. "You're a client and we have a professional relationship." She had to get that out there, because farfetched as it might be, if anything did happen she wanted him as willing to do it as she was.

"I respect that but it's only a barrier if we want it to be." Hunger and need swirled in his dark eyes.

"But that's where I am right now. This chemistry might be nothing more than a memory. Can we just take things one day at a time? Focus on your problem and my part in this situation? If something happens, well, we can deal with it then."

The crazy thought flitted through her mind that she might be the one to cross the line. That she might be the one to push it, just because he was so, so hot now and her lady parts were sending her urgent signals.

For a very long moment Blake didn't say anything and she was almost afraid to breathe. What if he said no? What if he even demanded Avery replace her?

But then he smiled, a slow curve of those sensuous lips. "I can do that." He wrapped his fingers around her hand, infusing her with a warmth that was almost erotic. "But that doesn't mean if we want each other we have to ignore it."

"I hear you, but—" She nibbled her bottom lip. "Can we just put it on the back burner while we deal with your problem?"

He nodded. "As long as you know it's still at the top of my list. Sam, this electricity between us won't disappear just because we tell it to. Sooner or later we're going to test those waters. Just sayin'."

"Thank you. I think." She swallowed some of her ice water, which at the moment she badly needed, and sat back in her chair. Her body was hot and hungry and filled with need, and she absolutely had to get hold of herself. Especially since she saw the same thing reflected in Blake's eyes. "So. Let's talk business. That's front and center, and why we're here, after all."

They paused while the waitress took their lunch orders. Then Sam pulled out her cell phone, called up her emails, and put the phone on the table.

"Avery sent the file to both my phone and tablet listing everything she briefed me on earlier. I'd like to get the details directly from you, though, on some of this. Then you can tell me what it takes to be a personal assistant."

"Good thing I ordered a big lunch," he teased.

They ate slowly, and as he talked Sam got a clear picture of the man he was now. She realized how far he'd come from the hot teenager and his cock of the walk attitude. Here was a man who'd grown into his own skin, who after a lot of hard work had achieved success. And just when he could finally enjoy it, some asshole was threatening to take it all away. Well, not on her watch. Her Vigilance agent self kicked in.

"I didn't really think anything about it when the first note showed up," he told her. "Writers—just about anyone in the public eye—get stuff like this all the time. You wouldn't believe how many crazies there are out there."

"I know Avery asked you this but just to satisfy me, is there anyone you have contact with who might be doing this?"

He shook his head. "None of my personal friends, but I've met so many people I've just had peripheral contact with. This could be any one of them."

She studied his face. "What about your former PA? Avery's notes said she quit without any warning."

Blake started to answer but the waitress arrived with their food. When she left, he just shook his head.

"Avery asked me the same thing. Annemarie was with me for four years, from the lean times to the good. She had enough skills electronically to suit my needs but I can't see her doing anything like this. Anyway, this is someone with mental problems and I can promise you, that's not her."

She thought about asking him what his real relationship with her was, but the tone of his voice when he answered her questions held no hint of sexual attraction, at least on his part. She was stunned at the feeling of relief that gave her. She really needed to watch herself here. She was conflicted. One minute she wanted to jump his bones, the other she wanted to put up an invisible wall between them.

Crazy much, Sam?

She had him take her though a typical day—travel, signings, ancillary activities. The hours he set aside to write. And what he did between, such as where he took his meals, what he did for relaxation. She made notes on her phone as he talked.

"This person could come from anyplace in your life," she told him. "The more information I have, the easier it will be for me to be on the alert, to notice things and hopefully pinpoint the source. Also to play the part of a very efficient personal assistant."

"Sure. It won't be that difficult." His laugh was rough with little humor. "I never thought my life would be turned upside down like this."

Sam shrugged. "I don't think any of us do. Unfortunately for you, it's one of the hazards of celebrity." She waited while the waitress cleared their plates and both refused coffee.

"I want a cup of French press from Fresh Roasted," he told her.

She grinned. "Who doesn't?"

"I want to—"

He was interrupted by the sound of a chime echoing from his pocket, signaling an incoming text.

"Sorry. I thought I'd put the phone on mute. This is my personal number so I need to get it."

"No problem. Go ahead." She wondered for a fleeting moment if he was connected with some woman. Then she gave herself a mental smack, reminding herself it was none of her business, regardless of their earlier conversation.

He pulled the phone out of his pocket, looked at the screen, and his face tightened in anger. He swiveled his head, looking everywhere on the porch. Then he stood up and tried to see through the big glass windows to the interior.

"Blake? What's going on?" When he didn't answer her she said, "Sit down and tell me what the problem is."

He held the phone out to her. "Take a look."

A message had popped up on the screen. *"I know what you did."*

Then the phone chimed again. *"You can change your number all you want, but you can't get away from me."*

As she was reading it the chime sounded a third time and yet another text scrolled up.

"Bodyguards won't help you."

And just like that the little crackles of electricity they were both ignoring, the dance her hormones kept trying to do, flat out died. Samantha Quenel, girl with a crush, disappeared and was replaced by Sam Quenel, super bodyguard. Every nerve in her body went on full alert.

"Sit, please," she repeated. "You're doing exactly what he wants."

"But—"

"Sit down, Blake." She tried not to shout, but her words came out louder than she wanted. She swallowed and inhaled a slow breath.

"I can't believe the fucker followed me here." He sat with obvious reluctance. "I can feel him here. Jesus, Sam, I swear I can feel his eyes on me. That fucker is here someplace."

"First of all, if he's so tuned in to your schedule he hits all your tour stops, it's a given he goes wherever you do. That means following you to Arrowhead Bay."

"But—"

"That means he knows about your meeting at Vigilance, which is how he knows you have security now. Looking for him here isn't going to help.

It will just give him the satisfaction of knowing he got to you. Anyway, it's possible he checked you out, then moved out of sight to send the text."

Blake clenched his fists. "So he sat here, watching me? Watching us? Laughing his ass off?"

"I don't think he's doing much laughing, but yes, he probably watched you for a while."

"He's spying on me." Every muscle in Blake's face tightened. "Do you know how that feels?"

"I do. But again, he wants to get a reaction out of you. That's the point of the whole thing. Of doing this out in public."

"You think he's hung around to watch every time he's left me a note? Sent me a text?" His hand closed around his water glass so tightly she was afraid he'd crack it.

Sam nodded. "Whenever he could."

"But I looked around every time and never saw anyone." A muscle twitched in his cheek.

"Blake. Listen to me. You wouldn't know if he—or she—was there anyway, unless it was someone you know."

"Which makes it highly unlikely it's Annemarie. Which it isn't."

"Unless she's got someone doing this for her." She pushed back from the table and stood. "Just sit tight for a minute."

Tension radiated from his body. She was worried he might decide to stomp through the restaurant and ask everyone if he could see their cell phone. "Where are you going?"

"To the ladies' room. I want to do a casual look around. I can get a better read on the crowd than you can."

"But what if he's watching you?"

"So? Women go to the restroom all the time. It's a known fact. Just hang on, okay?"

On the way to the ladies' room she casually looked around the room, searching for someone by himself—or herself—doing their best to look relaxed and at ease. But the few singles she spotted were either reading or sitting at the bar chatting with the bartender. Of course, that didn't necessarily mean anything. She'd seen people blend into a place so innocuously that they were easy to overlook.

Right now, though, what they needed was to get back to Vigilance and check out Blake's phone.

"Nothing made my senses tingle," she told him when she was seated at the table again. "He could still be hanging around here, though. Just in case, signal very casually for the check."

"We're leaving?"

"We're going back to Vigilance where we have technical support. I want one of the guys to take a look at your phone and see if they can find anything. Those guys could track an angel in hell, I swear."

"I'd like to find this asshole, drag him out in the street by his hair and beat the crap out of him."

"I can't say I blame you." She sipped ice water while they waited for the check. "Arrowhead Bay is a small town, so you think it would be easy to find a stranger, someone who would stand out in a crowd." She frowned. "Except—"

"Except for all the boat traffic we get," he finished for her, "and then the snowbird influx. Not to mention people heading south who drive through here because they aren't rushed and they find the interstate boring. This person could be any one of them."

Blake rubbed his jaw.

"This is just one fucking mess," he growled. "I find myself looking at everyone whenever I go anywhere wondering if this asshole is standing next to me silently laughing his ass off."

"I won't lie to you. Anything is possible. But that's why you have me. So I can do the looking." She watched as he signed the tab. "One more thing. I also want to pick up my car."

He frowned. "Because?"

Sam laughed. "Maybe because I'm a big girl and like to have my own car with me." Then she sobered. "Kidding aside, I have gizmos in mine that you don't."

As they walked to the parking lot, she continued to scan everyone around them, looking for any sign that someone was paying unusual attention to them. Everything looked normal, but she'd been doing this long enough to know that didn't necessarily mean anything. The invisible antennae she'd developed in the military and then with Vigilance were vibrating at full strength. Whoever this bastard was, he or she wasn't far away.

Another vehicle was parked blocking their view of Blake's car, so it wasn't until they got past it that everything amped up. The first thing they saw was the slashed tires.

"God damn it." He slammed his hand on the hood so hard she was afraid he'd break a bone or two. "Fucking son of a bitch."

Sam walked around to the driver's side and wanted to do some swearing herself. Someone had spray painted that side of the car with black paint.

I know what you did.

The distress that was obvious in his expression made her give one of his hands a quick squeeze, ignoring the jolt of electricity that raced along her arm.

"Don't touch anything," she told him, took out her phone and speed dialed the office.

"What's up?" Avery asked. "How did the lunch go?"

"Would have been better without the crap that happened. Listen, we've got a situation here."

"Such as?"

"It looks like Blake's fan has followed him to Arrowhead Bay. He got a text on his phone while we were eating. Someone also slashed his tires and sprayed that message on his car."

"Damn," Avery swore.

"No kidding. Is Mike around? Can you send him over? We need wheels and I want to get this car towed back to the office. When we get it back there we can print it, although I don't think this guy is stupid enough to leave any trace of himself."

"You're probably right. Okay, let me get Mike over there and have someone call for the tow truck." She paused. "Watch yourself. Whoever this is might be miles away but my gut tells me he's somewhere close enough to observe the results of his handiwork."

"No argument there."

"And Sam? I have information for Blake on his former PA, so come right into the office when you get back here."

"Good or bad?" she asked.

"Neither. Just sad."

"Oh." She glanced at Blake, standing with his hands in his pockets, muttering to himself. "Should I prepare him?"

"No. I'll handle it. Just get back here."

"Fine. I'll be watching for Mike." She slid her phone back into her jeans pocket.

"Who's Mike?" Blake was staring at his car as if he wanted to blow it up.

"Mike Pérez. Another of our agents, also between assignments." She ran over the arrangements with him. "Blake, listen. Knowing for sure your stalker followed you to Arrowhead Bay changes the game plan a little."

He frowned. "How? In what way?"

"Knowing you hired Vigilance gives him momentum to up his game and push your buttons even harder."

He grunted. "I don't know if that's possible. If I get my hands on him I'd cheerfully wring his neck."

"I know, but we don't want him to know that he's gotten to you." She kept her voice calm and reasonable. She could see he was doing his best to control his frustration and she didn't want him to blow unless they were completely alone. "That will frustrate him and that could lead to him making mistakes as he takes bigger and bigger risks."

"That's what I'm afraid of," he snapped. "Not for me, but for people around me, especially my readers. I don't want someone else getting hurt because some maniac has a grudge against me for I don't even know what."

He shoved his hands in his pockets and kicked at a stone.

Sam said nothing, amazed that he was as much under control as he was. But then she noticed the taut line of his body, the twitch of a muscle in his jaw, and realized his control was far from real. She slipped on her sunglasses and scanned the parking lot, a tiny thread of unease winding through her.

Whoever this was could have sent the texts, attacked the car and then driven off, but her instincts told her otherwise. This idiot was out there somewhere watching them, and was damn good at hiding himself. Blending in. Waiting for Blake's reaction. That was half of his satisfaction, to watch Blake's reaction. She'd make sure to drill him on exactly how things would go from now on whenever they set foot in public.

She pulled out her cell again and while ostensibly taking pictures of the car from all angles, she managed to catch most of the parking lot without being too obvious. She also caught what she could of the marina parking lot next door.

By the time she was finished, Mike Pérez had pulled up close to them in a black SUV. He climbed out and stood there studying the car for a moment.

"Damn. Someone is definitely unhappy with you," he told Blake.

"Don't I know it." Blake kicked one of the slashed tires. "Fuck. Just fuck."

Mike turned to Sam. "Want me to do a look-see around the lot just in case?"

"Just in case," she repeated, "although I think whoever this is has left already. I did get pictures of all the cars, even part of the marina lot. I want to enlarge them at the office and study them to see if anything looks suspicious. I figured he'd want to stay around to check out the results of his artwork."

"He could be just out of your line of sight," Mike pointed out. "Or even hiding in one of the cars. I'll take a look, then we'll get down to business."

"When we get the car to the office I want it printed, even though I'm sure it's a fool's errand. Any you find probably won't belong to our mystery nut."

He shrugged. "No matter. I called for the tow and the truck should be here any minute. Take the SUV and get back to the office. Avery's waiting for you."

"Okay." She turned to Blake, still rigid with anger, his jaw clenched so tight she worried it would crack. "Let's get to it."

As she drove them back to the agency, she went over in her mind the best way to tell him of some other changes, such as her intention to move into his parents' house with him, even if she had to sleep on the couch. She knew Avery would suggest it if she didn't. If this stalker was escalating, leaving Blake there by himself was a bad idea. When they went back to Tampa, he'd better have a guest room for her. And on the road the door between their adjoining rooms would always be left open. Stalkers like this didn't let closed doors stop them.

But as she drove them back to Vigilance, she was far too aware that her bigger worry wasn't protecting him. It was protecting herself and her heart. Time to call on that good old military discipline she'd learned.

Chapter 4

The stalker sat in his motel room, scrolling through the pictures on his cell phone. He'd managed to take them without anyone paying attention to him. It was amazing how invisible one could make themselves, and he'd perfected that art.

He wasn't surprised Morgan had hired security. Okay, a bodyguard. The jackass was right to be worried and afraid. If he thought hiring Vigilance would be a deterrent, he had another think coming.

He'd looked up Vigilance on the Internet but there was little about them to find, just a few words about their incredible setup and unequaled skills in all areas of security. It was such delicious frosting on the cake to do this right under their noses. He nearly laughed out loud at the thought.

The stalker had cyber skills that could counteract anything Vigilance put in play. The only thing he couldn't control was the bodyguard, but he had plans for her, too. Later, at the appropriate time. Everything had to fit into the plan, and the plan could be easily adjusted when you were as smart as he was.

Besides, what he had in mind for Blake Morgan couldn't be fixed by just upping security. His electronic skills were coming in handy as he moved his plan forward. He could hack into anything that was out there, no matter how well protected people thought they were. And disguise himself beneath layers of dark protection.

Leaving the messages for Morgan gave him a hot thrill. In almost every case he'd been able to conceal himself somewhere, using high magnification binoculars to see Morgan's reaction when he got the message. A few times he'd even been able to take photos. The shots were so good he thought about sending a couple of them to the man.

Cloning telephones was so easy it was laughable. He'd gotten Morgan's without the man being any the wiser or paying any attention to the person sitting near him in the coffee shop. Presto! He had the cell number. Ditto when he cloned another that he used to send texts from.

He'd have to ditch the phone and get another soon. He was sure the stupid female Vigilance had assigned to him would insist on taking Morgan's cell back to the office and letting their techs go to work on it. Of course, the number they'd get from it would only lead back to that woman who had no idea who he was. Poor Sarah Jo Murphy or whatever the hell her name was would probably have a fit when she was accused of sending threatening texts.

He'd love to be able to watch when they went to talk to her. Maybe she'd be angry at Morgan, thinking he had something to do with this. The more people he could turn against the man, the happier he was. And this was only the beginning of his campaign.

He took apart the phone he'd used to send today's text, removed the SIM card and flushed it down the toilet. Then he crushed the phone itself beneath the heel of his boots. He brushed the shattered remains into a plastic baggie and sealed it. Somewhere out of town he'd stop, open the bag, and scatter the remnants on the side of the road. Goodbye, phone.

No problem, though. He'd bought more than two dozen burner phones, knowing he'd need them, aware that he couldn't use any one for too long. And he'd made sure to buy them in a bunch of different stores in different locations. No matter how often they checked Morgan's phone to see who was texting him, he could stay one step ahead of them.

Sometimes he got so excited at what he planned for the conclusion he almost wet his pants. He could just see it now, the big scene. And he'd already written the note to share with everyone, telling them all just what a thief and a faker Blake Morgan was. At the last signing, the sight of those people fawning all over the man had made him nauseous. Didn't they know this whole thing was a lie? That he was a fraud, a user?

God, how he'd hated seeing that smug bastard sitting in the restaurant today, sharing an intimate meal with a gorgeous woman. It didn't matter that the woman was his new security. He didn't deserve her. He didn't deserve any of it. The stalker opened the leather briefcase he'd placed on the small table and took out one of the notebooks. Drinking one of the many soft drinks he'd bought at a big box store, he leafed slowly through the pages. It was all there, written out carefully in neat, very legible script.

He'd gone over it so many times he had it almost memorized.

Then he booted up his laptop and accessed one of the files on the hard drive. They both covered the same material but he wanted to have the originals in *her* handwriting. For one thing, they were his authentication. For another, he loved reading the way she'd expanded on and developed the written notes.

He couldn't wait until it could all be made public, but he had to control himself. He battled so many conflicting emotions and right now he needed to put a leash on them. He was building a carefully constructed campaign that would do the most damage to Blake Morgan, and if he rushed things the conclusion would lose its effect. Wringing Morgan's neck now would only give him momentary satisfaction.

Still, when he thought again of what brought him to this, a fit of rage seized him and he swept the empty soda can and a cheap vase off the table. They crashed to the floor, the carpet blunting the sound of the shattering vase. Now he knew what murderers meant when they said they were driven to commit their crimes.

He took a deep breath to calm himself down. Lack of control would get him no place.

Follow the plan. That way you'll cause him the maximum amount of suffering and destroy his stolen career.

Okay, then. He needed a task to focus on. He needed to find out who the bodyguard was, what her skills were, and maybe what their relationship was.

He pulled his laptop over and uploaded the pictures he'd taken today. He'd managed to highjack some very sophisticated facial recognition software that would help him identify the mystery woman. No matter how camera shy someone was, everyone got caught at some time or other.

While the program was running he planned his afternoon. Morgan and that female would be busy at Vigilance for a while, so he'd check to see where the man was staying. There were really only two choices—the B and B or the home of his parents. He'd scope out both of them, just to see how that would fit into his plans.

He was mulling over possibilities when the bell rang on his laptop, signaling success with the program. Yes! There she was, the bodyguard. Samantha Quenel. And she was also from Arrowhead Bay. Had Morgan dated her when they were younger? Were they rekindling an attraction from long ago? Oh, yeah, he'd bet she'd be guarding the man's body alright. Probably in bed.

Anger rose in him again, as he thought of the two of them, naked and rolling around on the sheets. That man didn't deserve to have anyone, not after what he'd done. If Samantha Quenel fell for the man's line of bullshit, the stalker would take great pleasure in showing her exactly what a shithead the man was.

But not yet. He had a plan and he was determined to stick to it. Of course, he also wanted to take advantage of unexpected opportunities. He swallowed a smile as he thought how nice it would be, if Morgan was staying at the house, to ruin something personal and cause him a little more grief. He deserved all he could get and more. He suddenly remembered when he'd researched the man, he'd learned his mother collected antiques. Excellent.

Oh, yes, he'd destroy something important to them just as Morgan had done to him.

I'm smarter than they are. I'll always be two steps ahead of them... until we get to the big finale.

He checked his watch. If he hustled his ass, he could get there before they were through with whatever they were doing at Vigilance. He had already scoped out the house. Getting in wouldn't be a problem. Not for him.

Mentally he rubbed his hands in glee as images ran through his mind. His rage slowly abated as he threw himself into this new project.

I know what you did, and I'm going to make you pay for it.

* * * *

"I'm tired of this guy fucking with my life," Blake growled as he handed over his cell phone to Avery.

"It won't be as bad now that you'll have Sam with you," Avery soothed. "She'll keep watch on everything around you."

"I might be better off just hiding in a hotel room," he grumbled.

"That's not very realistic," Sam pointed out, "and won't be necessary now."

"It's apparent he's got a lot of tech savvy." Avery gave him a sly grin. "But not as much as we do. If there's anything to be found, our guys can find it. I promise you."

"I'm not complaining," he told her. "Just mad. Damn it. I'll do anything to catch whoever this is. But what's the deal here? Sam says every time my phone is compromised we're going to ditch it and fire up a new one with a new number? Is she right?"

Avery nodded. "We're hoping to drive this person nuts while tracking whoever it is."

Blake snorted. "I hope it doesn't drive *me* nuts while we're doing it. What a load of crap." He rubbed his jaw.

"Luckily, based on what you told me earlier, you don't have too many people to notify each time. Most of the world contacts you through your public number so this only affects what, five or six people?"

Blake swallowed a sigh. This was getting to be more and more complicated. "Maybe a couple more but I guess not all that many."

"Besides, if your stalker has to keep chasing down your new number electronically, he might get tired of it, try something else and make a mistake. I've seen it happen too many times."

He knew that. He was just irritated at the way his mysterious stalker was screwing up his life. He should be concentrating on the remainder of his tour and working on his next book.

"Henry asked me why I thought whoever this is doesn't use the phone with my so-called public number on it. He'd know I can't keep changing that one."

"What did you tell him?"

"Exactly what you told me earlier today. That he likes showing me he can get past whatever security steps I put into place. That no matter how many times I change phones, he can still reach me. It's like a game to him. The other would be too easy. Besides, I get so many dozens and dozens of calls and texts, he could get lost in the shuffle and not taken seriously."

"It still makes sense to me," she agreed.

"So what do I do for phones?" He raked his fingers through his hair. This guy was jacking the hell out of his life. "Run out and buy one every time mine gets hacked?"

Avery grinned. "That's where we come in." She opened what looked like a shoebox on her desk. Inside, each nestled in its own little cradle, were ten phones. "If you buy these in a store, you just pay for the minutes, and the phone comes with a number. When you finish with the phone, you throw it away and the number is history."

"But not with these," he guessed.

"No." Sam grinned. "We use these a lot. Our guys here program the numbers into them but they also install a little gizmo that hopefully allows us to ping back whoever is hacking you. Give us their location."

Blake just shook his head. "Man, I read about this stuff when I'm doing research for a book, but it's another thing to actually have it part of your life."

"Hopefully not for long." Avery closed the box. "Here. These are all set to go. Now." The smile disappeared. "Sit down, both of you. I was planning to call you and get you back here, anyway, because I have an update."

Blake dropped into a chair in front of the desk. "The way you say it doesn't sound good."

Avery shook her head. "No, I'm sorry, it isn't. We finally located Annemarie."

"Where is she?" He leaned forward. "Did you ask her about this? Did she have an idea who this might be?"

"I'm sorry. The news is not good."

"Don't tell me she's involved." He slammed his hand on the arm of the chair. "I won't believe it."

Avery shook her head. "She's not involved. I hate to tell you this, but she's dead."

For a moment he couldn't speak. All the blood seemed to drain from his head and he couldn't make his mouth work.

"Dead?" He finally got the word out. "Annemarie dead? That's impossible. You must have gotten it wrong."

"No, I didn't, and I'm so sorry, Blake." Avery handed him a sheet of paper. "Here. I printed out all the details. She was killed in a one-car accident on a very rainy night."

"But where? How? What—" Why couldn't he make his brain work?

"According to the report," Avery told him, "she was in Maine, not far from Houlton. Do you know if she had family there or anything? Or was she visiting someone? The police report doesn't say."

"I have no idea." He felt sick to his stomach at the idea of Annemarie dead. "I told you she never discussed family or even friends. And I'm sorry to confess my ignorance by telling you I don't know where in Maine Houlton is."

"It's up near the Canadian coast," Sam told him. When everyone looked at her, she shrugged. "I had a roommate in college that came from Houlton. I visited her a couple of times before we lost touch with each other."

Blake drew in a long breath and let it out slowly. Annemarie dead? How was that even possible?

Because people die, idiot.

He closed his eyes and saw an image of Annemarie. She had been so enthusiastic for most of their four years, keeping him organized with ruthless efficiency, always with a smile on her face. What in hell had driven her to run away without a word of warning? And what would the next body blow be?

He glanced at Sam, saw her watching him with sympathy and...and something else. If only he could wrap his arms around her, put his head on her shoulders, and weep. And then take comfort from her body. He swallowed a hysterical laugh when he thought about the severity of the situation and yet his body was demanding that he lose himself in this woman he was feeling more for by the minute.

He looked at the sheet of paper. "Damn. This happened less than a week after she quit. I can't believe no one notified me."

"If you weren't listed as her person to call, then they'd have no reason to. Unfortunately, there's nothing in the report to indicate who that person was."

"But everyone knew she worked for me," he protested. Then he stopped. "I guess not. PAs aren't the most publicly visible people. Tell me what happened," he demanded.

"You know as much as I do." Avery nodded at the sheet of paper. "I only know what's on the report. She was driving late at night, in a bad thunderstorm. At the moment we have no idea where she was headed. The assumption is she was driving too fast and lost control of her car. It skidded off the road into a tree. The report says she died on impact."

Annemarie dead! No. Not possible. He shook his head, barely able to comprehend it. She had been so vivacious, so full of life.

"Are they sure it was an accident? Maybe this maniac who's after me had a hand in this."

Avery shook her head. "Nothing indicates it, but I'm calling the state police anyway to double check. They were the ones who filed the report."

"Please." He took a moment to pull himself together. Dead! He could hardly absorb the word. "Get me all the information you can including who claimed the body. There must have been someone they notified. Someone who—"

Avery held up her hand. "I've given you all the information I have so far. Of course we're looking into it further. But I at least wanted you to have this information right away."

"Thanks." He closed his eyes, conjuring up the last image he had of Annemarie. She'd been running around her hotel room, throwing stuff into her suitcase, driving herself and him nuts and not giving him any information about why she was leaving and why right then.

Then a thought popped into his head. "What about her apartment? Someone had to terminate the lease, close it up, get her stuff. Right? All that information is on my other cell phone." He paused. "Which is in my briefcase that I left in the SUV."

"I'll get it," Sam told him and jogged out of the room.

Neither Blake nor Avery said a word until Sam returned with the case. Blake took out his other cell phone and scrolled through his contacts until he found the entry for Annemarie and handed it to Avery. She copied down the information and handed the cell back to him.

"I realize you're really shaken by the news about Annemarie, but I have one more piece of business we need to go over. I had a nice conversation with your agent. He gave me all the details about the remainder of your signing tour." She tapped her tablet and studied the page it brought up. "His office has done a good job with all the arrangements, but we need to change that up."

Change things?

"Why?" he asked. "His assistant always works it out so everything goes smoothly."

"We'll be handling those from this office instead. We won't do them ahead of time, either. If whoever this is can hack into passenger manifests and hotel registrations—which, by the way, is entirely possible—we want to give him as little lead time as possible."

"Henry usually emails me with all this info," he pointed out. "Annemarie made sure I got to where I was supposed to be when I needed to be there." Just saying her name made his heart ache. "Who will be my point of contact now?"

"That will be Samantha." Avery smiled. "Your new personal assistant. You've got a week before you leave. That should be plenty of time for you to bring her up to speed on everything you need from her."

"I'm sure I can handle it," Sam told them.

"Good." Avery made a note on her tablet. "And Sam will be staying at your parents' house with you. I assume that's okay? As your bodyguard, she needs to be with you at all times."

He almost said that's what he wanted, too, but he bit his tongue. Despite Sam's belief they had to take this slowly, he knew doing just that was going to be hell.

Avery opened the box on her desk. "Let's get you set up with one of your new phones and then I think you two should get out of here."

She selected one of the phones and peeled off the little sticker on the back with the number. She checked to make sure it was good to go, gave Blake the sticker, and told him to memorize it.

"Okay, Avery. I think we're all set here." Sam touched Blake's shoulder. "Come on, big man. Let's get out of here."

He wanted to tell her his brain was falling apart. Instead he just pushed himself out of the chair, and picked up his briefcase.

"Thanks, Avery. For everything." He was still shaken by the news. "You'll check all that stuff about Annemarie, right?"

She nodded. "I will. Go on. Get out of here."

His suitcase and messenger bag were waiting in the hallway when he walked out of the office.

"I was so pissed off back at the restaurant I forgot all about them." Great. Good thing his head was attached. "This guy is really screwing with my brain."

"That's what he wants," Sam pointed out. "I'm going to help you make sure that doesn't happen."

"Yeah?" He shook his head. "How do you plan to do that? Get me a new brain? Sam, I've got all these signings coming up, ending with a big one at the end. I have to be on my game."

"And that's why you have me," she reminded him. "Come on. Let's get going."

He followed Sam out to the parking lot, trying to absorb the fact that someone had really turned his life upside down. Annemarie was dead. He was being stalked. He had an itch he couldn't scratch for his new bodyguard. What in the hell would be next?

Chapter 5

Blake was silent as they drove away from Vigilance. Sam knew he was still digesting Avery's news about Annemarie. She thought about swinging by Fresh Roasted for their special coffee, then wondered if maybe a slug of bourbon was more in line with what Blake really wanted. It was obvious Annemarie's death had been a real blow to him.

He blew out a breath. "I have to get my head screwed on right. I owe it to my readers. And I don't want to be in a position of making excuses for my piss poor attitude."

"Be glad you've got some time to digest all of this. And maybe before you have to leave we'll have all the answers."

"Wouldn't that be nice," he grunted.

Sam reached over and gave his arm a squeeze, and nearly jerked her hand back at the jolt of electricity that simple contact created.

We're taking it slow, she reminded herself. Seeing what's really there. But with each passing minute she was afraid she'd be the one to break the rules rather than Blake.

"I need to make a stop at my place first," she said. "Just long enough to pack a suitcase and get some other things I'm going to need. And don't worry," she assured him. "I've learned how to travel light."

At the little cottage where she lived she insisted Blake come in.

He frowned but followed her inside. "You don't really think whoever this is will do something to harm me if I wait in the car, do you?"

"No, because I don't believe he's even halfway through his little game." She shook her head. "I can promise you he's got a lot more tricks up his sleeve, and probably a spectacular finale." She waved at an easy chair. "Have a seat. I'll only be a few minutes."

"Something to look forward to." Blake dropped into the chair, leaned back and closed his eyes. "I just wish I knew what the fuck I did that was so terrible it prompted something like this."

"It could be something so insignificant you'd never think of it," she called from her bedroom. "Let me get everything together here. When we get to your place, we'll do a little mental exercise I learned a while ago and see if we can dig anything out of your memories."

"You think I haven't tried to do that?" he snapped.

"I'm sure you have," she soothed.

She did not want to get him riled up. He was dealing with enough as it was, but she was sure somewhere hidden in the recesses of his brain was the trigger for this whole thing. Checking to make sure she had what she needed, she closed her suitcase, zipped it shut, and carried it to the living rom. Next came her laptop with its carrying case and the little gizmos she kept in there, like thumb drives if she needed them. She gathered up her cords and charger, stuck them in the case and zipped it shut.

"Okay." She smiled at Blake. "Done. Let's get going."

"Already? I thought Annemarie was the only woman who could pack that fast."

"Six years in the military trains you good. Come on. Let's get out of here."

"I forgot you were in the military." Blake pounced on that as soon as they were back in the car. "Military police, if I recall what Avery told me."

"For part of it. Maybe I'll tell you about it one of these nights." Or maybe not.

She glanced at him again, not happy with the pinched look on his face or the tension vibrating from his body. Without saying anything she decided a trip to Fresh Roasted and its companion store, Fresh from the Oven, was in order after all.

"You don't need to do this, Sam. I'm good. I'm not a kid who needs a trip to the candy store to take the edge off."

But he looked like someone who had been run over.

"Then it's for me, and I'll share. Wait here. I'll be right back."

When she returned he was sitting rigid in the front seat, eyes staring straight ahead.

"You think he's watching us right now?"

"If he is, let's not give him the satisfaction of thinking he's got you on edge. Here." She handed him one of the go cups. "This should help steady you. Their coffee will fix just about anything."

"Unnecessary but thanks." He blew on it to cool it a little before taking a swallow.

"No problem." She put the muffins on the console. "For later."

She backed out of the parking spot and headed toward the Morgan house. Again they rode in silence. When they got to the house and were settled in, she vowed to make him talk about this situation with Annemarie. She knew her death was devastating. But she needed him on full alert if they were to figure out how to deal with this maniac.

"I'll check to see if there's room in the garage for your car," he told her when they pulled into the driveway. "I don't know if they took one of their cars and left it in Tampa when they boarded the cruise ship or not. Let's get inside so I can check."

But he sat for a moment in the car, just staring at the house. Sam wondered what was going through his mind. Was he glad to be back here, even under the circumstances? He'd said he was glad to be here with her. She wished she could trust his feelings. And hers. She *wanted* to trust them, because holy hell, she wanted him in the worst way.

At last, with a sigh, he climbed out of the car, grabbed his suitcase and messenger bag and carried them up to the porch. She followed right behind him, waiting while he pulled out his key ring and unlocked the door. She had always loved this house, even when she wanted to kill Blake. With its wide porch and decorative shutters, it had the same Key West look as Vigilance and many of the other houses in Arrowhead Bay.

"Let me go in first," Sam told him, nudging him aside.

"Why? This is my parents' home. Surely you don't think he'd do something here?"

"I think this person has no boundaries. Besides, I'm not taking any chances with your safety. Wait right here."

She pulled a gun from the small of her back and eased into the house. Ignoring her orders, Blake followed in right behind her. He dropped his stuff on the floor of the foyer.

"Even though I don't live here anymore," he told Sam, "it still feels like home."

"That says a lot about your parents, but I thought I told you to wait outside."

"Yeah, that's not happening. Besides, he's had plenty of chances to kill me if he wanted to."

"I hear you, but—" She had turned and taken two steps into the living room when she stopped short. "Shit."

"What is it?" Blake pushed her aside. "Fuck, Sam. I can't believe this. Damn it all to hell!"

Every visible surface of the room had a white sheet of paper on it. She walked over to one of them and stared down at it.

I know what you did and you'll be punished for it.

Oh, God. The anguished look on his face shot straight to her heart.

"Don't touch anything," she told him. "I've got this. Go in the kitchen and sit down while I check the rest of the house. I mean it, Blake. I don't want to have to worry about you. Then I'm calling Avery."

He took two steps in that direction, then came to such an abrupt stop she barely avoided colliding with him.

"Shit. Sam, come here and see this. I do not believe he did this."

What now, she thought, and looked at the spot on the floor where he was pointing. Centered on a plain sheet of the same paper were shards of what had once been a statue or some other china piece.

She wasn't sure what she was looking at, except the broken pieces of a knickknack. When she rested her hand on his shoulder she could feel his tension vibrating. "What is it?"

He took a deep breath and let it out slowly. "It's a Lladró statue my mother got when she and my father took a trip to Spain. She collects things like this. God. How the hell am I going to tell her about this? She loves this stuff." He looked closer. "There's a piece of paper in the center of it wadded up in a tiny ball."

He started to reach for it but she yanked his hand back.

"Leave it. I'm calling Vigilance and getting a team over here."

Sam checked everything, including the linen closet, grateful she didn't find anyone or anything. Then she put her gun away and walked into the kitchen where Blake was sitting in a chair at the table, head in hands.

"Who the fuck is doing this?" He sounded as much bewildered as mad. "And why? I swear, Sam, I've never done anything to hurt anyone. At least not knowingly. Certainly not anything that merits this kind of reaction."

Again she lifted her phone to make her call, but before she could hit the speed dial number the signal for an incoming call rang. The Vigilance number popped up on her screen.

"Yeah, Avery? I was just about—"

"Where are you?" Avery interrupted.

"At the Morgans'." Sam frowned. "Why?"

"We've got a big problem, Sam. We're no longer dealing with just a stalker here. This guy just upped his game in a major way."

"What do you mean?" Sam tightened her grip on the cell.

"Just listen and don't repeat anything I say until you hear it all. I had let Sheri know about Blake, since we really don't know what this stalker is going to do. About an hour ago she got a call from Sharon Kennelly. She and her husband live in the house behind the Morgans. Sharon came home after a late lunch with friends and found her husband beaten unconscious in the back yard. Sam, he's in pretty bad shape. Sheri called me as soon as she got to the scene. She's convinced it has something to do with Blake's situation. It's all just too coincidental."

"I see." Sam kept her voice under control so she wouldn't send any signals to Blake. She glanced out one of the back windows toward the Kennellys' house. "Is that what all those people are in the back yard for?"

"Yes. EMTs took Grant to the hospital right away. He was unconscious and they said he was lucky he wasn't dead he was in such bad shape. Sheri sent one of her officers with them and he took Sharon Kennelly. He'll stay on site guarding Grant until we assess the situation. I don't want to leave the man unprotected. He'll also try to get a statement if Grant regains consciousness before Sheri gets there."

"I hear you." She was aware of Blake coming up behind her now now, could almost feel his eyes boring holes in her back. "I was just about to call you, anyway. You need to get someone over here. Now. Our mysterious friend broke in here and decorated the living room with a slew of messages. And this time he's added a little something to it."

"Like what?"

"Like some personalized damage. Can you get someone here to print the place and bag the stuff?"

"I'd bet money Grant Kennelly spotted him somehow, went to see what was going on and the stalker attacked him. Hold on." Sam heard voices in the background, then Avery came back on the phone again. "Sheri's still there and I'm coming, too. Oh, and find out when Blake's parents are expected back. We'll station someone at the house until this thing is taken care of."

"I'll see you when you get here."

Sam disconnected and shoved the phone in her pocket. Blake was staring outside at the activity.

"What's going on, Sam?" His voice was tight with tension. "What's happened now? If it has to do with me, I want to know."

"That was Avery. She's on her way over."

"For this?" He pointed toward the living room. "This doesn't seem like something she'd need to see for herself." When she didn't say anything, he growled, "Come on, Sam. Tell me. We can't have any secrets here. What the hell is going on? And why are there people all over the Kennellys' back yard? Did she happen to say anything about that?"

Sam took a deep breath. "Let's sit down at the table for a minute."

"I'm fine standing," he snapped. "Just spit it out."

She studied his face, checking to make sure he wasn't about to fall apart. "We think that when your stalker broke into this house to do his damage, your neighbor in the back saw him and went to check on him. Blake, he was beaten up pretty badly. According to the EMTs, it's a miracle he isn't dead."

"What?" Every bit of color drained from his face and his eyes widened in shock. It took him a minute to speak. "Grant Kennelly was beaten nearly to death? Are you fucking kidding me?"

Sam was afraid he might pass out. She had to fight the urge to throw her arms around him, press her body to his and whisper soothing words in his ear. To give him comfort the best way she knew, except this was neither the time nor the place. But she was pleased when he reached for her hand and gripped it tightly.

Sam shook her head. "Sheri got the call about an hour ago. She'll be over here in a minute, as soon as Avery arrives. She'll tell you all about it."

"Where is he? I want to see him." He started toward the door.

Sam held up a hand to stop him. "He's at County General. And you can't see him for a couple of very good reasons."

"Yeah?" The look he gave her was a mixture of rage and hostility. "And what would they be?"

"For one thing," she told him, in a voice she hoped would calm him, "he's unconscious and being examined to see how bad the damage is. Sheri said it was pretty bad."

Sam watched the rest of the color leach from Blake's face.

"Jesus," he whispered.

"For another, you can't do him any good. You have to protect yourself right now." And that was her concern. His safety.

"Isn't that a little self-absorbed? Grant nearly got killed because of me. I want him to know how sorry I am. And his wife." He raked his fingers through his hair with his free hand. "Sharon. God. She must be a mess."

"An officer is staying with Grant and Sharon's sister is coming from Sarasota to be with her. Sheri will take care of them. My concern is keeping you safe. That's what you hired me to do, remember?"

"Maybe I should have hired someone to take care of the neighbors, too."

"Blake." She took one of his hands in both her of hers, glad when he didn't pull away. "No one could have foreseen this. It's all being handled. We were caught with our pants down this time. Everything was focused on you personally and Avery knew your parents were out of town. Our bad. We'll be more on top of things after this."

Blake suddenly looked as if all he air had been let out of him. "I can't imagine what the hell I've ever done to bring this on myself."

On impulse, she lifted his hand and placed a kiss on it.

So much for not sending the wrong signals.

"Vigilance will find out. They always do." She tried to find words to reassure him. "Blake, I am so very, very sorry. I know that doesn't help, but I promise you, we'll get this bastard."

"I hope before he destroys my entire life and everyone around me." He snapped his fingers. "My folks. They'll be back from their cruise shortly. I can't leave them here unprotected."

"All taken care of," she assured him. "Let me know exactly when they plan to return. Avery's going to assign someone to keep an eye on them until this is all over."

Blake snorted a laugh. "I'm sure they'll love that. My dad will probably have twenty-seven fits, but he'll be happy that my mother will be safe. But how do I explain that something I did caused all this and I don't even know what the fuck it is?" He sighed. "But okay, as long as they are protected he can get as mad as he wants." He looked out the window at the back yard. "There's a ton of cops out there. I didn't think the Arrowhead Bay force was that big."

"It isn't. I mean, there's hardly ever any crime except speeding, shoplifting, and the occasional domestic abuse. Sheri has an arrangement with the county sheriff to provide people when it's needed."

"Like today," he said, his tone edged with bitterness.

"Yes, like today."

She'd tell him to sit down and try not to think about what happened, but that would sound stupid. She wanted a way to make him better and take away the pain that etched lines in his face. She could feel his pain herself, was searching for the right words to say and not doing a very good job. A knock on the door interrupted her thoughts and she hurried to let Avery in. Right behind her was her sister, Sheridan March, Arrowhead Bay's chief of police. They both looked very grim.

"How about some details?" Sam asked, then stood back to let everyone in. "Can you fill me in on everything?"

"Yes. Fine. Let's check what your stalker did first." Avery stopped at the entrance to the living room and took in every bit of the scene. "Wow! Whoever this is wants to make sure Blake gets the message." She shook her head when she spotted the destruction of the statue. "And he continues to personalize it." She turned back to Sam. "Where's Blake?"

"Blake's right here." He walked in from the kitchen and stood next to Sam. "Hello, Sheri. How about filling me in on everything? Is it true this bastard beat the shit out of Grant Kennelly?"

Sheri nodded. "At least that's what our theory is."

"Grant knows my folks are away. If he saw some stranger trying to get in he'd come over to check it out. Are you running this investigation yourself?"

Sheri shook her head. "Normally I would, but this has much larger implications. If in fact it's Blake's stalker, I want people experienced with this and with more resources on it. The county sheriff is sending a detective who will be lead on this. Plus we get to use the county resources. Those people in the yard are from the medical examiner's office and from forensics."

"I assume the yellow tape is around where Grant was found?"

"Yes. We're looking for footprints, impressions, anything we can pick up. We're taking grass clipping everywhere there's blood spatter."

Sam tugged him away from the window and the scene in the yard. "You don't need to see that. Come on."

"I want to know everything. This happened because of me. Grant sure didn't expect to get beaten all to hell for his troubles."

"Our theory is it happened on your back porch. Then he was carried unconscious across both yards, right through that row of bushes. The earth is damp. I think Grant must have watered earlier today. Anyway, the added weight of carrying a guy that big made the attacker step harder into the damp earth and we've got a couple of good footprints. At least we'll know what size shoe he wears," Sheri said.

"Sheri's people are doing a canvass of the area," Avery added, "to see if anyone noticed strange vehicles or anything. Just anything out of the ordinary. We know he was at the Driftwood. He probably saw you drive away and followed you."

"Followed?" Blake interrupted. "I thought you said we were clean."

"I was watching for anything like that," Sam interjected, "but with the tourist traffic it was hard to tell."

Blake frowned. "How did he know how much time he'd have?"

"If he did follow us to Vigilance," Sam pointed out, "he probably figured he'd have enough time for his mischief while we were there."

"But why go to my parents' home? They have nothing to do with this. Just to find another way to stick it to me?"

"Probably. He may have managed to learn they were out of town and thought you'd be staying there."

"And he didn't worry about being seen?"

"I'm sure he had some kind of disguise. Think about this. The guy is very good at making himself invisible. Unremarkable. Someone nobody would notice. That's how he gets away with leaving these messages for you."

"I want to know whatever you find," Blake told them. "Anything at all. This is even more personal for me now."

"I'll let you know the minute I know." Sheri shook her head. "When Avery told me you were coming to meet with her about a stalker, I don't think either of us had any idea he'd escalate this far."

"I didn't, for sure." Blake emptied what was left of his coffee in the sink and turned back to look at them. "Who found Grant?"

"Sharon Kennelly, when she came home from lunch with her friends. She—"

"His *wife* found him?"

"She knew Grant was home," Sheri continued, "but she didn't see him anywhere and he didn't answer when she called his name. She went into the yard to see if he was out there, and found him unconscious in the hedges."

Blake looked ready to pass out and Sam felt sick herself. For a woman like Sharon Kennelly to find her husband in that condition would be a real shock.

"And he was stuffed into that hedgerow?" Blake closed his eyes, a sick look on his face.

Sheri's features set in a hard look. "Yes. She almost missed him but he was wearing a bright yellow golf shirt. It caught her eye."

"It makes me sick that Grant Kennelly got caught up in this psycho's attacks on me."

Again Sam had to fight the urge to touch him in some way, to assure him he wasn't alone in all this. "You okay?" she asked him. "Want a drink?"

"No, I'm not, and no, I don't want a drink." He shook his head. "Thanks anyway." But he looked totally shell-shocked.

"How about a fresh cup of coffee, then?"

"Yeah, okay. Coffee's good. Jesus!" He blew out a breath. "I can't believe this." He looked at Avery. "Do we know how Grant is? How bad it is?"

Sheri shook her head. "Not yet. They're still running tests and taking X-rays. We know he has a couple of broken bones, maybe a broken nose. A concussion most likely, but as yet we don't know how bad it is, and won't until he comes out of it. My officer called me from the hospital to bring me up to date. As soon as I have a report I'll let you know."

"I want to cover any expenses their insurance doesn't. That's nonnegotiable. I don't care how you do it but make it happen."

Sheri nodded. "I'll take care of it with the hospital administrator."

Sam took his empty mug and went to brew the coffee, even knowing he probably wouldn't drink it.

"You'll be seeing them poking around your yard, too, Blake," Sheri said. "We're looking for anything we can find."

He banged his hand on the counter. "Damn it all to hell. Who is this fucker? Why is he so fixated with me?"

"That's what we're going to find out," Sam assured him. She hated the deepening lines of stress in his face and the misery in his eyes.

Sheri headed toward the front door. "I'm going back to the Kennellys to see what we've come up with there. Avery, my fingerprint guy will be here as soon as he's finished at the Kennellys. Sam, you make sure you have eyes on Blake at all times."

"That's my job."

"Yes," Avery answered. "Keep your eye on your client at all times and your gun always at the ready. There's no telling what this psychopath will do." She gestured toward the back door. "Unless we find evidence to the contrary, we're going to assume the stalker got in the house that way. Probably picked the lock."

Blake leaned against the counter, making a visible effort to pull himself together. "You know, writing about this stuff as fiction is a lot different from the reality."

"By the way." Avery pulled out her cell and scrolled through her notes. "We traced the number those texts came from today. It belongs to a woman named Sarah Jo Murphy who lives in Plainfield, Minnesota."

Blake's eyebrows rose. "Minnesota?"

"Yeah. She was shocked as hell when a cop showed up on her doorstep and asked to see her phone. She had just returned from a trip with two friends but they were all over the East coast on a three-week trip. It could have happened anywhere. The police checked out her background thoroughly and cleared her. She's not the one sending you the messages."

"Jesus." Blake raked his fingers through his hair again, a gesture Sam had come to realize he did when he was frustrated or upset.

"Let's talk about fingerprints," Avery said. "We've got yours but we don't have any from your parents to eliminate them."

"My dad was in the military and my mother worked as a nurse in a psychiatric facility years ago. They'd be in the system, right?"

"Yes. That will help."

A knock sounded at the back door and Avery went to open it. When she came back she had a tall, thin man with her.

"Guys, this is Jerry, Sheri's tech. She and I decided we didn't need people tripping over each other. Since he's already here printing the back door and anything out there the stalker might have touched, we decided he'd do your house as well. It's actually all one case and this is more efficient."

Less than five minutes passed before Jerry stepped in from the living room and handed Avery a small baggie with a wrinkled piece of paper in it.

"This was crumpled up and sitting in the remains of that statue. We took pictures of everything before I bagged it."

Avery carried it to the breakfast table, smoothed it out, and read. Then she looked at Blake. "A love note from your stalker."

"Let me see what else the asshole wrote." He reached for the little baggie.

"No touching. Just come take a look."

He walked over to the table and stared at the wrinkled paper. Sam stood next to him, reading with him. Even in its badly wrinkled shape the words were legible.

Sam frowned. "What the hell?"

I know what you did. I will destroy everything in your world because of it, just like this statue.

"It's handwritten," Sam pointed out.

Avery nodded. "Yes. I think he couldn't resist the temptation and he didn't have a printer with him. We'll get the people at the sheriff's forensics office to analyze the printing but I don't hold out a lot of hope. This guy is turning out to be wicked smart."

"He's not that smart if the only thing he could do with Grant Kennelly was beat the crap out of him," Blake pointed out. "Smart would have been to say, oops, mistake, and leave without calling any more attention to himself."

"Don't sell him short. I sense this is all new to him, but he's very, very bright. And he may have gotten off on the violence."

Blake just stared at the note, an angry red flush creeping up his skin, and his entire body tightened. When Sam touched his arm, she felt the tension in his muscles.

"Do you think he knew my mother collects this stuff? Has he dug so far into my life?" He looked from one woman to the other. "How is he getting this information? My God, is there no part of my life that's safe?"

"Let's dial it down a little." Sam tried to sound as calm as possible. "This could just have been an opportunity that presented itself. We'll get this bastard. I promise you. Before he does any more damage."

"Any more damage?" He brushed away her hand and began to pace. "You mean before he actually kills someone? Because I'm pretty damn sure that since he thinks he got away with violence once, he won't hesitate to do it again. Can you promise that?"

"I—"

"Blake, we'll get him," Avery assured him again. "We always do. Meanwhile, I have an assignment for you. I know you've been over it all with me, but tonight how about sitting down with Sam and going through it again. Only this time let's do it a little differently. Tell her how you came to be a writer, what you did before, what your journey has been like since your first book was published. It's possible something will pop up you'd forgotten all about."

"Yeah, sure. Okay."

"And with that I'm out of here. Sam, I'll touch base with you later. You know to call if you need anything at all."

"Got it covered."

The door closed behind Avery.

"How the hell did I acquire a psycho like this?" Blake asked. "It's bad enough he's after me, but to half kill my neighbor in the process is just... is just...damn it!"

"Come on, Blake." She closed her fingers over his arm, trying to ease the tension. She was afraid if he didn't take a breath he'd have a stroke. "Why don't you show me where I'll be bunking? Then let's see if your folks have some wine stashed away. I think we both deserve a little stress reliever, and we can talk about how you came to be Blake Morgan."

She tugged on his arm and he turned toward her. When he did, his gaze locked with hers so intently she couldn't catch her breath. Hunger and need swirled in his eyes.

"I can think of a better stress reliever," he growled, before she could say a word. "Please don't say no. I need you, Sam. Right now. Just you."

She couldn't refuse him, not when her own body responded in an instant. From the moment she'd walked into Avery's office and seen him, from the minute he'd apologized to her and made her aware the chemistry was still there, she'd known she'd have to make this decision sooner or later. Her own dreams all these years had primed her for this.

What happened to putting things on the back burner? I think I am about to make a big mistake here and I can get hurt.

But then he pulled her body flush against his, so tight she could feel every bit of him, from the hard wall of his chest to the thick cock pressing against her mound through the denim of his jeans.

And she lost the argument with herself.

In the next instant, he was claiming her mouth with a desperation that could only have come from the pressure and tension of the day. He was like a man possessed, needing to wipe away everything, block everything out as he immersed himself in her.

If that kiss fifteen years ago had been hot, this one was scorching. Devouring. And she melted into it holding nothing back.

His tongue was liquid fire along the seam of her lips, licking the surface then forcing her to open for him as he thrust inside. He didn't have to do much forcing, though. She opened for him willingly, knowing this was what he needed but even more what she was willing to give. She took his tongue inside, rubbing her own over it in an erotic dance that seared every part of her body. He tasted like coffee and sunshine and sin.

She dug her fingers into his shoulders, holding on to him for balance as he set fire to every nerve in her body. The hell with all the rules and regulations, all the limits of discipline. They disappeared in a cloud of smoke. The only thing that mattered was this man, now, and the way he made her feel. And his need. Something to counteract the blows he'd taken today.

With his mouth still devouring hers, he slid his hand down her back, tracing her spine then squeezing one cheek of her ass. The movement pulled her even closer to his muscular body, if that was possible.

She wanted to protest when at last he broke the greedy kiss, but then he slid his warm lips along the line of her jaw and tiny shivers raced along the surface of her skin. His kisses, as he trailed them along the tender skin beneath her jaw and down her neck, were almost frantic. He finally placed a hot one in the hollow at the base of her throat, where she knew her pulse was beating like a mad thing, taking a tiny bite before moving his mouth.

When finally he lifted his head, she opened her eyes to find his very hungry gaze locked with hers. Those whiskey brown eyes had darkened to pools of chocolate, the tiny flecks of gold in the irises like flames. With one swift move, he lifted her in his arms, cradling her against his chest.

"This has been brewing for a long time, Samantha Quenel. You have one chance to tell me to stop." His voice was harsh with barely controlled passion and need. "Just one."

But for the life of her she couldn't find the strength to do it.

Chapter 6

If Avery finds out about this I'll be out on the street or doing security on Easter Island, but I don't care.

Sam just couldn't make herself care. Not when the long-suppressed dream of a love-struck teenager was about to come true. Maybe it was just a foolish leftover from her teen years but the circumstances had stayed with her all these years.

Besides, she told herself, Blake needed this right now. Needed *her.* She could push all her insecurities into an imaginary closet for the time being. This didn't mean anything more than the fact she was offering him comfort when he needed it.

Yeah, right! Lie to yourself much?

If only she hadn't made so many bad choices in the past.

But she couldn't make herself say no, so she just wound her arms around his neck and nipped his chin.

"Okay, then."

A stairway led off the little foyer and Blake took the steps two at a time. Pressed against his body, Sam inhaled his scent, a heady combination of earthy outdoors and pure male, breathing it into her system already on sensual overload.

He nudged open the second door on the right and carried her into what was obviously his bedroom. She caught a glimpse of the room. A double bed of dark wood was centered on one wall, flanked by two nightstands. On another wall was a desk with shelves above it still holding a collection of books and high school memorabilia. She could tell Anne Morgan had chosen not to make any changes in the room her son had grown up in.

That was all she had time to absorb because Blake stood her next to the bed and began an assault with his mouth again, on her chin, her neck, behind her ears. He grabbed the hem of her shirt, yanked it over her head, and tossed it to the side. The heat of his hands spread through her as he cupped her breasts, squeezing them and pressing his thumbs against the nipples. His mouth was on hers again, hot and insistent, and this time he nipped lightly along the outline of her lips.

Sam felt the tension vibrating in him, the urgency to wipe it all away—today, the past weeks, the notes, and now the brutal assault on his neighbor. Whatever he needed at this moment she would give him, no matter how hot and hard and fast.

But then, abruptly, he lifted his head and took a step back.

Sam frowned, searching his eyes, seeking a clue as to what was happening. "What—"

He held up a hand. "No."

She stared at him. "No?" Her insides knotted and a chill raced through her. Did he suddenly regret everything he'd said at lunch? Did he think he was making a mistake? Oh, God, it was happening again. What an idiot she was. "I don't understand. I thought—"

"I meant no, not this way, like some animal." He shook his head. "Not like this." He blew out a breath. "You might not believe me, but I've thought about this for too many years to go at it like a dog in heat."

"But I understand," she protested. "You've had a rotten few weeks, topped off by a really rotten day. It's okay, Blake. Really." *As long as you don't leave me hanging like this.* "If we're finally going to do this, please don't walk away."

The kiss he gave her, just a brush of his lips over hers, was soft as the kiss of a butterfly.

"Oh, we're going to do this alright. Make no mistake. But we're going to take it slow, and easy, and enjoy every single minute."

He sat her on the edge of the bed and knelt before her.

"One inch at a time," he told her. "That's how I want to see you. I've waited a long time for this and I don't intend to hurry it." Then he chuffed a short laugh. "At least I hope I can take my time."

She noticed he didn't offer to put her shirt back on. Not that it mattered. She was so hot anyway she didn't need it to keep her warm.

He slipped off the short ankle boots she wore and set them to the side. Then he cradled each foot in turn, stroking the arch with his thumb, a sensual gesture that sent shivers through her. Even more so was the feeling when he slipped his hands inside the legs of her jeans and rubbed her calves with his thumbs.

She couldn't tear her gaze away from his face and the hungry look in his eyes. Yes, hungry. That was the only word for it, as if he wanted to eat up every inch of her. Just the thought of it set up a hard throbbing in her sex and made her nipples peak. She wanted to squeeze her legs together but Blake had placed himself squarely between them.

He watched her carefully as he ran his thumbs up and down her skin. "So soft," he murmured. "I'd love to taste every inch of you." He looked up at her. "Maybe I'll do just that."

Before she could say or do anything he rose to his feet and yanked her close to him. The heat and hunger in his eyes burned its way inside her, hitting every pulse point and every nerve. Sam couldn't remember ever being wanted like this before, by anyone. She stood, unable to move, while he eased her jeans over her hips and down her legs, helping her to step out of them. With a very light touch he brushed his knuckles along the lace at the upper edge of her bikini panties. As utilitarian as she dressed for work, underneath it all she refused to give up her sexy lingerie. And Blake's obvious appreciation made it all the more worthwhile.

She waited for him to slide her panties down her legs but instead he focused for a long time on her breasts and the pink satin and lace bra that contained them. Her nipples were so hard she was sure they were almost poking through the fabric.

Blake cupped them in his palms and brushed his thumbs back and forth over the hard points. Her breasts ached for his touch and her sex throbbed so intensely she wondered why her entire body wasn't one big pulse.

He moved his big, warm hands down her arms, across her midriff and then to her back. With a deft flick of his fingers he unclasped the bra and added it to the pile. Cupping the mounds in his palms, he brushed his fingers back and forth across the tips already so stiff they were almost painful. When he gave them a light pinch, she sucked in a breath and curled her fingers into her hands. Her legs were shaking and she wasn't sure she'd be able to stand up much longer.

Thank the lord Blake moved his hands to her arms, then her shoulders, then to cup her face again. If she'd thought the kiss before was hot, this one was off the charts. His tongue was a live wire, setting her mouth ablaze everyplace it touched. She gave it back as strongly, absorbing the taste of him. By the time he broke the kiss she was shaking with need, and he'd barely touched her!

Nudging her gently, he pushed her back until she was sitting on the bed. With hands she realized were shaking almost as much as hers, he eased the tiny panties down her legs and off. When he parted her thighs and stared at her sex, she suddenly realized what the phrase "eating me up with his eyes" meant.

Blake drew in a deep breath. Then, parting the lips of her sex with his thumbs, he bent his head and slowly licked the length of her slit.

Oh, sweet Jesus!

She nearly came right then. His tongue was hot and slightly rough and he damn sure knew what to do with it. He stroked her wet flesh, tracing lines on either side of her clit before pausing to take a nip of the swollen bud.

"Aaahhhh."

The sound rolled out of her mouth before she realized it. She tried to thrust her hips up at him, to silently urge him to do more, faster, harder. But it was obvious he had his own agenda.

When he lifted his head to look at her, his lips were wet with her juices and hunger was stamped on his face.

"I've waited fifteen years for this, Sam. I'm taking my time."

And he proceeded to do just that, licking and lapping, nipping at her sensitive clit, running the tip of his finger around her opening. When he thrust his tongue inside her she nearly came off the bed. Blake Morgan was a man who knew how to pleasure a woman, and she didn't even care how he'd gotten this way. She just didn't want him to stop what he was doing.

He slipped one finger inside her, curling it so he hit that sweet spot that drove her crazy. Then he added a second finger.

More! She wanted to scream the word at him. *Give me more.* His slow, steady pace was driving her out of her mind. She gripped the bedclothes with her fists.

She almost yelled *No!* when he removed his fingers from her wet heat, but in another second he replaced them with his tongue, and his fingers went to work on her clit. God! She could feel the release building inside her, stronger and more intense, until her entire being was focused on that one thing. At that moment he pinched her clit, hard, and she tumbled over the edge, the force of her release shaking her.

He stayed with her all the way, wringing every last drop from her, slowing his strokes as her body began to ease from the grip of her orgasm. Finally she unclenched her hands, felt her entire body go lax. Blake eased his tongue from her body and placed a soft kiss on her clit before raising his head.

He rose to his feet, his eyes still glued to her naked body as he stripped off his own clothing. He paused only long enough to grab a condom from his wallet and drop it on the nightstand.

"I didn't expect I'd need any more." He lips curved in a half smile.

"And do you?" She watched him carefully. "Expect to need more?"

Again that heat flashed in his eyes. "Oh, yeah. A lot more. But I don't think I'll buy them in town here. I'm probably already the subject of more gossip than I want."

"Blake, listen." How did she phrase this? "We aren't...This isn't..."

"I wanted to see if this chemistry is real. It is. Maybe this won't go anywhere at all, but I really want to try. Sam, you starred in so many of my dreams I wondered if I was in an alternate universe and it was real, not imagined."

"You dreamed about me?"

Now why was that so hard for her to understand? Hadn't he had a starring role in her own dreams all these years?

He came down over her, his face so close to hers she could count his eyelashes.

"More nights than I can tell you, and that's no lie."

She nibbled her bottom lip. "But what if that's all we've got between us?"

He brushed his mouth over hers. "Then we'll enjoy the hell out of it while it lasts. Sam, I don't want to push you into anything. And I certainly don't want to screw up your situation at Vigilance. I don't imagine sex with a client is on the usual checklist."

She burst out laughing. She couldn't help herself.

"No, it isn't. But let me worry about that." She tried to read the expression on his face. "This was a long time coming, Blake, if you'll pardon the pun. Like you said, this may be all there is between us. We have no idea where it's going, or if it's going. I can still do my job while we satisfy our curiosity. I promise you that."

"Good." He placed a kiss on each of her breasts.

"But I don't want you to feel—"

He touched a finger to her lips. "You let me worry about what I feel. And right now, what I feel is extremely hard and painful if I don't get inside you in the next ten seconds."

Naked, he was as magnificent as she'd always imagined except her teenage dreams did not do justice to the mature reality. She figured he had to do more than sit in front of a computer all day, because he was fit and toned. His pecs and abs were hard, the muscles of his arms and legs defined. The hair sprinkled on his chest and scattered on his forearms and legs was a shade darker than the hair on his head, and so soft she wanted to rub herself all over it.

She tried to slide her hand in between his legs, to wrap her fingers around his hot, throbbing cock and feel the soft sac of his balls, but he shook his head.

"Later. After."

She stared at him, wishing he'd just get on with it. "After what?"

"After I'm inside you."

He knelt between her legs and lifted them, spreading them wide to give himself both an unobstructed view and a clear path. He placed the head of his shaft at her opening and slowly eased himself in.

"Look at me," he commanded as he entered her with a slow stroke, his passage eased by the slickness of her walls.

Again she looked directly into his eyes, and what she saw there made her catch her breath—need, desire, and something else. Something close to desperation. She wanted to make that last disappear. Wrapping her legs around his waist, she locked her ankles at the small of his back. Their bodies now so tight together they moved as one.

As his strokes grew harder, as the tempo increased, she swore she could see right into the heart of his soul. Every nerve in her body fired as she met him thrust for thrust. When they came, together, it was with the force of an explosion, tremors shaking them both. She had no idea how long they lay there, connected, until she finally unwound her legs from his waist and let them fall to the side. Blake placed a soft kiss on her lips and another on the hollow of her throat. Did he feel the hammering of her pulse through the thin layer of skin? Or know how completely he had turned her inside out?

Kissing her one more time, he eased his body from hers and went to dispose of the condom. The perspiration on her skin was drying, taking her body heat with it, so she pulled up the covers and waited to see what he did. Should she get up, act like nothing happened, thank him for some stupendous sex, or what? That one night with him so long ago, that one incredible kiss, had fed years of daydreams, even as she'd hated him for the way he'd treated her afterward. She would take her cue from Blake. That would be the safest thing.

But good lord. Unexpectedly he had touched something deep inside her. If she wasn't careful she could be in big trouble here. The last thing she needed was to fall in love with Blake Morgan. Their shared past and her personal history was a road strewn with rocky bumps. Want and need battled with common sense and a little bit of fear.

Damn!

When he came back into the room, unselfconscious about his nudity, he lifted the covers and slid into bed beside her. He pulled her against his body, spooning himself around her, one hand cupping her breast. Silence stretched between them. Finally, Blake cleared his throat.

"Sam, I—"

She shook her head. She couldn't have a discussion with him now. "No talking, okay? It was…beyond great. Can we just leave it at that for now?"

"Just as long as you agree it was good." Hunger still swirled in his eyes. "Damn good, and I'm not going to let you forget it. Now." He stroked her hair. "Right now I think we can both use a little nap, don't you?"

Sam knew at some point they would have to talk about this, and she wasn't even sure what she would say. Meanwhile, a nap sounded good to her.

"Mm-hmm."

She closed her eyes and rested her head in the curve of his neck, but she didn't fall asleep for a very long time.

* * * *

The ringing of Sam's cell phone woke them. At first, she had to remember where she was, whose bed she was lying in, and who was spooned against her, one arm around her, hand cupping her breast. Then in an instant it all came back. Blake. The events of the afternoon. And the unbelievably spectacular sex.

No time to reflect on that right now, though. The job was calling. She fumbled for her phone and saw it was Avery.

"Hey, Avery, what's up?"

"Couple of things. First an update on Grant Kennelly."

Sam sat up in bed, pulling the sheet up to her breasts and doing her best to ignore Blake's warm hand insinuating itself between her thighs.

"Yes. How is he?"

"Okay, but he's got a long recovery ahead of him. As the chief law enforcement officer on this, Sheri was able to get the details for me. He has a broken jaw and a bad concussion. Looks like the guy pounded his head on the concrete of the porch on top of everything. He also took a punch to the chest right over his heart so they're monitoring that." Avery's sigh carried over the connection. "Tell Blake I spoke to the hospital administrator about Blake paying Grant's bill. He'll have to jump through some hoops to do it because of HIPAA, but there are some appropriate ways to do it. As soon as I have the info I will forward it to him so he can make arrangements."

"Good. That will help, although I'm not sure anything can make him feel better about this. He still blames himself."

"And I'm sure telling him it's not his fault doesn't have any effect."

Now it was Sam's turn to sigh. "You got that right. Anything else?"

"No. Just wanted to check in. Take care of him."

"That's my top priority," Sam assured her before hanging up.

"Okay." Blake pulled her back down to hm. "I know you were talking about Grant. Tell me everything."

Sam repeated what Avery had told her.

He was silent for a long time, digesting the information. "I guess it never occurred to me someone else could be in danger from this guy. Sam, we have to find out who he is before someone else gets hurt."

"And we will. Meanwhile, let's get up, search for that wine and raid the refrigerator. I think it's long past dinner time." Her stomach chose that moment to grumble softly. "See what I mean?"

They both laughed, and the tension eased just a little bit.

"Yeah, I see," he chuckled.

"Let me take a shower and we'll see about eating." She started to slide out of bed.

"Wait." He tightened his hold around her.

"What for?"

"You were right earlier. I don't know where this is going. Yet. But it's more than a roll in the hay to me, Sam." He nipped her earlobe.

"And like *I* said, let's just see what happens. Maybe we'll fulfill that teenage dream, and that will be enough. But whatever happens, I want both of us to be sure."

She wanted to believe that so badly, but that hurt teenager kept getting in the way. Not to mention the memories of her other bad decisions. Well, she'd think about them later. Now she just wanted to enjoy the residual good feeling.

Then he grinned at her. "But think of the fun we can have figuring this out."

She laughed softly, turned around, and brushed a kiss over his lips.

* * * *

When they brought their luggage upstairs, Blake didn't even give her a chance to put hers anywhere but his room. He knew even though what they'd shared had been nothing shortly of cataclysmic, Sam was probably still uncertain of what this was between them. That was okay. She wanted to be sure and so did he. In the middle of all this madness she was the one bright spot.

Baby steps, he tried to tell himself. *Remember, baby steps.*

He urged her to shower in the other bathroom, however, afraid that if he got naked with her right now they'd never make it downstairs. He was in the kitchen standing in front of the refrigerator when Sam came up behind him.

"How are you fixed for groceries?"

Blake chuffed a short laugh. "Take a look. Leave it to my mother to make sure we don't starve."

She looked over his shoulder, to the fridge stuffed with every variety of groceries they could need and burst in laughter. "I guess we won't have to worry about what to eat."

"Yeah, that's my mom. She still thinks I don't eat right. Of course, when I'm into a book, sometimes that's the case." He spotted what he was looking for and pulled a bottle of Riesling out of the second shelf. "I'm pretty sure we can use this, right?"

She nodded. "I'll make us some sandwiches to go with."

As nice as the day was, under normal conditions he'd suggest they take everything out on the patio to eat. But he wasn't sure he could sit out there without imagining Grant Kennelly's bleeding body stuffed under the hedgerow. Instead they took the sandwiches, the wine, and two glasses to the table in the breakfast nook. Blake filled both wine glasses and lifted his toward Sam.

"To you, Sam, just for being here and keeping me sane."

He watched, waiting, until she touched her glass to his.

"We'll get past this, Blake." Her lips curved in a warm and gentle smile. "I promise you."

They each took a sip of wine. Then Blake picked up half of his sandwich, took a bite and chewed thoughtfully.

Sam studied him for a long moment. "Listen, Blake, I—"

"Sam, I want to tell you—"

They looked at each other and just like that the tension eased.

"Ladies first," he told her.

She let out a tiny sigh. "I just wanted to say that this afternoon was really great."

"I agree." He swallowed some more wine and tried to collect his thoughts. He was feeling his way here, no pun intended. "We waited a lot of years to see if the chemistry from that one night is real, and was something beyond high school. Something that would get past my being such an ass to you. Circumstance, fate, whatever you want to call it, brought us together. I'd say we at least made a start. Let's leave it at that for now. Okay? No pressure here."

"Yes." She said the word slowly. "I agree. I'm not rushing anything. We have to be sure."

He nodded. "But I just have to say this. I've carried the memory of that date—that kiss—around with me for a long time."

A memory that was never out of his mind. He had a limited time to see if this worked, to convince Sam that it could, and he didn't intend to make any mistakes.

"I have, too." She said the words reluctantly.

He nodded. "I just want to be sure you know I'm not just looking for a roll in the hay."

She smiled. "I get that, Blake. We're good."

"Okay, then." That would have to do for now.

"Besides, first and foremost I have a job to do here."

"And I don't want to get you crosswise with Avery. Fraternization and all that."

"She trusts us to handle things and be alert. Anyway, lately we've had a couple of assignments turn into permanent relationships and it worked out okay."

He reached across and took one of her hands. "Then let's see where this goes, and take it from there. So. How about telling me how you ended up being a high-risk security agent?"

"Oh, well, that will require a little more wine." She refilled both glasses. "So let's see. Where should I start?"

"How about the beginning."

"Okay." She swallowed a bite of her sandwich and washed it down with a sip of wine. Once upon a time..."

He listened while she told him about her four years at Florida State. Studying criminology, of all things, she told him and laughed. She sat on a bench one day wondering exactly where she wanted to go with it when she learned military recruiters were on campus.

"I was graduating, had no clear plans except I wanted to go into law enforcement." She grinned. "And the recruiter was really cute."

"So you joined the Army to get a date with the recruiter?" He winked.

"Not exactly. And it was the Air Force."

He stared at her. "The Air Force? For real? I didn't know you liked to fly."

"I do, but that's not why I joined. I just saw a great chance for advancement."

Blake cocked an eyebrow. "So what did you do in the Air Force?"

She shrugged. "This and that. After four years I could apply for the Ravens, which was really cool."

"What are the Ravens?"

She grinned. "I could tell you what we did but then I'd have to shoot you."

He frowned. "No kidding?"

"Yes, kidding. Just pulling your leg. They're part of the Air Force Security Forces. We provided security for the Air Mobility Commands, and that's just too complicated to get into right now."

"Where did you provide the security?"

She shrugged. "In all the fighting zones. For dignitaries, special passengers, and some very expensive airplanes the people might want to steal or destroy."

Now that he *really* didn't want to think about. Not about Samantha serving in the midst of the wars going on overseas.

"How long were you in for?" He kept trying to visualize her in an Air Force uniform.

"Eight years. Four until I could get into the Ravens and a four-year commitment for that. And don't look at me like that," she warned. "I was well trained for what I was doing."

He had no doubt about that.

"So when your contract was up you decided to stay in the same business, so to speak?"

"So to speak." She fidgeted with her glass, twisting the stem. "I really didn't know what I wanted to do. My family wanted me to be in a more secure environment. I guess they were done with being glued to the television for bad news."

"And after that?"

"I came home to hang out with my folks while I looked around." She took another swallow of her wine. "Avery had moved Vigilance here a couple of years before that. Someone must have told her about me because she invited me to lunch one day and we clicked."

"It's obviously working out."

She nodded. "Avery's great. So is everyone there."

He had so many questions he wanted to ask her. Questions about her friends. Questions about men in her life, which he probably had no right to dig into. But suddenly he wanted to know every single thing about her, including what kind of movies she liked and if she was a baseball fan or did she like football. He hoped that even with the situation they were in, he'd still have the opportunity to find out. Because today might have begun as a stress reliever but it ended up being way more than that. He hoped that the upcoming trip would be the beginning of something for them.

If only they could find the fucker that was screwing with him.

Blake chewed the last bite of sandwich, swallowed, and drained the rest of the wine from his glass. This had all been a nice respite from the reality of what was happening. A respite that he needed and that was important to him for a lot of reasons. It was nice sitting here with Sam, talking, learning little things about each other. It almost made him think none of this crazy stuff had happened at all.

Almost.

And then reality intruded again.

They had both placed their cell phones on the table next to their plates. Now Sam's went off, its distinctive tone the sound of a foghorn. They looked at each other, the softer mood broken.

Sam looked at the name on the screen. "It's Avery again. Maybe they found out something." She hit Accept. "Hey, Avery. What's up? Anything new to report?"

Blake waited with barely controlled patience while Sam nodded, said "uh-uh" a few times, and finally hung up.

"Well?" he demanded.

"Sheri called. And no," she said quickly when Blake opened his mouth to ask if they'd caught the guy. "They did, however, find a few neighbors who remembered seeing a pickup parked in your driveway. They didn't think much about it because it has some kind of commercial name on the door."

"Removable signs," Blake guessed.

Sam nodded. "No doubt. Pickups are up pretty commonplace these days, especially around here. And people are so used to seeing service people of all kinds they don't pay much attention to it."

"But if we know it's a pickup, we can keep an eye out for it from here on out."

Sam shook her head. "That would be nice, but no. You can bet the first thing he's going to do is swap vehicles. I'm sure this one isn't his. He had to fly in here from someplace, if he's hitting you at all your tour stops. You don't know, he could even have flown in to Tampa on the same plane you did."

Blake's sandwich suddenly felt like a lump of cement in his gut.

"Are you kidding me? On the same plane?" A chill raced along his spine. "You mean he could have been that close to me?"

She reached across the table and grabbed his hand. "I just said maybe, because anything is possible. You need to be aware of that."

He squeezed her hand but then leaned back in his chair, his brain spinning with the whole situation.

"I'm thinking maybe we should get out of Arrowhead Bay sooner rather than later."

"And go on to your next book signing early?" She shook her head. "That would accomplish nothing except give him lead time there to cook something up."

He ground his teeth in frustration. "I feel trapped, Sam, like I have no place to go. Like I have a big black X on my back. I want to take this trouble away from Arrowhead Bay but I don't want to bring it with me someplace else. And that's not possible, is it?"

"No, unfortunately. But there are still things we can do."

"Like what?"

She held up four fingers and bent one down. "For one thing, staying around here has its advantages. We've got immediate access to Vigilance and all its bells and whistles, as well as more manpower if we need it." She bent a second finger. "We're in a location where we know every nook and cranny, better than your stalker. Makes it easier for us to be aware of anything out of sync."

"Except for today," he interrupted.

"Except for today," she agreed. "But that came out of nowhere. You can be damn sure that won't happen again." Another finger. "Third, he's probably expecting you to leave here and may even be making his arrangements to hit your next stop ahead of you." She bent down the last finger. "Plus, it gives Avery time to dig through all those names you gave her and maybe identify some possibilities. People we can be on the lookout for."

"I know you all keep saying that, but truth to tell, I can't imagine anyone I know doing something like this."

Sam snorted. "You know how many people have said that and been wrong? Not too long ago we had someone kidnapped by a man who supposedly was her father's best friend."

He stared at her. "Are you kidding me?"

She shook her head. "Not even a little. So we both need to be hyper alert at all times. Don't assume anything about anyone just because you know them. You never can tell what goes on in someone's brain."

He looked at his phone. "At least I haven't gotten any text messages since we switched phones."

"Right, but that's because we haven't been anywhere that he could get close enough to you to clone it and get your number."

He swallowed the bitter taste in his mouth. "There's a comforting thought."

"You want comfort? Lock yourself up until we catch whoever this is. And even that is no guarantee." She reached across and touched his hand. "I'm just trying to make you understand all the aspects of this. It's my job to see that nothing happens to you, and I need your help to do that."

"I know." He turned his hand over and wrapped his fingers around hers. "And I'll do my best not to give you grief."

"I'll count on that." She smiled. "And maybe I have some extra incentive to keep you safe."

At once memories of what happened in his bedroom came alive in his brain and his cock swelled to painful proportions. He thought it would be great if they could spend all their time in bed. Maybe the stalker would get tired of him. Every word Sam had said to him at lunch was burned into his brain. He knew the connection was there, in spades. But getting her to trust it was another matter altogether, something he planned to work on. He'd take it one day at a time with her and hope like hell when this book signing tour was over and the stalker was history they could make plans for the future.

"What else did Avery have to say?"

"They've already eliminated a number of names on the list, especially those people who have daily routines that would be disrupted if they were flying all over the country stalking you." She swallowed the last bit of her sandwich. "She did say, however, that it was strange that Annemarie Schaefer seemed to have no family at all. Her parents are both dead, she has no siblings—at least that we can find so far—and her mother and father both appeared to be only children."

"What about friends?" He frowned. "How was I so self-involved that it didn't occur to me she lived in a vacuum? Who does that?"

"You'd be surprised. Besides, you had more things to worry about than Annemarie's personal life."

"Yeah," he grunted, "selfish ass that I was. I kept her busy all the time. All I was concerned with was getting my stuff taken care of."

"I'd say that just means you were focused and depended on her to take up the slack so you could do your thing. Don't keep beating yourself up, Blake. This is not your fault."

"So you say. Try telling that to Sharon Kennelly."

"Okay, look at me. Guilt is normal in a situation like this, but you have to deal with it. *We* have to deal with it, difficult as it might be. You have a career you've worked hard to establish and a signing tour to prepare for. Let's tackle it one thing at a time. Getting you rattled is exactly what this jerk wants. Anyway, they're going to continue digging, because to Avery this is like a puzzle she needs to solve." She rose and picked up their plates. "Why don't I get my tablet, pour us some more wine, and you can start schooling me on what's required to be your assistant."

"Sounds like a plan." He knew the grin he gave her was positively lecherous. "Except you might have some additional duties that weren't on Annemarie's list."

She stopped with the plates in her hand and turned back to him.

"Just so you know, I might need a lot of practice in those 'extra' duties."

He nodded. "I'm counting on it."

Chapter 7

The stalker could hardly keep from laughing out loud. Who did these Vigilance people think they were, believing they could fool him? He was ten steps ahead of them. Smarter than they were. And he'd bet good money his electronics were every bit as good as theirs. Hell, maybe even better. His degree in computer engineering and ten years developing surveillance software gave him the skills he needed now. Hell, if he could hack the United States government, he could certainly hack Vigilance, no matter how superior they thought they were.

Perhaps that gave him the greatest satisfaction of all, the knowledge that all their so-called state-of-the-art electronics couldn't keep him out. He was lucky to get a reservation on their same flight, but if necessary he'd have deleted someone else's to make room for himself. So what if some stranger showed up at the airport and discovered he had no seat on the plane?

Before Morgan had hired his bodyguard, he'd done an electronic search of all the hotels in Charlotte using a program he'd written. *She* had told him they always made the hotel reservations way in advance so searching for them was easy. He'd learned where Morgan and the woman were staying, and in a suite, no less. Of course, that prick had more money than God. He could afford it.

Money he hadn't earned honestly. Money that belonged to someone else.

The thought made his stomach cramp and anger wash through him. If not for the asshole, she'd be alive today, and probably a celebrity.

He deliberately clamped down on his rage. It affected his thinking and he had to stick to the plan. He couldn't make a mistake, not when it was working so well.

He had never believed himself to be a violent person, at least he hadn't thought so. That made it all the more amazing to him at how easy it had been to beat the shit out of that old man. The idea of going to the Morgan house had been spur of the moment, after he learned the man was not registered at the B and B. He'd seen it as an opportunity to create more mischief and misery for the asshole.

He'd thought his disguise had been perfect, a cable service repairman with orders to work on their system while they were away. He'd even used his laptop and portable printer to create credentials for himself. But no, the old fart had insisted he was calling the cable company. Said the Morgans would never let anyone in their house while they were away. He'd wanted to pull out his trusty knife he always carried and slit the guy's throat, but knifing was always chancy. If they didn't die right away they might still have time to scream for help. Instead, he gave him the full power of his fists, an uppercut to the jaw that knocked him out at once. Then he added some insurance by banging his head on the concrete porch and kicking him before picking him up to carry back to his own yard. Man, that felt good. He could have kicked the shit out of the old guy all day long.

He'd never known that physical violence could be so satisfying, even sexually stimulating. He'd gone back to his hotel room, stood in the hottest shower possible, and brought himself to an incredible climax. More than any other woman had done for him.

Hiding the old man in his hedges had used up a few minutes. Then he'd had to be quick about his work, unable to take as much time as he'd wanted. But at least he was sure he got the message across.

He'd considered taking a different flight from Tampa to Charlotte, but the urge to watch Morgan had been too great. Besides, the man had never seen him. Probably didn't even know he existed. And the stalker was becoming a master of disguise. They'd never seen him following them to the airport or even given him a second glance at the gate. Why should they when they had never seen him? Of course, he'd arrived five minutes before boarding and then made sure to sit in the back of the plane. They hadn't noticed him walking down the aisle, dressed in his sloppiest clothes, baseball cap pulled low on his face.

While they went to pick up their rental car in Charlotte, he'd cabbed to the hotel and checked in. The trick was leaving the envelope for Morgan at the front desk without anyone identifying him or describing him. In his room, while he changed clothes, he ran the program to see what suite they'd been assigned. When nothing came up under Morgan's name he tried the bodyguard. Did they think he wouldn't find all this out? He was too fucking smart for them. But it frustrated him that Samantha Quenel's name popped up with no room number associated with it. Had they worked out a deal with the hotel not to list the suite number in the registry? That was the only thing he could figure out.

Well, no problem. He'd move to Plan B, pulling out one of the many disguises he'd brought with him. Today it was a wig with longish hair, totally different than his close-cropped cut. He took off the jeans and plaid shirt he'd flown in, an outfit, by the way, that the clerk nearly turned up his nose at. Instead he pulled on tailored black slacks and a grey shirt.

The clerk at the front desk barely gave him a glance when he asked if he could leave the envelope for his friend who was checking in today. The man just nodded, took the envelope and propped it up where it was sure to be seen.

Back to his room, another quick change and then he was hanging out at the lobby coffee bar, nursing the tall coffee he'd just bought. The fact that little tables and chairs encouraged people to hang around made it just that much easier for him to watch people coming in. Watching for Morgan to arrive. He wanted to rub his hands with glee.

This is for you, my love. All of it. I'll lay it all on Morgan's shoulders. He has no idea how sorry I'll make him. They'll know everything when I finish with him.

* * * *

The flight for Blake had been anything but relaxing. Despite Sam's assurances, he still had the feeling someone was watching him. It took a lot of discipline to keep from looking over his shoulder all the time and checking people around him. Finally, when they were seated at the gate, he'd slipped on his sunglasses. Hiding behind the dark shades, he could keep checking the area for anything that tickled his senses. Of course, all his senses were slightly out of whack due to the stalker, so he could have been seeing trouble where there wasn't any.

He was pretty sure he was driving Sam nuts, but he'd never been in this situation before. Like he'd told her, living it was a lot different than writing about it.

"It's apparent this guy has massive cyber skills," Sam told him. "He had to have hacked into the passenger manifests to see what you reserved and what hotels you were staying at. Avery says it's the only way he could have all the information from the first leg of this tour. How else would he know anything except the city and store? You can be sure he did the same thing this time."

"Great. Just fucking great."

"I know you've got that hinky feeling." She nodded. "I completely understand."

He'd tried to relax, but his brain would not shut off. For one thing, his parents had returned from their cruise while he was still in town. They were devastated to hear about Grant Kennelly, and Blake felt like ten kinds of shit.

"It's not your fault," his father kept telling him each time they spoke. "You aren't the psycho here."

"But I obviously did something that set this all in motion."

"Blake, listen to me. I'm sure every one of us has done something at some time or other that a slightly off-balance person could take as a major crime. It's very difficult to know how someone will react to something you don't even know you did."

Blake knew his father was right. Still, he couldn't shake the feeling of guilt that dogged him. And it had rolled around in his mind all the way from Tampa to Charlotte.

When they picked up the rental car he kept checking the immediate area nonstop while Sam completed the paperwork.

"We're going to be prepared for him, no matter what," Sam assured him as she drove into the city.

"I hope." He was glad that she was driving since he was too edgy.

"Let's get registered," Sam said as they pulled up to the hotel. "Then I'll come back for the car and park it myself. I'll tip one of the bellman to keep an eye on it for a few minutes, just in case."

"Good."

They carried their own bags into the lobby. Sam stepped up to the desk with her Vigilance credit card. The reservations were in her name, just in case.

"Oh, yes, Miss Quenel." The clerk pulled the information up on his computer. "A suite with two bedrooms, just as your office requested." He busied himself entering her information then coding two key cards for them. "Oh, and your friend left an envelope for you."

Blake froze. He had no idea how Sam managed to pull it off as casually as she did, but she smiled at the clerk and said, "Thank you. Do you know which friend? Did he give you his name?"

"No." The clerk frowned. "He said you were expecting this, so I just assumed...I'm sorry, but if someone chooses not to give their name I try to be courteous and not ask."

And it could be a serial killer instead of a friend, Blake thought. Not much security here.

"Did he say if he'd be back and when?" Sam asked.

The clerk shook his head. "No. He just asked if I'd make sure you got the envelope."

"Oh, of course." Sam was cool and collected. "Well, I'll read his note. Maybe he won't be able to join us after all. Thank you for making sure I got this."

"No problem. I hope you enjoy your stay. Please let me know if there is anything we can do for you."

"Thank you, I will."

She used two fingers to slip the envelope into the tote and picked up her bags. Nodding at Blake, she set off toward the elevators. He followed her with his own luggage but when he would have said something to her she shook her head.

"Let's just put the stuff in the suite," she said. "Then I'll run down and park the car."

He was ready to bite nails by the time they reached the suite. But even then, Sam touched her finger to her lips, then held it up signifying to wait one minute. She opened her tote and took out something that looked like a handheld wireless radio. She spent five minutes checking out the living room and both bedrooms. Then she tossed the gizmo back into her tote and blew out a breath.

"Okay. Now we can talk."

"What's that little thing you carry with you? What were you doing?"

"It detects hidden microphones and cameras."

Blake was stunned. "You think he knew what room we'd be staying in and bugged it before we got here?"

She shrugged. "Anything is possible. He obviously knew the reservations were in my name so that ploy didn't work too well. We aren't discussing secret plans but others often do, so it's standard for Vigilance agents. Never take a single thing for granted."

Blake forced himself not to freak out. "Nothing is going to keep this guy away from us."

"I think we can agree on that."

"I want you to open the envelope." He didn't think he could hang on to his patience another minute. "Now."

"Yup. Just what I'm about to do."

She lifted it from her tote and placed it on the little desk near her. Using the letter opener from the desk, she slit the envelope and eased out the contents.

"Another envelope?" *What the hell?*

"This one's got your name on it." Sam held it up. "Obviously he came prepared for anything. This is a guy who from all appearances has incredible hacking skills. He has to be pissed that the hotel isn't listing your room number."

"But how does he even know who you are? Just because he saw us together doesn't give him that information."

"Child's play for someone like him. He could have taken my picture, maybe at the Driftwood, and run it through facial recognition software. If he's able to get all this other information about you—about us—that would be easy enough for him to do."

"So what does it say?"

Holding it by the edges, even though they both knew the chance of fingerprints was slim to none, she laid it out on the desk.

Blake stared at it. "Fuck."

I know what you did and soon everyone else will. Even if I have to kill someone to prove it.

"Yeah," Sam agreed. "What you said. Alright. Let me take care of the car and then we'll get with Avery."

Blake did his best to keep it together while she was gone. Damn! He didn't like her running around by herself with that nut job out there. Then he had to remind himself who the professional was here.

He paced, constantly checking his watch. It felt like an hour by the time she let herself back into the suite at last. He shoved his hands into his pockets to keep himself from grabbing her again. Instead he just said, "Well?"

"I can't say for sure if he's hanging out or not. Nobody the least bit questionable rode up or down with me in the elevator. And I don't think the mommy with the two little girls who rode the elevator in the parking garage with me are who we're looking for."

Blake hunched his shoulders. "I agree. But what about in the lobby? Wouldn't he be looking to see what we do next?"

"I did my usual look around as if I was trying to find someone. Even went up to the coffee bar, described a fictitious woman and asked if she'd been around. That I was supposed to meet her."

"And?"

She shrugged. "And I can't tell if he was one of the people sitting there or not. There were four men, all average, any of whom could be him." She tossed her purse on the couch. "Anyway, the car is parked and locked. We'll see if there are any mementoes left for us when we go to get it tomorrow."

"You know the chances are better than even there will be. He seems to be everywhere, leaving notes everyplace." He rubbed the back of his neck. "And I could still swear he was on the plane with us."

"Then he didn't check any luggage and he got a super speedy cab to get here before us, check in, and leave the note, because we got through the rental car desk in record time."

He frowned. "You're sure he's staying here?"

"Of course. Otherwise how could he be right in the thick of the action? But we're alert and watching for him."

At that moment, his newest cell phone chimed. Blake looked down at the screen. Unknown caller.

"It's him." He held out the phone to Sam. "Look."

"Okay," she soothed. "But it's just a message like before."

"Just a message?" He ground his teeth. "He wants to drive me nuts."

She nodded. "Most likely. Pull up the message."

You can't run away or hide. I know what you did.

Blake wanted to smash the phone on the floor but Sam pried it out of his hand.

"We'll send this to Vigilance and activate another one."

"At this rate, we'll be out of phones before the tour is over," he grumbled.

She smiled at him. "But remember, we can always get more. Okay, let me take care of business here. I'm going to set up my laptop and get Avery on Skype."

Avery was on another call when Sam texted Vigilance to get her boss set up. But ten minutes later there she was. Blake didn't know how she did it. She had to manage at least a dozen situations like this or worse, yet she looked calm and composed.

"Let's have it," she said after the greetings were out of the way.

Sam told her about the envelope at the desk, about it being addressed to her with another one inside. Then she held up the sheet of paper with the note on it.

"Alright," Avery said. "Here's where we are. Whoever this person is, he has incredible cyber skills. He could have hacked into our system to get his information, but I'm not willing to go there yet."

"Damn." Blake wanted to throttle someone. "And he says he doesn't care if he kills someone to get his revenge. Jesus."

"Yes. That concerns me, because maybe it's not an idle threat. Sam, I'm going to meet with whoever of the team is around and see if we can come up with a plan of some kind. Blake, we've been in worse situations and come out on top. I'm going to ask you to trust me and Sam—especially Sam—to make sure he doesn't carry out his threats."

"Maybe if I knew what I'm supposed to have done I could figure out who it is."

"You know," she said slowly, "this may not even be connected to Blake Morgan the author, but Blake Morgan the person. It could be something that happened a long time ago. That's why going over and over everything is important."

"Swell." He couldn't keep the bitterness from his voice. "Maybe I hit someone's kid in kindergarten."

Avery's lips curved in a tired smile. "Believe it or not, people have been killed for less. Just shake your brain and see what else falls out."

"We'll do it," Sam assured her. "Listen, tomorrow's a full day. Blake's got a spot on the local morning show, then an interview with a reporter and then in the evening the book signing. Plus he's going to show me how to deal with his emails, now that I have his login information."

"Be sure to keep the ones that make you itch in a separate folder and email them back to me."

"Will do. I'll of course have my phone on if you need me."

"Tomorrow, then."

The screen went blank.

"We need to call the bookstore," he told Sam. "Annemarie always called the day we got into town, checking the arrangements and asking if there was anything more they needed from me."

"Let's do that next, then. You have the number?"

He nodded, pulling it up on his cell. "And here's the manager's name. Ask her if they're all set. If there are presolds I need to sign and should I come early for those. If there is anyone special I need to meet with first."

"Like who?"

"If it's a chain bookstore, sometimes the regional manager is there. That's good because it can open the door to his other facilities."

"I would think by this time they'd be standing in line to host you."

He laughed. "Maybe if I was Tom Clancy. Anyway, if she asks you something you can't answer, just tell me."

"Okay. Here goes."

She dialed the number, got the manager on the line, and went through the routine. While she listened to the woman she made notes on her tablet. Finally she hung up and looked at Blake, showing him what she'd written. "She said everything's fine and they're looking forward to it," she relayed. "They've had a lot of calls from people checking the time and also a lot of hits on the Facebook page. They're expecting a big crowd."

"Good. That's why I write books, so a lot of people will read them."

"So, this is all okay?"

He nodded. "Routine. But I always need to check."

"What else would you usually be doing in the afternoon now? We got here a day ahead because of your interviews so what would you be doing with your time?"

"Research."

She cocked an eyebrow. "Research?"

He nodded. "Like we discussed. Annemarie used to help me. I'd give her a list of topics and she'd start digging for information."

"Do you still have any of the folders where she bookmarked pages? Copied stuff? How did she do that?"

He actually found himself smiling. "Yes, Mom. I still have them. She saved it all on her hard drive in the appropriate folders, then copied the folders to a Dropbox we share. Shared," he corrected himself.

"Show me the Dropbox. I want to see what's in there."

She sat down at the round table by the window. "Bring your laptop over here and let's see."

It took him less than a minute to boot up and get to the Dropbox account he'd shared with Annemarie.

"See? Just like I said." He opened one folder, then another. "Everything's there. I can go back to it any time I need to."

Sam peered at the screen. "Okay. Email me the link and the password now, so I'll have them."

They spent the afternoon dealing with that and some other business he had to take care of.

Sam spoke to Henry and reconfirmed the appointments for the next day, then handed the phone to Blake. He assured the man that yes, he'd be on time and on his best behavior.

"Aren't I always?"

"I just want to be sure this whole business with the stalker isn't throwing you off your game," his agent told him.

"Maybe I'll use it as part of the plot for my next book," he joked.

But he forgot that Henry seldom joked.

"You know, that's a damn good idea. Be sure to take plenty of notes, will you?"

Sam gave him a strange look when he disconnected the call. "I thought he was supposed to be your friend."

"He's my agent," Blake corrected. "He sees the possibility of sales in everything."

She gave a mock shiver. "I'm not sure Henry and I would get along too well. Listen. It's almost seven o'clock. I—"

He looked at his watch. "So it is. Damn! I must have bored you to death for hours."

He was glad when she smiled and shook her head. "Not at all. I actually find this all fascinating. So much of what we do at Vigilance is reflected in your plots. When this is over let's get Avery to give you the full tour of the agency—the techno stuff, how we plan missions, how she hands out assignments. All that good stuff."

"I'm sure there's a lot she can't share with me," he pointed out.

"True. But I'm sure she'll tell you what she can. Anyway, as I started to say, I don't know about you, but I'm starving."

Blake wasn't all that hungry but he knew he had to eat.

"I should warn you. That happens when I'm into a project. I write and forget about everything else."

Her smile made him think of her naked body beneath his, the feel of her skin and her delicious scent. It seemed that every minute he spent with her, he became more and more connected to her, more emotionally attached. He wanted her to trust their relationship. Trust *him*.

Too soon. Take it slow and easy.

"Then I guess I'll have to be your watchdog as well as your guard dog. Want to go downstairs and get a bite?"

"Not really. Our unknown friend might be hanging around. Let's order room service."

They ate a leisurely dinner, deliberately staying away from any conversation about what was happening between them. Still, neither of them could ignore the electricity that crackled between them. Then he coaxed Sam into watching one of his favorite action movies with him. And finally it was close to midnight and time for bed.

"Let me just say this," he said, "so all my cards are on the table. Avery reserved a suite with two rooms. Great. I can use the living room to work. If you think I'm asking or expecting too much too soon, I won't be happy, but I understand how you feel. You can't trust this yet. But I won't be able to sleep unless you're next to me, so only one of those bedrooms is going to get slept in."

And only one of them was.

Chapter 8

Despite the intensity of the night before, they were up very early in the morning. Sam was pleasantly sore in a number of places, and she'd discovered something besides the fact that Blake was an incredible, giving lover. Keeping him at an emotional distance was going to be a lot harder than she thought. She was uncovering the many layers of Blake Morgan, and each one pulled her emotions more than the other. If she wasn't careful those emotions would blow up and she'd find herself in a bad place. But how did she learn to trust him after all this time, when her memories flashed a warning to her brain and her heart?

Carefully, very carefully.

She'd expected the shallow teenager to be the same as an adult, but things were exactly the opposite. The adult had little in common with the teenager except his good looks. She worried that her heart might be in real danger here.

First things first. We have a big day ahead of us.

They opted for room service again for breakfast. Sam wanted to keep Blake as relaxed as possible, and sitting in the open where their stalker might be right next to them was not the way to do it. Blake was edgy and jumpy, going through an entire small carafe of coffee himself, and Sam didn't think it was because of the stalker. She was shocked to discover that he had a mild case of stage fright.

"Not with the readers," he told her. "Not in bookstores. I love my readers, even in big crowds." He chuckled. "Especially in big crowds. But the media scares the shit out of me."

She wrinkled her forehead. "Why? You're so confident about everything else. What can some poor reporter do to you?"

"Some poor reporter who's looking for a scandalous hook to make his story rise above all the others. Like some of the research I use is nothing but lies, or my publisher inflates my sales. Or, hell, I don't know. I beat my dog."

She chuckled. "I didn't know you had a dog."

He gave her a weak grin. "I don't. But you know what I mean."

She straightened the knot on his tie and rubbed her hand against his smooth-shaven cheek. God. He always smelled so very good. She was in such big trouble here. How did she distinguish between the fulfillment of a teenage wish and something much more mature? How could she make herself trust this? It wasn't like they were teenagers anymore, and Blake was doing his best to show her in every way how he felt.

Worry about that after you save his ass.

"Okay." He drew in a breath and exhaled slowly. "I'm as ready as I'll ever be. Lead on, Macduff."

"Why don't you wait for me in front of the hotel?" she suggested. "I'll go and collect the car and pick you up. You should be safe inside."

"You think there'll be another message on the windshield," he guessed. "If there is I want to see it."

"You don't need—"

"To see them all? But I do. I want to keep seeing everything this asshole sends."

"But Blake—" she started again.

He shook his head. "It won't be any worse that what I've already seen."

"You don't think you've been upset enough by them?"

He shook his head. "I know you think you're helping me by keeping this shit away from me, but the cat's out of the bag with the message shit, so let's just go get the damn car." One corner of his mouth lifted in a hint of a grin. "Anyway, maybe if I focus on him I won't have such a bad case of stage fright."

She gave up. He was, in fact, right. Hiding the messages from him wouldn't do anyone any good, least of all him. Better for him to see them and be aware.

"Okay. But if there is one, do *not* look around. Leave that to me. I can do it without being quite so obvious. And if he's watching, we don't want to give him the satisfaction of seeing you react."

"Fine. Let's go."

She threw everything she'd need in her tote, including her small purse. Blake hefted his messenger bag and they headed out of the suite. In the parking garage, they took the elevator to the third level and walked to the car. She spotted the folded sheet of paper under the wiper blade at once.

"Don't touch it," she warned Blake and drew a pair of latex gloves from her tote.

"He'll see you doing this," Blake warned.

"Good. And while there's slim to no chance we'll get any prints, if he *is* watching I want him to see we have procedures in place."

She unfolded the sheet of paper and held it so they both could read it.

I know what you did. Deny it all you want, but before long you'll pay for your sins.

"I'm getting sick of this fucking shit," Blake spat. "He's knows what I've done? Why the hell doesn't he tell me? Am I supposed to be a mind reader?"

Sam was beginning to think about squashing this guy herself. She didn't know how Blake was holding it together, especially with the public appearances he was making. And in that moment she saw him as more than the high school hot jock, the teenage sex god, the man who had fractured her heart. He became a man suffering unnecessarily but holding his shit together. A man who seemed to have unbelievable inner strength.

So maybe he wasn't that teenage asshole anymore. Maybe it really was time for her to give him a chance. Maybe the real Blake was someone she could depend on and...she choked...fall in love with.

Don't jump in feet first. Remember your history.

But she might, in the end, have little choice in the matter.

"No," she told him, "you're supposed to be consumed with guilt about something and so not need an explanation."

Sam refolded the paper and slid it into a pocket of her tote. As casual as her attitude was, she still scanned every bit of the area she could see. She was mostly trying to see if anyone was sitting in their car and watching—or pretending not to watch. She couldn't spot anything, but the itch at the back of her neck told her the stalker was somewhere in the vicinity.

"Get in the car," she told Blake. "Just nod your head at me. Don't say anything or look irritated. Pretend it doesn't bother you. Can you do that?"

"Of course. I'm a great actor. I was in the senior class play in high school. Remember?"

She actually smiled, which she hoped would irritate the crap out of the stalker.

"I sure do. Taffy McDaniels was the heroine." She snorted. "Who names their daughter Taffy anyway?"

He tried to match her humor. "People who like candy?"

"I guess."

As they drove out of the parking structure, circling from one floor to another, she kept a sharp eye out for anyone following them. But a car had pulled out in front of them and two joined the line in back of them as they reached street level, and it was hard to tell if any one of them was the stalker. She turned on the GPS on her phone, entered the address of the television station, and edged into traffic.

"I'm glad we left early enough to give us some leeway," she said, trying to ease the tension radiating from him. "You never know how bad traffic in a city will be."

"We'll be there in plenty of time." He sat looking straight ahead through the windshield, drumming his fingers on his thigh.

"I'm curious." She moved over a lane to get away from slow-moving traffic. "If you hate this so much, why do you do it?"

He lifted one shoulder and let it drop. "My agent and publicist say it's good for my image. And when it airs the day of a signing, statistics show it increases the crowd."

"The price of fame?"

"I guess." He leaned back and closed his eyes.

"Are you okay?" she asked after a minute.

"Just centering myself. Digging up the public version of Blake Morgan."

She left him alone for the rest of the ride, only nudging him when they pulled into the station parking lot. The lot was gated and guarded, which pleased Sam.

"I guess he could always bluff his way in here," she said, "but let's hope the setup deters him." She parked in one of the visitor spots close to the building. "Show time, kiddo."

He sighed. "Yeah. Okay, let's do this."

Sam was fascinated watching the process once they got inside. She'd been security for a number of people, from politicians to rock stars to people of great wealth. Somehow, though, even with the rock stars, she'd never been part of a visit to a television station. Everything they'd done had always been on site of a performance.

When Sam gave their names, the girl at the reception desk smiled so wide Sam thought her cheeks would crack.

"Oh, yes, Mr. Morgan. We're very excited about you being here today." She looked at him shyly from beneath lowered lashes. "My boyfriend is a huge fan of yours. If you wouldn't mind, I have one of your books here. Before you leave could you sign it to him?"

"Sure. Let's do it now."

"Oh! Oh, thank you." The girl lifted it from the shelf beneath the desk. "His name is Scott."

Blake scrawled a message and signed his name, then handed the book back. "Did you want a picture?"

"Oh, my God!" Her eyes widened. "That would be so wonderful."

By the time she'd used her cell phone to take two selfies, a man was heading out into the lobby.

"Bridget, you wouldn't mind sharing Mr. Morgan with the rest of us, would you?"

"Oh!" Bridget blushed bright red. "Of course not. I am so sorry, Mr. Moretti."

"That's okay. But I need to claim him now." He held out his hand. "Alan Moretti. I'm the station manager."

Blake did the polite greeting thing, introducing Sam as his personal assistant. Then she and Blake followed the man out of the lobby into the bowels of the building. Sam did her best to look as if this was all routine to her while they herded Blake through makeup, introduced him to several people on the set, and made them comfortable in the guest waiting room.

"Fifteen minutes," Moretti told them. "Someone will come and get you. Would you like coffee or anything in the meantime?"

They both refused politely.

"Okay, then." He turned on the television set against one wall. "You can monitor us from here. We do some news items first, the weather, a rundown on what's happening today. Then you're up as our first guest."

"Good enough."

Sam watched Blake, admiring him. He looked so relaxed you'd never know he considered this one of the seven major kinds of torture. But when Moretti left the room, Blake's posture immediately became rigid and he cracked his knuckles. He avoided looking at her and appeared for all the world as if he'd withdrawn into himself. He might have been going to an execution instead of an interview.

Then the television show came on, the opening graphics filling the screen with the theme music playing behind them. She reached over and touched Blake's arm.

"They'll be coming for us any minute," she reminded him.

"I know. I'm ready."

She only hoped he meant it. "Just remember, I'm right here with you."

Then the door to the room opened and a young man in a polo shirt with the station logo on it greeted them. Blake was out of the chair, all smiles and shaking the man's hand. She wondered how in the hell he did it, and made it look so easy. Her admiration for him continued to grow.

"Jeff Groman," the man said. He shook Sam's hand, too. "We're ready for you, Mr. Morgan."

He led them down a hallway and into the studio. Sam took in the cameras stationed at different positions and the number of people moving around, doing whatever it was they did. Bright spotlights lit the set, half of which was the familiar news desk set up, the other half a conversation area with a couch and two chairs.

"Miss Quenel?" Jeff touched her shoulder and pointed to a director's chair. "We've got a seat for you over here. Or if you prefer, right here is a good place to stand. We find that most of the people who deliver our guests prefer that."

Good, because she had no intention of sitting someplace where she might not be able to move fast if needed. Not that she expected this nut job to attack Blake here in the studio. First of all, he'd have to find a way in. But her motto was "alert, always ready." It had never failed her.

She watched as Jeff Groman guided Blake to the conversation area, situated him in the armchair, and fitted him with a microphone. People moved around, speaking into their mics, changing the lighting, getting ready. Then Dan Gilardi, the host who'd be interviewing him, joined him, sitting at the end of the couch closest to the chair, introducing himself. Getting him comfortable.

And then it was time. The director cued them, counting down from five, and they were live.

Sam had been holding her breath, although she wasn't sure what for, and finally released it when she saw things were going well. Gilardi asked Blake all the usual questions: where he got his ideas, what kind of research he did, how he put his stories together, if his characters were based on real people. If she hadn't known better, she'd have thought this was a walk in the park for him. He was relaxed, smiling, friendly.

God. The man was incredible. Stressed out, upset about Grant Kennelly, never knowing when the stalker was going to strike again, yet there he sat, cool as a cucumber, relaxed as if he was chatting with a friend. She'd seen the behavior of a number of other high-profile figures and her admiration for the man Blake had grown into took a giant leap forward. She wasn't ready yet to hand over her heart by any means, but she was seeing a side of the man that surprised her.

Finally Gilardi talked about the book signing that evening, the location and the time.

And then they were finished. The lights over that part of the set went off and Gilardi rose and shook hands with Blake. Alan Moretti, who had come on to the set to watch the segment, moved forward.

"Great interview," he enthused. "I can see why your fans love you."

Blake grinned, relaxed now that he was out of the torture chamber. "Thanks, but I think it's my books they love."

"Speaking of books, we brought some into the guest lounge. Would you mind signing them for the staff?"

"Of course not."

Half an hour and another round of handshakes later they were done and back in the car.

"Whew!" Blake leaned back in his seat. "I'm always worried I'll put my foot in my mouth and say something that will give my agent or my publisher a fit."

"I don't know why. You did great up there."

"Thanks. Hope this afternoon's interview goes as well." He pulled his cell from his pocket and scrolled through his notes.

"We're meeting this guy for lunch, right?"

"Yes. Henry texted the info to both of us." She edged into another lane of traffic.

"Anything from Avery today?" he asked.

"Not much, but I'll bring you up to date on what we do have. How about if we grab a cup of coffee someplace and I can go over it with you?"

They found a small coffee shop that suited their purpose and carried their drinks to a table at the window. Sam had tried to park close enough so she could keep an eye on the car and see if anyone approached. Unfortunately, the sidewalk was crowded with people, so periodically it was lost to view.

Blake blew on his coffee, took a sip, and leaned forward. "Okay, give. Does she have anything new? And anything else on Grant's beating?"

Sam took a hit of her own coffee, black with an extra shot, and scrolled through her phone for Avery's message.

"They collected a ton of prints but we don't know yet if any of them belong to your stalker. Vigilance is running them through our system and Sheri's detective is running them through IAFIS, the national fingerprint database, but so far nothing. We do know that he's a large man, so that's something."

"How do you figure that?"

"Grant Kennelly is pretty heavyset. This guy carried him from your parents' back door to the Kennellys' hedges."

"Oh, right." He swallowed some coffee. "So I should start being careful of heavy men with big feet?"

She swallowed a smile at his grumpiness. There was nothing funny about this at all.

"Avery's got them combing through every part of your life since high school, especially once your first book was published. You never know who's jealous of your success or what triggers something like this. I do have to say you've had a lot of interesting people in your life."

He barked a short laugh. "No kidding. Get after Henry, too. I was lucky enough to sign with him in the beginning. He could probably tell you about some idiots who might fit the bill."

"Oh, rest assured, we had Henry send us a list right at the start. But the machine keeps chugging. Whoever this is, Vigilance will find out." She checked her watch. "We'd better get going. You don't want to be late for lunch with the reporter."

"Yeah, because I'm really looking forward to it so much."

She cocked an eyebrow. "You know, every personality I've worked with eats this kind of stuff up. They can't get enough of it. I thought celebrities craved the media."

He nodded. "Most of them do. But twice I saw friends of mine crucified for the sake of a good story, hung out to dry for no reason at all. I can't help wondering if I'll be next in line. And with this stalker business? I'm gun-shy about everything."

"One of the things Avery does is train her people to handle the media. We have a lot of high-profile clients, so there's always a lot of media contact. I won't let them set a trap for you. I know how to redirect the conversation."

His lips curved in a tired smile. "Annemarie was good at that, too."

"Annemarie sounds like a real paragon." Oh, hell. She hoped that didn't sound as waspish as she thought. "Sorry, I didn't mean for it to come out that way. I gather she was an incredible help to you."

"She was. That's why I was shocked when she just left the way she did." He ran a hand over his face. "And why I'm still struggling with the news of her death."

"When we get to the car," she reminded him, "don't react to anything I do. The stalker is sure to be watching and I don't want to give anything away."

He lifted an eyebrow. "Anything like what?"

"If there's a new message, you'll see." When she bent down to pick up her purse, and she was out of sight of the window, she slid a folded piece of paper inside her sleeve. Then she led the way out the door.

Blake spotted the note first as they approached the car, a folded sheet of paper placed beneath the passenger side windshield wiper.

"Damn it to hell." He gritted his teeth. "This bastard is all over me and we can't get a smell of him."

Sam wasn't too happy herself. Whoever this was had to have waited for the right opportunity when a crowd obscured the view of the car to leave the message. But that meant that he was close to them, keeping an eye on them, watching them. The itch between her shoulder blades told her she wasn't wrong.

"Don't let him see you're angry," she told Blake in a quiet voice.

"What do you mean? Is he watching us? Where the hell is he?"

He started to look around but she put a hand on his arm and squeezed, hard.

"I'm sure he is, and he's watching for your reaction. You won't be able to tell who it is because he obviously does disguises well. And just looking for a large man won't do you any good, because there seem to be a lot of large men walking around here right now."

"But—"

"He could be in any one of these storefronts, looking out the window, glancing over people's heads. Waiting. Watching. Do not give him the satisfaction."

"If I see him, I'll kill him," Blake growled.

"And that would certainly make good material for our reporter friend who's waiting for us, right?" She reached for the folded paper, then shielded her movement so she could switch it with the one in her sleeve. "We're going to give him something to think about. Maybe he'll get mad enough to make a mistake."

Without unfolding it, she crumpled the paper into a ball and tossed it in the trash can by the lamppost.

"What the hell?" Blake tried to retrieve the paper but she pushed him away.

"Get in the car."

"But—"

"Get in the damn car, Blake. For once can you just listen to what I'm telling you? Please?"

She could almost see the steam coming out of his ears but he got into the car, snapped the seat belt in place with far more force than was necessary. She watched to see if any cars pulled out behind her and when none did, and they were away from that street, she slid the real note from her sleeve and handed it to Blake.

"Here. I'm not worried about fingerprints anymore. Vigilance has enough to work with between what you left them and what they lifted from your parents' house. Open this and read it."

"What is this?" he growled, unfolding it. "Sam? How the hell did you do this?"

"A sleight of hand trick Mike Pérez taught me my first month at Vigilance. He'd used it to smuggle a document out of a meeting. What does it say?"

"Shit."

"It says shit? That's all?"

"You know that's not what's on here. Damn it, Sam, he watched the television spot this morning."

"Well, of course he did. He's your number one fan right now. So read it to me."

> *"You made a big mistake this morning. You don't appreciate the right people. But you'll pay. Soon everyone will know what you've done."*

Blake handed the folded note back to Sam.

"You'd think if what I'd done was so hideous I'd remember, wouldn't you? Damn it, Sam. This is driving me nuts."

"Well, pull yourself together, because we're almost at the restaurant. Get through the interview then we can crash in the room until the signing tonight."

The restaurant had a parking lot at the side. With no spaces available at the curb, Sam considered herself lucky that she scored a spot right against the wall. She made sure the front of the car kissed the concrete, which was the best she could do.

She slid her hand through Blake's arm as they walked to the front of the building. "Okay, let's go make you more famous."

Chapter 9

The stalker sat in his car, watching, his rage slowly building. Damn it to hell. Did nothing go his way? It was that damn bodyguard who was screwing up everything. *She* was the one calling the shots. Otherwise he was sure Blake Morgan would be completely rattled and afraid by now. Almost killing the neighbor should have pushed him over the edge. Instead it gave him an unexpected rush. He could hardly wait to do it again.

Of course, he'd have to choose carefully. A random episode would mean nothing. And it also had to have the right effect on the signing tour. He didn't want the tour cancelled. He had something spectacular planned for the finale. No, he wanted one that would send a message to that piece of scum, one that showed him how close he was and that he could do this at will. It couldn't be connected directly to Morgan by the public, though. It was important for the tour to continue, for him to be able to implement his plan at the different stops along the way.

He smiled, thinking of the steps leading up to the finale, each one destroying the man a little more until at last they reached the ultimate act of revenge.

But that bitch kept interrupting his plans. Like today, when she crumpled his note and threw it away without even reading it. For a moment rage had blinded him. How dare she dismiss his notes like that, as if they meant nothing. They meant everything, each one carefully crafted to lead the piece of shit one step closer to reality. He'd wanted to retrieve it from the trash can, but it was across the street and the sudden surge of traffic had made it impossible.

And he didn't want to hang around to get it. He had other things to do. Plans to make. He grabbed his tablet from the seat beside him and brought up the tracking program. He'd managed to place a tracking device on the car Morgan and the woman were using, laughing silently at how easy it was. He'd just dropped something behind the car and when he went to retrieve it, stuck the little device in place. It was important for him to know everyplace they went so he could move forward with each step of his plan.

Remember, he kept telling himself, the point for now was to unnerve him. Throw him off his game. Make him take a good hard look at things and realize someone knew what a fake he was. How he'd lied and fooled the public all this time.

That interview this morning had enraged him. The stalker had listened carefully but the man had ignored the most important part of his career. The thing that had *made* his career. The reality behind Blake Morgan. But no. He'd left it out. Deliberately, the stalker was sure.

Well, not for much longer. Soon everyone would know the truth about what he'd done.

Soon.

* * * *

As soon as they were back in the suite, Blake stripped off his jacket and tie and tossed them on a chair.

"I need a drink. Preferably a big one." So many different emotions were seething inside him he couldn't make himself settle down. Lunch had been fine, and the reporter no worse than others he'd met with. But the note was making him twitchy, along with the certain knowledge that the stalker was seldom far away from them.

Sam grinned. "Good idea, but how about after the signing tonight?"

"How about—never mind. Where's that note?"

"Right here." She held it out to him.

> *You made a big mistake this morning. You don't appreciate the right people. But you'll pay. Soon everyone will know what you've done.*

He scraped his fingers through his hair. "Mistake? What kind of mistake? I answered all the questions honestly and politely. And who don't I appreciate? My readers? I thanked them a bunch of times." He looked over at Sam, who was sitting at the little table with her laptop. "I don't know what the hell this guy wants from me."

"And that's really the sticking point here," she told him. "If we could figure that out, we might know who we're dealing with."

"Anything new from Avery?"

"Yes and no. Yes, an email but no, nothing of value. They've run all the prints from your parents' home. The only stray ones they found belong to the woman who cleans for them once a week."

"We could have figured that," he pointed out. "Whoever this is, he's not stupid enough to leave prints anywhere."

Sam looked over at him. "You know, at first I wondered if this was some jilted female in your past out for revenge."

"I told you," he snapped. "You won't find anything like that. Have I had relationships? Some, but nothing very long or lasting. And every single one of them ended amicably."

She laughed. "You must have some magic touch, Morgan. Surely there's some woman out there who believes you strung her along and then dumped her."

He was beside her in two strides, cupping her cheeks in his hands.

"Listen to me, Sam. Please, listen to what I'm telling you." He blew out a breath and crouched in front of her, taking her hands in his. "I know we agreed to take this slow and see what happens, but I need to tell you this. I'm sorry if you think it's too soon. I've lived with the memory of that night and what might have been for a long time. No other woman ever got to me the way you did, despite how young we were at the time. The more I'm with you, the mature Samantha, the more I'm coming to believe you're the only one for me. Can you believe that? Please?"

Yes, Sam, please believe me.

Maybe he was wrong to tell her this so soon, but he couldn't keep his mouth shut any longer.

He lifted her hands and kissed each of them, then cupped her face again and brought her mouth to his. God! Her lips were so soft and she tasted so hot, a flavor that rushed into his system and heated his blood. He took the kiss deep trying to show her how he felt about her, what he felt *for* her. He only broke the kiss when he needed to breathe. He lifted his head and found Sam looking at him with a stunned expression.

"You were more than just a date to me, Sam. I know that sounds stupid, considering the age we were at the time. But think about this. Think about how it's been when we make love."

"Blake, please. I'm not anywhere near ready to deal with this yet."

He held her face between his palms. "Listen to me. Did you at all believe the things I said the other night? Or how it is when we make love? Yes, Sam, made love. How can I make you believe I'm not that immature teenager anymore? I haven't been for a long time, and I won't stop saying it until you believe. So jilted lovers after my ass? I've never been with a woman long enough for her to consider herself one. Period."

She ran her tongue over her lips, wetting them and making him want to kiss her again.

"Okay." She blew out a soft, slightly ragged breath. "No angry women after you. Got it."

"And get this, too." He kissed her again, short and hard. "As soon as this tour is over and we catch this fucking bastard, my number one priority is making sure you know we're going to build something here."

Some unnamed emotion flared in her eyes, but in a minute it was gone. Maybe it was the nature of the situation he was in, but he had become desperate to hang on to her, to create a future with her. She grounded him in a way no one ever had.

"Um, okay." She wrapped her fingers around his wrists and locked her gaze with his. "We'll see."

"Sam, I—"

She touched the tips of her fingers to his lips. "One of these nights when I can talk to you in the dark, I have to tell you another reason I'm so skittish. I—" She bit her lower lip. "I haven't always made the best choices with the men in my life, so I'm not sure I can tell what's real anymore. I couldn't stand it if I made a mistake where you were concerned. We need to be sure we aren't just living out some teenage fantasy."

He wanted to tell her this was no mistake, that what had happened before in her life didn't matter, but he knew it mattered a lot to her so he'd just have to help her work through it.

"The past is the past," he said slowly, "but I hear what you're saying. When you're ready, lay it all out on the table so I can brush away those fears. Now—" He rose to his feet. "What else from Avery?"

"They're going through the names you gave them of everyone you could think of who might have the tiniest grudge. That was some long list you gave them."

Blake's mouth curved in a wry grin. "You said to include everyone."

"Including the author who argued that you had better placement at a book signing. Holy hell, Blake, are people really that petty?"

"You'd be surprised. This is a very competitive business. We're all after the same consumer dollars with massive amounts of product they can choose from. That's why I keep doing these interviews. Not everyone gets on that circuit and it pays to take advantage of whatever you can."

"I'm beginning to think writers are worse at this than actors or musicians, both of whom I've had the unpleasant task of providing security for."

He shrugged. "Maybe."

"At least Vigilance is eliminating people, which is something." She set her laptop aside. "So what's your routine while you're waiting for the signing?"

He looked at his watch. "We've got four hours to the event. I try to get there about fifteen minutes ahead of time."

"And in the meantime?"

In the meantime, I want to strip you naked and take you to bed, immerse myself in your body until that's all I can think about.

"What I'd like to do will have to wait until we get back here later. I have some research I need done for my latest book. And I'm going to try to get a chapter done today. This business with the stalker has really thrown me off my schedule."

"Would you have been writing during the week you were off?"

He nodded. "I have a deadline looming and I'm behind."

"Then why don't we both get busy?"

Blake sent her the list of things he needed researched, then grabbed his own laptop, sat down at the table across from her, and booted up. He had two email addresses, just as he had two cell phones, one for private and one for the public. Annemarie used to answer his public emails but when she left, his publisher assigned someone to do it for him. He usually breezed through it, just in case there was someone he wanted to touch base with himself.

Then he pulled up the personal ones. He clicked first on the one from his cousin, Robin, who was one of his biggest cheerleaders. She had even gotten her book club involved and they read each of his books when they came out. She had attached a document that the message said was something he'd enjoy reading. But when he opened the document he was stunned. Although the header indicated Robin's email, the attached document definitely wasn't from her.

"Killer! I know what you did!"

He nearly knocked his chair over backing away. "What the hell?"

Sam looked over at him. "What's up?"

He turned the laptop around so she could see.

"Don't touch any of the keys. I want to send this to Avery. But let me text her first, so she knows it's coming."

"What good will that do?" he demanded. "They can't trace the source."

"You never know what they can do."

"Does that mean he hacked my cousin's computer, too? Shit."

Sam shook her head. "No. I don't know all the ins and outs of cyber warfare, but I do know we've had situations like this before. Our guys have a way of tracking back to the source." Then she hesitated. "Well, sometimes."

"Before you send that, minimize it and let me check my manuscript. I don't know if the document in this email carries a virus that will allow him to hack into it or not. But if this guy can do that he can get into my hard drive and my files."

Blake clicked over to the folder where his current files were stored, sick to his stomach when he saw it was completely empty.

"God damn motherfucker." He slammed his fist on the table.

"What?" Sam hurried to his side. "What's wrong?"

"See this folder?" He pointed to the screen.

"I do. There's nothing in it. Oh, God, Blake. Is that where your manuscript is stored?"

"Yeah." He wiped his hand over his face, as if he could wipe away what he was seeing. "Let me check something else."

He clicked on the icon for his cloud storage, typed in his password and opened it. At first everything looked okay. He opened some of the folders and the files were still there. But then he went to the one for his work in progress and it, like the one on his hard drive, was empty.

"God, Blake." Samantha stared at his screen. "What are you going to do?"

"First of all, I'm smarter than this idiot. I wasn't prepared for this, but I do know computers can crash, and even cloud storage can be hacked. Watch this." He reached beside him for his messenger bag and pulled out a thumb drive. "Hard backup just in case."

"No. Stop." Sam closed her fingers over his wrist. "Don't plug it in there."

"Why the hell not? Sam, I need to get some work done."

"Let's plug it into mine to check it. I'm calling Avery. She may want us to ship this laptop to them so they can run diagnostics and see if they can pick up whatever virus or viruses this guy is using, or programs to mess with your stuff."

"What am I supposed to do without my computer?" God. He was getting so far behind. He'd have to get Henry to have a talk with the publisher.

"We'll take care of it. You've got your manuscript and that's what's most important. Just let me give her a call. Please."

More than anything Blake wished for that drink now. He drummed his fingers on the table while Sam talked to Avery, trying to make sense out of what they were discussing. Finally, when he was about to grab the phone himself, Sam disconnected the call.

"Okay, here's what we're going to do. It's obvious this guy's cyber skills are way up in the stratosphere, and we can't leave you electronically unprotected."

He frowned. "I don't understand. What can we do?"

"Vigilance has contacts in several cities that we use for various things." She grinned. "You know, all our jobs aren't in Arrowhead Bay."

"I know that." He bit down on his impatience.

"So we're going to see someone here in Charlotte that Avery's worked with for a long time. He'll get you all fixed up."

"What about sending this laptop back?" he asked. "And transferring all the material on it?"

"He'll take care of that," Sam assured him. "Including shipping the laptop, just in case your stalker decides to follow us around. Just shove everything back in our bag."

A headache was starting to build at the base of his head. He dug into his messenger bag for some aspirin and tossed down three of them with a glass of water. Then he packed up his bag, grabbed a soft collar shirt, and switched it for the one he was wearing.

"Tonight's shirt and tie again," he told Sam. "Right now I need to be comfortable."

As if a different shirt could fix what was happening.

When they pulled into the driveway of a house in an upscale residential area of Charlotte, rather than a store or office in a business area, he wasn't the least surprised. He was learning that nothing in this business was ever as it seemed on the surface. And despite the turmoil of this situation, he intended to find time to keep notes on all of this for the future.

A man who could have been forty or sixty, in black jeans and a T-shirt, let them in.

Sam made the introductions. "Blake, this is Fred."

Fred just nodded, listened to what they wanted, and went to work. Blake watched everything the man did, fascinated, and took mental notes. Two hours after they arrived they walked out the door with a new laptop filled with every kind of security possible. His files had been restored from the thumb drive and he had a cloud storage account with the no-name security company.

"Can I go to work for the CIA now?" he joked as they pulled away.

"No." Sam chuckled. "But you could audition for Vigilance."

Blake looked at his watch. "I don't think I'll be getting much work done this afternoon."

"Do you normally eat before a signing?"

"No. Well, just something light. Some kind of snack. Annemarie used to order something up from room service. And I need to shower, shave, and get dressed."

"Then as the new Annemarie," she said in a light voice, "I'll find an appealing snack and get it up to the room for you."

On the ride back to the hotel, everything seemed to suddenly coalesce and slam into him like a big black rock. He thought he'd been pretty together up to this point, dealing with everything rationally, even when he wanted to rail and scream and find this guy and chop his head off. He'd done his best to maintain a calm appearance all afternoon, but inside he was shaken.

He leaned his head back in the seat, trying once again to make sense of everything. He thought of Grant Kennelly, a nice man who was only watching out for his neighbor, beaten half to death because he got in the way of the stalker. The situation shook him badly. Avery fed them daily updates and thankfully, the doctors predicted a full recovery, although it would be a long one.

The notes, their language getting bolder and bolder, were unsettling him more than he let on. The knowledge that the asshole had been watching them the whole time they were in the coffee shop—coffee shop? The asshole was watching them all day!—distressed and unnerved him. And now this thing with his laptop. The fact that this stalker could access his emails and his files that he thought were so protected really rocked him. He thought not being able to write this afternoon was probably a blessing in disguise, since his brain was so fractured by this whole situation. He probably wouldn't have been able to write a coherent sentence.

He was still trying to straighten out his brain and make some sense out of all this when they walked back into the suite. He couldn't even concentrate when Sam asked him to make a choice from the room service menu.

"Whatever you choose is fine." He set his messenger bag down on the couch.

"Blake?" Sam walked over, stood in front of him and placed her soft hands on his cheeks. "Blake, look at me."

He managed a half smile. "You're the only thing I want to look at."

"That's nice, but just look into my eyes and listen to me."

He drew in a breath and then let it out slowly, hoping it would settle his whirling mind.

"Okay. I can look at you forever."

"Then look and listen. Don't let him get in your head like this. I know it's hard, but that's what he wants. That's why he's doing everything the way he is. He wants to turn you into a quivering, shivering mass before he finally unleashes the big one."

He gawked at her. "The big one? Hell, Sam. What the fuck do you think he's got in mind?"

"The beatdown on Grant was an unexpected treat for him. An accident of fortune that allowed him to rattle you even more."

"It wasn't fortunate for Grant." Blake snorted.

"Of course not. And it's one more thing for you to deal with." She stroked his late day scruff. "The more he can put you on edge, the more he can shake you up, the happier he is. He wants you destroyed. But I promise you when he gets to the end of his campaign he will have something huge planned."

"And I don't even know the fuck why."

"Not yet, but we'll find out. Meanwhile, you have readers who aren't part of this. They know nothing about it and tonight a significant number of them will be standing in line to listen to you and get you to sign their books. They're who you have to focus on right now."

He cupped her face in his palms and brushed his lips against hers. He loved the way she tasted, like ripe fruit, and her faintly floral scent that always tantalized him and made him hard just by inhaling it.

He grinned at her. "I know what would really relax me," he teased.

"I'll bet it would, but let's save it for later. Okay?" She gave him a quick kiss and took a step back. "Now go shower while I order up some snacks."

"Get something more for yourself," he suggested. "You don't have to wait to eat until later."

"I'm good." She planted a very light kiss on his mouth. "Now go on. Shower and change."

Every gesture like that, every intimate touch, continued to give him hope that when this tour was over they'd have the solid basis for a future. He'd walked away from her once. He wasn't planning to do it again.

With that in mind, he pulled himself together while he showered and dressed. By the time he was back in the living room, nibbling on the finger food Sam had ordered up, he was feeling good about the coming event tonight. That good feeling lasted until they went to get the car and found the latest note tucked under the windshield wiper.

I know what you did, and soon everyone else will, too. Take care of those near and dear to you. Your time is coming.

Chapter 10

Sam took a picture of the note, then texted Avery and sent the picture as an attachment. Avery texted right back.

"Just help him keep it together tonight. Take pictures of the crowd. Maybe the creep will show.

They wouldn't know who he was, but she and Avery had discussed doing this at all the stops. That way if there was someone who showed up each time they'd have a face to focus on.

On the way to the store she did her best to calm Blake down and help him gather himself for the book signing. She hated to see him so rattled, but she could hardly blame him. This guy, whoever he was, knew exactly how to stick the knife in and twist it.

She'd spent some of the time in Arrowhead Bay doing a lot of reading about Blake Morgan. The world could find out anything it wanted to know about the man just by doing a global search online.

She'd learned he was well respected in the industry, that his books got excellent reviews and that with the fourth book he'd finally hit the best-seller lists. When she checked his social media pages she discovered he had thousands of Facebook likes and more than fifty thousand Twitter followers. Scoping out his photo album on Facebook she discovered that he never posed with just one woman unless it was a reader, and that his readers apparently mobbed him for pictures.

She asked herself over and over how a guy who had grown up to be a decent human being could have acquired someone so vicious as this stalker. There was no hint, not on social media or in any of the articles she'd read, of anything he might have done to engender this kind of situation.

All this reading also gave her a clearer insight into the man he'd become. Maybe she could let herself believe what he said. God knew she wanted to very badly. Those feelings she'd kept buried all these years were battering at the wall she kept around them. But she worried things were moving too fast, not at all the way she'd insisted that day in the Driftwood. And then there was her past, and all the mistakes she'd made. How did she get beyond that?

God, what a mess.

But right now, she reminded herself, her focus was on Blake. She done her best to settle him before they left the hotel. Now she sensed him pulling himself together and donning the personality of the public Blake Morgan. When they exited the car in the parking lot behind the store, someone not familiar with him would see a man relaxed and ready to meet his public. Only Sam, or someone else who knew him well, would catch the telltale tightening of his jaw or the haunted look in his eyes.

Chelsea Hanover, the store manager, was waiting for them when they rang the bell for the back door.

"We're so excited to have you, Mr. Morgan." She smiled as she led them inside. "As I told your assistant, we've had tons of calls since your television spot this morning." She gestured toward the interior of the store. "And as you can see, you won't lack for fans tonight."

Sam wasn't sure what she had expected, but it wasn't the wall-to-wall people in the store, which was no small space.

"I'll do my best to satisfy them," Blake told her, his public personality covering him like a cloak. He took Sam's arm and tugged her forward. "This is my personal assistant, Sam Quenel. If you have any questions about anything, feel free to ask her. And she'll be taking pictures of the readers. I hope that's okay."

"That will be fine. They'll like that, especially if you tell them you'll be posting on Facebook. And I know there will be some who will want selfies with you."

He had talked to her about this. He didn't want to risk upsetting his fans and she agreed she'd supervise it.

The moment they were out of the little hallway and into the store proper, the noise level rose exponentially.

"There he is," someone called out.

Sam skimmed her gaze over the crowd. She figured the ages ran from early thirties to mid-seventies. Of course, thrillers appealed to all age groups so the crowd was a real mixture.

Sam had been to other book signings so she was familiar with the setup—a roped-off section with a table for the author, pens and water at his elbow. The books had already been purchased by the readers, who held them tightly as they waited their turn. Blake was introduced and he gave what he'd explained to her earlier was his usual presentation, calling for questions at the end. Then the rope holding back the line was lifted from the stanchion to let the first group of people move toward him, with two of the store employees guiding them to maintain order.

How does he do this? Chat, sign, take pictures, move on to the next one.

She had his messenger bag behind her against the wall, away from the crowd, so this time no one could leave a note. While Blake did his thing, she took pictures. She was constantly checking the crowd, mainly looking for a man who would be big enough and strong enough to carry Grant Kennelly across the yard. But she also kept her eyes peeled for anyone who gave off weird vibes. It wasn't outside the realm of possibility that the stalker had an accomplice.

Sam made sure she was never far from his side, continuing to take pictures of the crowd with her phone. At the end of the night she'd send them back to Avery. Vigilance could run them through their sophisticated facial recognition software. She didn't expect they'd get one to pop up with a label that said "stalker," but you never knew what you'd get out of one of these searches. And at the upcoming signings she'd do the same thing. If they were lucky they might spot the same face in more than one place.

Finally, the last person shook his hand, had their picture taken with him and left with their signed book. Blake put down his pen and flexed his hand, no doubt cramping from writing all that time. Chelsea Hanover asked if they could take some pictures of him with the display of his books and with some of the store personnel. Then his final chore—sitting in the office and signing the presolds, for people who could not make the opening.

"Thank you so much for doing this, Mr. Morgan." Chelsea shook his hand enthusiastically.

"My pleasure."

"Our regional manager wanted to be here. He's a big fan of yours. Unfortunately he had a business emergency that required his attention. He did, however, ask me to pass along that he'd be contacting your publisher about dates in some of the other stores."

"Tell him thank you very much. I'll look forward to it."

"See?" Sam nudged him with her elbow as they left the store. "It was a good night and you were a huge success."

"I'd like to think so." Blake breathed a sigh of relief. "I don't know what I was expecting," he told her. "Maybe some maniac to come running in screaming about whatever it is I'm supposed to have done. But it was just a normal book signing. Thank the lord."

"Do you always get a crowd this big?" She was curious about that.

"Usually. That's why Henry asked for the signings to be at larger stores." He chuffed a laugh. "On my first tour, I was happy to get ten people."

"Hopefully, all the rest of the signings will go as well."

Sam held her breath as they approached the car, but the windshield was blessedly free of any notes. She pressed the remote, opened her door—and took a step back.

Holy hell!

A book lay on the passenger side of the front seat. Not just any book, but the one he'd been signing tonight with a note folded on top of it. A knife had been stabbed through both items.

Blake had stored his messenger bag in the back seat and opened the front passenger door to climb in. The moment he spotted the little display, he took a step back. "What the hell?"

"Don't touch anything," Sam told him. "And don't try to get in."

"Fuck." He spat he word. "He's done it again."

Sam looked at him. "What do you mean? Has he left you a little, um, present like this before?"

"No, not that. It's in the stuff I told Avery about. He left one of his notes in my trunk, taped to the spare tire. Crap." He scrubbed a hand over his face. "Do you know that for a hundred dollars you can buy a little gizmo online that will unlock any car door?"

"Unfortunately, yes. They make for all kinds of problems." She set her tote on the ground.

"Damn it all to hell." He smacked his fist on the roof. "He used this new book. Is the knife supposed to mean he's stabbing me in the heart? Or I figuratively stabbed someone in the back? Or maybe, God forbid, he's planning to kill?"

"Careful," Sam warned. "He could be watching. And for God's sake, don't look around. He wants to see your reaction. Remember?"

"Hell."

"I think any of those choices are possible," she answered. "Or maybe none of them. With someone like this, where the reason behind everything is so vague, it's hard to make a determination. And I don't want to eliminate any possibility too soon."

"Shit." He let out a long sigh. "How did my life get so screwed up? Sam, I swear to you, I know I keep saying this, but no matter how much I dig through my brain, I can't think of a thing I've done to warrant this kind of stuff."

"It could be something totally insignificant to you, but so enormous to this person that he keeps blowing it out of proportion."

"Swell. Just swell."

"Be very, very careful here. Don't touch anything. Just stand back for a minute. The first thing I want to do is take a picture and shoot it to Avery. She'll call back soon, I promise you."

She could almost see the tension rolling off him in waves as she took her pictures and sent them off in a text to Avery.

"People coming." Blake inclined his head toward the back of the store.

She looked up as two of the salespeople walked out the back door.

"Lean on the car like we're talking, maybe discussing whether to go out to eat or something."

"Everything okay, Mr. Morgan?" one of the women called.

"Yes, we're all good. Thanks. Just figuring out if we're hungry or not."

"I can recommend some good places around here," the other woman chimed in.

"We've got it, but thanks." He waved at them.

Sam hoped they got the message.

"Oh, okay. Well, good night. Thanks again for tonight."

She and Blake waited until the women had climbed into a car and driven off.

"That was good," Sam told him in a low voice. "We don't want to get anyone else involved in this and start some kind of panic. Or worse yet, a gossip train."

"No shit. The next signing is day after tomorrow and we can't let anything derail it." He shook his head. "You never know what attracts people and what turns them off."

"Agreed. We don't want to give this guy any publicity until we have to. We should hear back from Avery in a second."

Even as she said the words, her phone chimed.

"Looks like he's making use of his little gizmo again," were Avery's first words.

"Yeah. Blake said the same thing."

"He's got balls. You have to give him that. He did this whole thing in a parking lot where anyone could have seen him."

"It's a strip center," Sam told her. "The bookstore is the anchor and the parking for it is in the back at the end. The store had a space for us right by the back door, so whoever this is took a major chance on being discovered."

"The knife disturbs me," Avery told her. "It's an indication that, as we expected, he's escalating. The problem with people like this who are unbalanced, once they get a taste of the excitement danger creates, they often find it hard to stop."

Sam let out a sigh. "Great. Just great. We'll be on the alert and I'll start vetting the bookstore sites better." She shifted the phone to the other hand. "We shouldn't stand here much longer. You want me to send this to you?"

"Please. Use the same person you met with this afternoon."

"That's my plan," she told her boss.

"How's Blake?"

Sam turned away and lowered her voice. "About how you would expect but keeping it together."

"Take care of him, Sam. I don't want him to fall apart."

"I'm on it."

She disconnected the call, shoved her phone in her pocket, and opened her tote.

"Now what?" Blake asked.

"Now we remove this very carefully and get it ready to overnight to Avery."

She took out a pair of latex gloves and a large plastic bag. After snapping on her gloves, she slid the book and knife toward her and eased it upright into the bag. Then she placed it on the floor in the back.

"You just going to leave it there?" Blake asked.

"Of course not. But the box I need to put it in is back at the hotel. Come on. Let's take care of this. Then we'll get something to eat."

Blake shook his head as he slid into the car. "I don't think I could eat anything. Not after this."

"Maybe a slice of pizza?" She had to get him to eat or he'd be sick.

"I don't know." He closed his eyes.

In the light from the parking lot she could see the lines of tension etched into his face. "We'll see. Let's do this first."

"Where are you going to ship anything this time of night? Everyplace is closed."

She grinned. "Our friend from this afternoon has many resources."

Blake glanced at his watch. "You're going to call him at this time of night?"

"The word is he never sleeps. Let's take a detour to his place. Then we'll revisit the food thing again."

* * * *

Blake wanted to wait in the car while Sam carried the sickening package into the house, but she vetoed that.

"You don't know if he's out there, watching, waiting for an opportunity to attack you."

"Before he tells me why he's doing all this?"

"It's not worth the risk. Come on, big boy. Let's get this done."

"Avery called," Fred told them at the door. "I know what needs to be done. Come on, Sam."

They left Blake sitting in the living room while Fred ushered Sam to a room in the back. Blake leaned his head back against the couch and tried to find some measure of calm. Most of the good feeling from the successful book signing dissipated with this latest episode. If he only knew who or what was behind this, but no matter how he beat up his brain, nothing came to him.

He wished he could just shut that same brain off for a few hours and forget about all this for a while. At the signing tonight, he'd found himself looking at the people who brought their books for him to sign and wondering if it was one of them. Or, like Sam, mentioned, was it someone who didn't come to buy a book but just to watch him, study his reaction to everything? The idea gave him the creeps and a tiny shudder raced over him.

He knew Sam would try to feed him, but the last thing he wanted right now was food. What he really wanted—needed—was to take a naked Sam to bed and lose himself in her exquisite body. Each time they'd been together the coupling had been close to frantic, as if they were trying to satisfy a desperate need. Something left over from the past. A desire to find out if what they'd carried around all these years was more than the vestiges of teenage horniness.

What he wanted tonight was to shut out all of this craziness, block the anxiety that dogged his every minute, and make slow, delicious love with Samantha. He wanted her to leave Sam in the living room and bring Samantha into the bedroom.

He felt as if he'd been sitting there, waiting, for an hour, but when she finally came to fetch him, he checked his watch. Only fifteen minutes had passed.

"Well?" he asked, looking from Sam to Fred.

"All set," she told him.

"I have a private plane flying someone's client to Fort Myers tonight. Avery will send someone to the airport to meet the plane and collect the package."

Blake lifted an eyebrow.

"Just like that?"

"Just like that."

Sam thanked Fred, and then they were back in the car and headed down the quiet residential street. Neither of them spoke on the drive back to the hotel, as if there was nothing to say. Blake knew they still had way more questions than answers, and he was sure Sam was as tired of the questions as he was.

"Food?" she asked as they reached the downtown area. "If you don't want to stop anywhere, the hotel has room service 24-7."

"Let's get inside first. I have the feeling that creep has eyes on us and I want to get out of his sight."

"No one followed us when we left the bookstore," she told him. "But I understand where you're coming from."

"But if you're hungry, feel free to order something."

"We'll see. Like you said, let's get inside first."

He did his best not to keep looking over his shoulder when they parked the car and moved from the garage to the hotel. He was glad it was just the two of them in the elevator going up to the suite. Before he even stepped into the hall he had his tie off and stuffed in his pocket, the top buttons on his shirt undone, and his jacket off and draped over his arm.

"I hope you're planning to wait until we get into the suite before going any further," Sam teased.

"Barely." He managed a wink.

She might have thought he was teasing but far from it. The moment they were inside and had dropped their things by the couch, he reached for her and took her into his arms.

"I don't want food, Sam." He wrapped her long braid around one hand and tilted her head back. "I want you. Naked. That's better than any food or drink you can order for me. That's all I need. Just you."

She stared back at him, her brilliant blue eyes now the color of a stormy sea with all the emotions swirling in them.

"That sounds…serious." She wet her lower lip with her tongue, and his cock immediately leaped to life.

"As a heart attack," he told her.

"We don't want any heart attacks here, do we?" She stroked his cheeks with her slender fingers.

"Definitely not." He couldn't take his gaze from her. "Could I interest you in a shower? Something to wash all this crap out of our lives for a while?"

He held his breath, waiting for her answer. She had to know how he was feeling. She had seemed to pull back a little. He was glad that right now she wasn't giving him a hard time about what he wanted. Make that needed. The more he was with her, the more he knew this was real. The trick would be convincing her. Her reluctance had to be about more than what happened all those years ago. He didn't know if she wasn't sure of him or herself, but he planned to figure out how to make damn sure she knew this wasn't just an itch he was scratching without scaring her off. When the time was right he'd make her tell him.

But not tonight.

"I think I could be persuaded," she said at last.

"Good."

Before she could change her mind, he swept her up in his arms and carried her into his bathroom. He didn't know what the one looked like in the other room, but this one was big enough to hold a dance in and the shower even had a convenient bench built into it.

He stood her by the vanity and very slowly removed each article of clothing, paying careful attention to every area of her body as he exposed it. He kissed his way down her neck and from shoulder to shoulder, drawing a light path with the tip of his tongue before lightly licking the valley between her breasts.

Her breasts! God, he'd never seen such wonderful breasts, round and firm with dusky pink nipples turning a darker shade of rose as he teased them with his tongue. On impulse, he sucked first one then the other into his mouth, tugging on them, grazing them with his teeth as he released them.

Kneeling, he undid the button of her slacks and eased down the zipper, pushing the fabric over her hips, down to her feet. He couldn't stop himself from smoothing his fingers over the tiny swell of her stomach or the angle of her hips. Her skin felt like the richest satin and her scent, a light floral, was driving all his hormones to charge ahead full speed. She braced herself on his shoulders as she kicked off her shoes and stepped out of the pool of material, then kicked it to the side. She was left standing in just the tiniest lacy blue bikini panties he'd ever seen.

When he took the lace edging in his teeth and dragged it down his eyes nearly popped out of his head. Both times he'd been in bed with her he hadn't paid enough attention to details, but tonight, that's what he was all about. Details. Like the fact that she obviously waxed bikini style, with a tempting strip of dark blond curls framing her delicious slit. Holding her hips to steady both her and himself, he drew a line down the wet length, delving in just slightly to tease her clit with the tip of his tongue. Then he did it again.

God! He could do this forever, but he had so much more of her to taste and explore.

"You still have your clothes on," she pointed out in a shaky voice. "Would you like some help taking them off?"

"I wouldn't say no to that."

He rose on legs just slightly unsteady from the desire coursing through him. He forced himself to stand still while she eased the fabric over his shoulders and down his arms. She mimicked what he'd done, peppering his shoulders and chest with soft kisses and pausing long enough to swirl her tongue around his nipples. An involuntary groan slid from him as every lick of her tongue sent a spear of fire straight to his groin.

When she dropped to her knees before him, as he'd done for her, the image was so erotic he was afraid he'd come before she even had a chance to touch him. He had presence of mind to reach into his kit on the vanity and pull out a string of three condoms before he lost his mind altogether.

"Optimistic?" Sam's voice shook.

"Hopeful."

She went back to work easing both his slacks and his boxer briefs down at the same time. Like her, he kicked off his shoes, managed to toe off his socks and kicked his slacks and boxers to the side. She danced her fingers down the line of hair that arrowed to his groin, brushing the tips over the thick nest. His balls ached with need and his cock was swollen and throbbing.

Touch me!

He wanted to shout the words, but he forced himself to stand quietly while she explored him. But when she wrapped those slim fingers around his shaft and gave the head a gentle lick he couldn't swallow the groan. She slid her fingers between his thighs, cupping his sac, while she took the length of him in her mouth.

Jesus!

He rocked back and forth, his shaft sliding in and out of her hot mouth, her satiny lips closing around him like an erotic vise. He knew he had to stop soon or it would be all over, but the sensations that swept through his body at her touch were so addicting he wanted them to go on forever.

"Shower," he gasped, urging her to her feet.

He reached in and turned it on, testing it until he was satisfied with the temperature. Then he took her hand, helped her inside, put one of the condoms in the soap dish, and took the bottle of scented bodywash the hotel thoughtfully provided. Pouring some into his hand, he worked it up into a thick lather and began applying it to her body.

He was mesmerized by her body, the gentle swell of her stomach, the curve of her hips, the roundness of her breasts. Her arms and legs were graceful as a dancer's and just as deceiving, their strength belying their delicate appearance. When he had finished with her front he turned her and began the same process with her back. He carefully kneaded each bump of her spine, and massaged the suds into the curve of her buttocks.

Very tentatively he slid his soapy fingers into the crevice between her cheeks, waiting to see if she would pull away from him. She tensed for a moment but then relaxed, braced herself against the wall, legs spread, and leaned back into his touch. He slid his hands around to her front, over her lips and down her stomach to find that hot, wet slit again. If he was hard before, Blake's dick was like granite now. He ached everywhere with consuming need. Just touching her clit with the tip of his fingers heated his blood and sent electricity to every nerve in his body.

"My turn," she whispered, turning around.

Her fingers were soothing as she smoothed lather over his tight muscles in slow, teasing strokes. Blake didn't know how long he could maintain his control, as close to the edge as her touch brought him. He gritted his teeth as she smoothed the soap over his body, swirling it in the hair on his chest and around his hard nipples. The light scrape of her fingernails across the flat, hard buds sent shards of fire straight to his balls and made the vein circling his shaft pulse and throb.

When she knelt before him he wanted to yell stop and plunge himself into her right then. Somewhere he found the tenuous threads of control to keep it together, but he didn't know for how long. Her strong fingers worked the lather into the muscles of his thighs, up to his groin, and wrapped around his dick until he had to bite his lip hard to keep from coming. Jesus! This woman did things to him, made him feel things, no other woman ever had.

But when she stroked him up and down, her hands slick from the foam, he closed his fingers over her wrist and moved her hand away.

"I've only got so much control," he told her in a hoarse voice.

He urged her to her feet and lifted her to the bench. If he was going to maintain any kind of control, he needed to take her edge off first. Because once he was inside her it would be a race to the finish.

With one of her legs resting on his shoulder, she was completely open to him. He sucked in his breath at the sight of her so pink and ready for him. Massaging her clit with his thumb, he slid two fingers easily into her waiting sex, loving the sound as she inhaled sharply. He cupped her head and held it in place, watching the change of expression.

He began a steady rhythm with his fingers, in and out, her inner walls clutching at him. She leaned back against the wall to steady herself, the heel of her foot digging into his shoulder as he increased the pace of thrust and retreat. She was so hot, so slick, so tight it took his breath away. Another rub with his thumb on her swollen hot button, another deep thrust with his fingers, and he felt the spasms begin inside her sex. He increased his speed, adding another finger.

"That's it. Come for me, Samantha. Come now."

She bore down on his hand and in the next second the spasms gripped her. He held her steady in place with his free hand while she rode the other. She was still trembling with aftershocks when he grabbed the condom, rolled it on, and with his hands holding her in place lowered her onto his raging hard-on.

Oh, sweet Jesus!

He saw stars as lightning flashed through his body and her slick walls closed tightly around him. Gritting his teeth to maintain some semblance of control, he pressed her until her back was against the shower wall.

"Hold on tight, darlin'. And don't let go."

He wanted to take it slowly, to savor every stroke, linger in that hot well of her body, but by now he was too aroused. Gripping her hips, he drove into her again and again, harder and faster.

"Look at me," he rasped.

She opened her eyes and he saw such a swirl of emotion in there he nearly lost it. He leaned forward, placed his mouth over hers and slipped his tongue inside. And that was all it took. One more hard thrust and he exploded, the muscles in his back tightening, his cock pulsing as he came again and again and again. And Samantha, despite the fact he'd made her come already, was right there with him, closing around him like a tight, wet fist.

When the last throb, the last spasm had died away, he eased from her. After disposing of the condom, he lifted her off the bench and gently rinsed both of them. He turned off the shower, helped her out, on to the bath mat, and grabbed big, fluffy, warm hotel towels for both of them. He stood her facing him while he dried first her body then his.

Neither of them said a word but both knew something irrevocable had changed between them. He thought he could spend the rest of his life doing this. Being with her. The fantasies he'd carried in his mind all these years paled into comparison with the reality. While she didn't say anything, he sensed the same feelings in her, only pushed back behind the emotional wall she'd erected. He was pretty damn sure she had no more idea how to deal with it than he did, but by God he was going to find a way.

Just as soon as they got rid of the crazed stalker.

Finally he carried her into the bedroom and tugged the covers back on the bed. When they slid in, he spooned around her, one arm around her cupping a breast, his cock nestled against her bottom. He was just on the edge of falling asleep when she spoke.

"Blake?"

"Uh-huh?"

"You were right. It was a lot better than eating or having a drink."

He laughed softly, kissed her cheek, and fell into a sleep where he dreamed of a naked Samantha.

Chapter 11

The stalker sat in his bedroom working to control his rage. Nothing had gone as he planned today. He had thought it all out so carefully, everything calculated to throw Morgan off his game before the book signing that night. He'd had hope when he saw how angry the man was in the parking lot of the Driftwood in Arrowhead Bay. But it seemed the more he pushed, the calmer Morgan became. Either the man hid his emotions well or he was so coldblooded that nothing bothered him.

Or Vigilance was coaching him, which was just as bad.

Angrily, he was coming to believe it was the latter. Otherwise how could he have done what he did, without even a twinge of conscience? He hadn't even shown the reaction the stalker expected when they'd found the Morgans' neighbor. What kind of man didn't rant and rave and go bananas when someone nearly got killed because of him? A decent man would have canceled the rest of his book tour.

But of course Blake Morgan wasn't a decent man. He was selfish, egotistical, and a people user. And *he* was going to make sure the world found out. But first he was going to destroy the man's career, then the man himself. It was no less than he deserved.

He lifted the knife from its place on the nightstand, stroking his fingers over the sharp blade. He'd carried the weapon with him in Arrowhead Bay just because he liked the feel of it hanging in its sheath from his belt. As he stroked the knife, irritation at today's events surged through him again. He had taken such care crafting this note, printing it out in the hotel's business center and placing it on the car when Morgan and the woman were inside the coffee shop. The possibility of detection out there on the street only added an additional thrill to the task. To have it thrown away was an insult to him he wouldn't soon forget.

But tonight was even worse. He had taken a chance and eased into the back of the crowd in the bookstore, just to get a glimpse of the miserable bastard rolling in glory that wasn't his. While everyone was enthralled with the man, the stalker had placed his "gift" to him in their rental car, using a knife similar to the one he had now. There weren't many places to hide in the parking lot where he could watch, but he managed to find one behind the dumpster and used his binoculars.

He cursed steadily under his breath when nothing he expected happened. Where was the horror he expected? The yelling and screaming? It was that damn bitch he was with, coaching him not to respond. He'd wanted to scream. Then they'd taken off for the same house they visited earlier in the day. He'd be too exposed if he followed them, but he could track them on his tablet with the dandy little GPS unit he'd placed beneath the car.

Who lived in that house? He'd done a search but the county records only listed the name of a company that apparently did not exist. Whoever this was had to be friends with Vigilance. What had they asked him to do with the "present"? He still had no idea what they'd done at the place earlier. And why hadn't there been a reaction to his hacking into the laptop? He'd deleted the man's damn files, and sent him a message that should have caught his attention. Why were they acting like nothing had happened? Was that why they'd visited the house earlier? He'd give his left nut to find out what went on in that place.

Fuck all. This just was not going the way he planned.

But one thing he did know. There was hardly a person who could top him in cyber electronics. Whatever they set up to trap him or block him, he could get around it.

He pulled up the photo again, looking at the sweet face on the screen. For *her*. He was doing it all for *her*. For what she'd been cheated out of. Maybe he should skip their next stop, give them a false sense of security. Yes, that was it. And he'd return with even better ways to torment the almighty Blake Morgan.

* * * *

Blake was more than relieved when the next stop on the tour went off without a hitch. There wasn't a hint of the stalker anywhere—no notes, no incidents. Nothing.

"Maybe he decided Washington D.C. was too dangerous a place for him to pull his stunts," he joked over breakfast in their room the next morning.

"Possibly," Sam agreed. "He might think there are too many opportunities for things to go wrong for him. But you can count on one thing. He's far from done."

Blake frowned. "You think so?"

She shook her head. "Think about it. We don't even know yet why he's doing this, what terrible thing you've done. He hasn't made his point yet, or gotten his revenge."

"I still wish I knew what brought all this on."

"And I wish I knew if he's planning to hurt someone again. He's tasted blood and it didn't throw him off his game. That's when you get a feeling how dangerous someone is."

"But that was an accident of circumstance," Blake pointed out.

"Yes, but he's got a taste of it. We need to be extra careful. The next one could try to point the finger at you."

His jaw dropped. "Me? Anyone who knows the least little thing about me would never think I'd hurt anyone."

"What is it I said? Desperate people do desperate things under the right circumstances."

"So what do we do? How do we prepare for it?"

Sam shrugged. "Just be as alert and prepared as we can be. Avery had a suggestion and I think it's a good one. We have reservations at the hotel in Philadelphia. We're going to leave them as well as the plane reservations, but we're changing stuff up."

"Like how?"

"The Philly date isn't for three more days. We're going to leave here this afternoon and get there two days ahead of time." She picked up her phone and scrolled through to her notes. "There are a couple of flights we can choose from today. Avery has checked what flights have seats available at the same time. She doesn't want to make reservations because he hacks into the airline manifests. If he gets the least smell of us leaving here early he'll do that and be prepared."

"So what's the plan?"

"Someone will met us with last minute tickets and get us the hell out of the terminal and onto the plane before anyone knows we are there. Hopefully we'll leave the stalker, who is sure to be watching for us, with egg on his face."

Blake broke off a piece of muffin and chewed it while he thought about what she said. "He won't be happy."

"But you'll be as safe as we can make you."

"Don't you think it's strange," Blake said, "that we haven't seen him or gotten any notes here in D.C.?"

"I do," Sam agreed. "But my senses tell me he's here. I can feel it. Maybe even staying in the same damn hotel."

"Then why haven't we heard from him this stop," Blake asked, "or gotten any notes?"

"He's playing with us. Maybe he thinks he's giving us a false sense of security while he gets ready for his next episode." She looked around. "I'm going to call Avery and have her send someone to sneak our luggage out of the hotel."

"What about when we get to Philadelphia?"

"We'll leave the hotel reservations as they are, but we'll be staying at a different place. Just like she did for us here, Avery's made the reservations in both places in the name of a phony corporation they use for things like this."

"How do we get away with not showing identification at the front desk when we check in?"

Sam laughed. "Leave it to Vigilance, okay? We often have to stash people who have to remain anonymous. The office will take care of it."

He chased the muffin with a swallow of coffee. "Okay. I guess I'll just trust you people to do what you do best."

Sam winked at him. "Because we are the best."

He wanted to tell her she was the best in his book, but they hadn't yet reached that point in their relationship. Things were good between them, but he could tell Sam still had her reservations. Maybe she still hadn't forgotten the egotistical boy who'd been such an ass. He was doing his best to prove he wasn't that guy anymore, but he figured it was just something that would take time. And maybe they wouldn't be able to deal with it until the stalker was caught and they could breathe easily for a change.

"Avery texted me before with an update on Grant Kennelly." She took a sip of coffee.

"And?"

"He's doing better. They moved him into a private room and Sharon is there practically all the time."

"I thought her sister came up from Sarasota."

"She left a couple of days ago when they were told Grant was stable." She set her cup down carefully. "Avery told them that since what happened was part of a Vigilance operation, the agency was covering what his insurance didn't."

"Good, because they'd never take it from me."

When they went to fetch the car, Blake approached it with every muscle in his body tense, surprised and only slightly relieved when there was no message under the windshield wipers. Then he reminded himself this was a different car. Vigilance had sent someone to play switcheroo with the cars, passing the new keys and a slip with the parking slot to Sam in the bar.

"I feel like I'm in a James Bond movie," he joked, automatically turning to look behind them as they climbed into the car.

"If you insist on checking the traffic in back of us," Sam told him, "use the mirror on the visor. Don't keep turning around to see if he's behind us."

"I wouldn't know if he was, anyway, so I don't know why I'm even doing it."

"Because it's a natural reaction." She reached over to touch his arm.

He gave her hand a quick squeeze. "Don't mind me. I'm just not used to being in a situation like this."

"Who is? And remember what I said. He's got something else up his sleeve."

"So I should expect something shocking in Philly?" He swallowed the sour taste in his mouth.

"Something, anyway." Sam looked over at him. "I'm sorry, Blake. I know you want to believe he's done, but—"

"I know, I know. I'm not really that stupid. Just hopeful. And I think you're right. He's trying to throw me off my game so he can come back with another whammy."

"Look." She skillfully maneuvered in traffic. "We have to be alert, but we're changing our itinerary and you should have a couple of days in Philadelphia to relax. You have the publicity thing again the day of the book signing, but maybe until then we can just play tourist. How does that sound?"

It sounded great to him, although he wouldn't mind just spending the two days in bed with Sam. It seemed the more he was with her, the more he wanted her. And again he reminded himself not to push, not to rush. He wasn't walking away this time.

"Do you think he was watching when we left to get the car?"

"Maybe. He could have been sitting in a parked car waiting for our reaction. Too bad for him we left in a different car from a different level of the garage, so there was nothing for him to see."

Still, Blake was on edge when they reached the airport. Sam pulled up to the departure check-in where a man stood with their luggage. He spoke quietly to her as he handed her an envelope, got in the car, and drove it away.

"Are you sure this isn't a movie?" He tried a little levity.

"Be nice if it was."

"So what now?"

She opened the envelope and pulled out two ticket confirmations. "We have the last two seats on a flight that leaves in thirty minutes. We need to hustle."

At the gate, Blake still had that uneasy itch between his shoulder blades. He kept telling himself he had to trust both Sam and Vigilance that they'd eluded the stalker, at least for the moment. He tried to sleep on the flight but his nerves would not let him settle down. Maybe they'd evaded whoever this was for the moment, but as Sam had pointed out, something worse was likely to happen.

At the hotel Sam connected with a woman who was waiting for her in the lobby and handed her another envelope. Then she got in the car he and Sam had just arrived in, and drove off.

"Just grab your bags and follow me," she told him. "This hotel valet parks all the cars."

"We don't have to check in?"

She grinned. "Already taken care of. These are the room keys. Come on."

"What about our car? She drove off with it."

"And we'll be using the one she arrived in. That way, at least for a couple of days, no messages left for us."

"I'll say this," he told her. "I'm sure getting my money's worth with Vigilance."

"We aim to please. Come on. No suite this time. There were none available. But we've got connecting rooms."

But as far as Blake was concerned, the only thing that would get any use in the other bedroom was the en suite bathroom.

* * * *

The stalker was in a rage. What the hell was going on? Where were these idiots? He'd been slouched down in this car ever since he saw them come down in the elevator. They had to be going someplace because Morgan had his messenger bag with him when they came down in the elevator. He hadn't made his presence known here in D.C., just to see if he could put them off their game while he worked on his plan for Philadelphia. According to the computer, they had two more nights here. Maybe they were going sightseeing, or maybe Morgan was researching a book.

Now they had just disappeared. But where? He'd hacked the bastard's phone to get his calendar and found nothing on the plate for today. He never left a day free, so why now? What were they doing? Did they think they could really outsmart him?

When he finally had to accept the fact that they weren't coming to pick up the car, he headed back into the hotel.

"Excuse me." He caught the attention of one of the clerks.

"Yes?" Phony smile. "May I help you?"

"Yes." He dug deep for his best company manners. "I have an envelope to deliver to the people in the Vigilance suite but I've forgotten the number. It's very important that I get this up to them."

"I'm sorry." Another insincere curving of the lips. "We're not permitted to give out room numbers."

"But this is very important. It's from his publisher." He was getting ready to throttle the clerk.

"If you will leave it with me," the clerk said, "I'll be sure he gets it. Or if you like, I can phone up to the suite and tell him you are here. If he says to send you up, then I can give you the number."

He wanted to bite nails. Morgan would know it wasn't from his publisher. He certainly wouldn't give permission for the stalker to come up to the suite. If he made more of a scene, the clerk would remember him, which was not good.

"You know what?" He dug up his own smile from someplace. "I remember the publisher told me Mr. Morgan would be writing this morning and he doesn't like to be disturbed. Let me just check and make sure he has to have it right away."

"As you wish."

He could feel the clerk's eyes boring into his back as he walked away, holding his cell phone to his ear while he pretended to make a call. He'd already made himself too memorable to the clerk. It was a damn good thing he wore a disguise that made him look totally different.

He had few options left to him. He could go back to the garage and keep watching for them to get their car. He could change disguises and hang out here at the lobby coffee bar, waiting for them to come down from the room. That would only work for so long, however. If he spent too much time there he'd call attention to himself.

Instead he went to his room to think, regroup and reorganize. Maybe try to see things from a different angle. They hadn't disappeared off the face of the earth. As he sat there drinking coffee and nibbling snacks, he realized he could come at this backward. It would take time and a sophisticated program, but he apparently had plenty of time and the program was already on his laptop.

Buoyed with enthusiasm, he accessed the hotel's registration database again and fed it into a special program he'd written to find the identities of people on a list. He'd written it for a client, a private security service. It was probably illegal as hell, but the client didn't give a shit and neither did he, especially after the fat fee he was paid.

He lifted the phone and ordered a bottle of wine from room service. Then he turned on the television. He might as well try to relax. If the program worked—and he had no doubt it would—at the end of the run when all other guests were eliminated—what remained would be the name under which Morgan was registered. They could only fool him for so long.

He closed his eyes and thought about the next steps in the process. Morgan had two more book signings before the big one. He'd be closing the tour in Tampa, a good decision by the publisher, and this signing would be a little different. Instead of being at a bookstore, it would be held in an event center in South Tampa, one that could accommodate up to three hundred people. The stalker had read all the details and looked up the event site. How lucky for him there was even a diagram to download. That would be the place for his final act of revenge. He would go out in a blaze of glory, making sure the world now knew how Blake Morgan had created a career on lies and thievery.

He would die there, but that was his plan. His life was empty now, fueled only by his determination to unmask Morgan. It would be his ultimate satisfaction and his ultimate revenge.

His room service order was delivered, and the program chugged along, sifting through the names. Then bingo! Two rooms registered to a corporation his program couldn't identify. It had to be them. Excitement coursed through his veins.

But why hadn't he seen them? He'd watched carefully from the lobby, knowing when they'd have to leave for appointments but he hadn't caught a smell of them. What the hell?

He wasn't sure if they'd be in their rooms right now or if they'd gone out someplace now that his obligations were taken care of. They'd made themselves so scarce it was hard for him to know what was what. He decided he'd put on one of his disguises and knock on their door. If one of them answered, he could just say he was sorry, he had the wrong room. But if no one answered, he'd get in and out quickly, leaving more messages everywhere like the last time.

He set the half bottle of wine aside for—hopefully—a celebratory drink later on. He pulled on a blond wig, jeans, a black T-shirt with an open collared shirt over it, and tinted glasses. He'd learned people focused on things that stood out, like the glasses, rather than on the person.

He also stuck his knife in its sheath and hooked it into his belt loop, adjusting his T-shirt and collared shirt so it was hidden. The last thing he picked up was the folder with all the messages in it.

He took the elevator down to their floor, waited until the corridor was clear and knocked on their door. He waited but there was no answer so after a full minute he knocked again. Still no answer. He slid from his pocket the master key card he'd stolen from housekeeping and swiped it at the door lock. When the light turned green he slid into the room, closing the door at once. He had to hurry. They could come back at any minute.

He searched through the room, and it only took seconds before he realized something was wrong. There were no clothes in the closet, no toiletries in the bathroom. He opened the door to the connecting room and searched every inch of it, with the same results.

What the fuck?

He went through both rooms again, opening every door, searching to see if they'd left some clue by accident, anything, but the rooms were clean as a whistle. Rage consumed him. He wanted to scream. But that would be sure to bring someone running, and he couldn't have that.

Damn, damn, damn. How had this happened? Where the hell were they?

Finally, his anger still simmering in his bloodstream, he took out his knife and began hacking at the bedclothes, first in one room then the other. Then he shredded the bath towels and finally the drapes on the windows. In his mind, he was slitting Blake Morgan's treacherous throat, then slicing through the flesh of that bitch now traveling with him. He imagined their blood flowing, draining from their bodies while he laughed in triumph. Then he took the packets of notes he had with them and spread them around the rooms. By the time he was finished he was exhausted.

He made his way back to his room and the wine waiting there for him. He had the information on their next plane reservation, as well as the one at the next hotel. But what if they took a different plane or stayed someplace else in Philadelphia? It was obvious they were trying to avoid him and get him off their trail. Well, he had plenty of tricks still in his bag. He had a surprise and he was going to pursue it, no matter what.

Maybe he should go to Philadelphia a couple of days early. He could scope out the store where the book signing was scheduled. See how he could blend in with the crowd. Maybe figure out a different kind of mischief to create.

He also needed to take time to compose the first letter he planned to write to the media. He'd test that in Philly. He wanted to grab their interest so they poked at Morgan about the kind of asshole he was. Spread it all over the news. Even all over social media, something he planned to do before long, but the timing had to be just right. Everything was intended to happen in steps. He wanted to drive the man crazy before he unmasked him to the world. It was only fitting to destroy him as he'd destroyed another human being. A wonderful, warm human being.

Already he could visualize the final destruction.

* * * *

The hotel in Philadelphia wasn't one Blake had ever stayed at before but he liked it as soon as he walked in. It was smaller than he was used to, although far from tiny, and it had more of an old-fashioned feel to it that he liked. He also appreciated the fact that there was no trace of them at the front desk. He was sure by now the stalker was over the top enraged, having lost track of them. At least it gave him a couple of extra days to breathe.

The first thing Sam did was take out the little gizmo again and go around checking everything in the room. She'd done it in D.C., too.

Blake studied her, puzzled. "Surely you don't think he found these alternate reservations and planted something to spy on us, do?"

"I never assume anything." Finished, she put it back in her tote. "I just don't want unpleasant surprises."

"But what could he hope to gain by planting some kind of device?"

"He could listen to us, find out what our plans are, any number of things. I don't intend to take any chances."

Finished with that task, she called the bookstore to check on the signing, then reconfirmed Blake's media appointments.

"I know Annemarie had to do more than this," she protested. "Just tell me. I promise I'm a quick study."

"I know you are." Absently rubbed his jaw. "But to tell the truth, I'm not in the mood for research or editing or anything else in that category."

She was in the middle of trying to persuade him to do a little sightseeing and hopefully unwind when her cell rang.

She looked at the screen then at Blake. "Avery," she told him. "Hey, Avery. What's up?" She frowned. "What? But who? And where is he? I think—"

Blake, impatient at hearing only one side of the conversation, took the phone from her hand.

"Avery? Sorry to cut in on your conversation, but what's happened now? More bad shit?"

"Hello, Blake. Nice to speak to you, too." Her voice was edged with a combination of irony and sarcasm. "I was in the middle of telling Sam that we've unearthed a possible candidate for the stalker. Why don't you have her put me on speaker so I can brief you both at once?"

"Who?" he snapped, when Sam had pressed the icon. "Who's doing this to me?"

"We don't know for sure," she pointed out. "But does the name Andrew Foley ring a bell?"

"Oh, yeah." He snorted. "He was pissed off because he lost out to me for best mystery of the year award at a mystery writers' dinner two years in a row. It's true he called me all kinds of names and threatened to ruin my reputation. You think he's doing this? I don't know about that. He seemed like all show and no go."

"We're dealing with events that happened last year and the year before," she pointed out. "Still recent enough to be raw. We've tracked down evidence that he's been badmouthing you to everyone he can. Called you a fraud and a few other unprintable things. I called to get your reaction, to see if you thought he might possibly be doing this."

"I can't think what I would have done that he thinks is worthy of all these notes. Sure, he was angry, and pissed off at me, but people lose awards all the time, and they don't go off the rails like this." Blake rubbed his jaw. "I guess anything is possible, though. Where is he now? What's he doing? I want to talk to him. If I can see him, I can get a good read on him."

"I don't think that's a good idea. I just wanted to touch base in case you could give me some personal feedback before we move forward."

"Avery." Blake ground his teeth. This was the first concrete name they'd come up with and he wanted the details. "If you don't tell me, I can find him myself. There are plenty of people I can ask. You should know that. But I want to talk to him myself."

"I just don't want you going off half-cocked."

"I'm not an idiot, Avery." Blake gripped the cell so hard he was afraid he'd break it. "Just tell me where he is, or I'll find out myself."

Her sigh carried across the connection. "He lives just south of Philadelphia. But Blake—"

"Here?" He wondered if this was an accident or fate. "He's right here? Son of a bitch. I want the address. I want to see that miserable bastard myself."

"Just calm down, please. See? Now you understand why I was reluctant to pass this along, especially considering where you are."

"Damn it, Avery," he snapped. "I—" He stopped, drew in a full breath and let it out slowly. "I will behave myself. I promise. But I might get more out of him than a stranger. Besides, I'm in a better position to assess if he's really the stalker."

Silence hummed along the connection and he could visualize Avery weighing all the pros and cons. "Alright," she said at last. "Put Sam on the phone. I'll give her the information. Along with strict instructions to ride herd on you."

Blake shoved the phone at Avery but he stood right next to her. He'd grab that phone again, if he had to.

"Uh-uh," she was saying. "Yeah. Got it. Got it. Okay. I'll report back to you."

"Okay." Blake pounced. "What's the address?"

"Avery's texting it to me right now." She put a hand on his arm. "Calm down, cowboy. We're not going there if you're planning to blow up at him."

Blake chuffed an impatient breath. "For God's sake, Sam. The man is trying to ruin my life. He leaves threatening messages. He's almost *killed* someone."

"Take a breath," she told him. "We don't know for sure that he's the one, only that his is the first possible name that popped up. If we go there, you have to follow my lead."

He shook his head. "I want to confront him. To demand he tell me what the hell is going on."

"And what if he's not the one? Avery only said he's a possibility. Let's go see him and scope out the situation. It may not be him at all. So calm down. We'll go pay him a visit and see what's what."

It took a supreme effort of will but he banked his anger and frustration and forced himself to calm down. She was right. And if he went at like a madman, all that would result would be a shouting match. Foley was good at that. He knew from personal experience. He'd do his best to tamp down his irritation but he needed some kind of outlet for all the anger and rage building inside him. This would take every bit of his self-control.

The drive to Andrew Foley's house took a little over forty-five minutes. The community was obviously upper middle class, quiet but not ostentatious wealth and success. The house was two-story, brick, not as large as some of the others in the street but with a well-tended lawn and shrubs. Sam pulled up in the driveway and parked facing the garage door. She turned off the ignition and looked over at Blake.

"You ready for this, sport? You got yourself under control?"

He clenched his fists. "I'm totally together."

She burst out laughing. "Yeah, I can see that. Okay, take some deep breaths and let's do this, but remember, don't let him bait you."

"I'll do my best."

The climbed the stairs to the porch and he rang the doorbell. In a minute, he heard the sound of shoes on what was probably the foyer, then the door opened. He'd met Marianne Foley when she'd come to the dinners with Andrew. He remembered her as being a pretty brunette, in her forties, who stepped back to allow her husband to bask in the limelight. At the moment, stress carved lines in her face and her eyes looked defeated.

"Hello, Blake." Even her voice sounded sad. "What brings you to our neck of the woods?"

"Hello to you, too, Marianne."

She looked at Sam. "I see you have a lovely woman with you."

They'd already decided to introduce her as a woman in his life, figuring that would make her less threatening.

"Yes. Samantha Quenel." He smiled. "We've known each other for a long time. We were in the area and I was wondering if I could come in and say hello to Andrew."

The pinched look on her face intensified.

"Oh, Blake, I don't know. You haven't been his favorite person for a while, you know."

He nodded. "That's one of the reasons I stopped by. I would love to be able to bury the hatchet and at least be cordial acquaintances."

Marianne stood there, twisting her hands, the picture of indecision.

"Marianne?" The name sounded like a roar from inside the house. "Who the fuck is out there?"

She looked at Blake. "He's...not doing well today. Maybe you—"

"God damn it." In the next second Andrew Foley appeared behind his wife. He glared at Blake. "You! The bastard who ruined my life."

"Andrew." Marianne tried to nudge him back into the foyer. "They were just leaving. I was about to explain that you weren't feeling well today."

"Not well?" He snorted. "I haven't been well since he stole those two damned awards from me."

"Please go back inside, I'll—"

"No. I want him to come in, so he can see exactly what he did to me."

At the words *what he did*, Blake glanced sideways at Sam to make sure she heard.

"Bring them in right now, Marianne. I need another drink to talk to this bastard."

He clumped away toward the back of the house.

"You'd better come in," his wife told them. "Otherwise he'll make my life miserable." She shook her head. "Not that it isn't already. Come on."

She stood back to let them enter, then led them in the direction Foley had stomped off.

Blake could tell Sam wasn't exactly eager to do this, but she entered the house with him. As they followed Marianne Foley, she took his hand and gave it a quick squeeze. Walking through the house he noticed that while it was immaculate and obviously expensively furnished, there was a very depressing air about everything. He wondered if this had been going on since that first clash over the award.

Foley was in his den, pouring three fingers of some kind of whiskey into a cut glass tumbler. In contrast to the rest of the house, the den was a disaster. Folders and papers were stacked haphazardly everywhere, along with a variety of books. A large computer sat on a massive walnut desk and it, too, sat in the midst of chaos. And the scent of alcohol clung to the room as if it was a permanent part of the air.

Foley himself looked at the long edge of ragged. He need a haircut, at least a week's worth of scruff covered his chin and his cheeks, and his clothes looked as if he'd slept in them. As Blake studied him, he began to think they were chasing their tails here. Unless Foley's wife was helping him, this man was in no shape to carry out the campaign the stalker was waging. He wasn't sure if he was even in any condition to travel.

"Sit, sit." Foley gestured to two armchairs, while he plunked himself down behind the desk. He took a healthy slug of his drink, rubbed his chest and looked at Blake with hate in his eyes. "Come to rub your big success in my face, asshole?"

Blake forced himself to be calm. "That's not who I am, Andrew, and I'd like to think you know it. I came to see how an old friend was doing."

"Friend?" Foley made a rude noise. "When were we ever friends?"

Blake reminded himself not to lose his cool. "I always hoped we could be friends. I had nothing to do with the way the awards were decided. If I'd had my choice, both times it would have gone to you."

"Yeah, yeah, yeah. Easy for you to say." Another big swallow of liquor. "You're not the one who had it stolen from them. Who told lies about someone to get it."

"I'm sorry you feel that way, Andrew, but let me assure you I never lied to anyone about anything. I have always had the highest regard for you and your work. If I had it to do all over again, I'd remove my name from nomination so you could get the award that you deserved."

"Ha! The only truth in that statement is that I deserved the award." He stood, and shuffled over to the bar, where he refilled his glass from the bottle sitting there.

"Honey, I think you should make that your last one for today." Marianne spoke from the doorway where she'd apparently been standing all this time. "You said you wanted to get some work done."

He whirled toward her. "Work? Fuck work. My publisher wants me off his list, my agent wants to dump me. Why even bother." He lifted his full glass in a mock toast to Blake. "I bow to the king, however he got the throne."

Blake mentally counted to ten. "I wish I could do something to make you feel differently. In any event, I can see that our presence here is only upsetting you. I'm sorry about this. I hope in the future we might be able to mend the broken fences."

He rose and held out his hand to Sam. Marianne Foley stepped back from the doorway, an expression on her face that was a combination of sadness and bitterness. He just wasn't sure if she was bitter about him or about what her husband was doing to himself.

"I'm sorry, Marianne. I guess coming here wasn't such a good idea."

"I probably should have been honest with you when I opened the door." She shook her head. "It's just so hard to know what will help and what will set him off."

"Go on, run away." Foley's heavy voice followed them out toward the foyer.

The next thing they heard was the sound of a glass smashing against something. Marianne flinched and opened the front door.

Blake started to say something, but then decided there really was nothing to say. They were both silent as Sam backed the car out of the driveway and headed down the street. Neither of them spoke until they were back on the main road back to the hotel.

"Holy shit!" The words popped out of Sam's mouth. "I mean it, Blake."

"Yeah, no kidding." He shifted in his seat, uncomfortable as the image of what Foley had become was front and center in his brain. "I know he was upset, and he's run his mouth about me for the past couple of years. But, I had no idea he had let it eat him up and destroy him like that."

"You can't take that on your shoulders," she insisted. "How many authors in every genre of fiction and nonfiction are up for awards they don't receive? Do any of them fall into the bottom of a bottle and badmouth the winner?"

"No." He scrubbed his hand over his face. "They don't. Foley's the exception to the rule, and it makes me sad."

"One bright spot," she pointed out. "We can eliminate him as the stalker."

Blake barked a short laugh. "That's the damn truth."

"I'd better call Avery and tell her she can scratch him from the list and see what else they're working on."

"She won't be any too happy." And wasn't that the truth.

"Something else to add to her list." Sam maneuvered through the busy traffic. "Especially since no headway is being made on Grant Kennelly's assault."

He looked over at her. "Nothing?"

"Not a damn thing. That detective's working overtime and he's got the full resources of the sheriff's office on it. If your mother wasn't so anxious to help them find this maniac I think they'd be in real trouble, as many times as they've gone over the house looking for a stray print, a stray hair. Anything. Same thing in the yard. Both yards."

"Whoever this guy is," Blake said, "he's a damn good stalker."

She sighed. "Yes, unfortunately. It's pretty evident he only got into this to right some wrong he perceives you've committed."

"Which I have no idea what the hell it is." He scrubbed his hands over his face. "And that scene with Andrew Foley today. Good lord. I had no idea the man had fallen so completely apart."

"I point out again that it's not your fault."

"Doesn't make it any easier." He leaned his head back. "I probably shouldn't say this considering what we just left, but I could really use a drink."

Sam giggled. "I think you can handle it. In fact, I'll take you someplace really neat for one."

"You know Philadelphia?"

"I did a bodyguard gig here for six weeks last year. I know just the spot for you."

Chapter 12

The stalker was ready to bite nails. Nothing was working here. Here he was, in the Philadelphia hotel where Morgan had rooms for this stop on the tour, and he couldn't find them.

The longer he thought about it, the more enraged he became. It was very obvious that they hadn't used the rooms registered under their names. Every registered guest was verified by his program. He began checking other hotels in the same city, for phony names or even a phony company name like they'd used in D.C. He'd check the suburbs if he had to. He couldn't let them just disappear from him. They had to be staying somewhere in the city.

He'd dig into airline passenger manifests next, just to make sure they were still booked on their original flight to Cleveland two days from now and hadn't changed their reservations. They couldn't use fake names for that, thanks to Homeland Security. And finally, hotel clerks be damned, when he found the right hotel, he'd find someone to bribe who could tell him what fucking room Blake Morgan and his so-called bodyguard were in.

What he needed to do was shake things up a little. Maybe it was time to send that letter. He'd wanted to do it closer to the end of the tour but damn it, if they kept flying under his radar he didn't think he could wait. Morgan had two interviews lined up in Philadelphia.

At an Internet café, he carried his coffee to a computer at the far end of the room and set himself up. It didn't take long to find the emails for the people he was targeting. He had the letter all written, he only had to type it into the computer.

He proofed it twice to make sure he hadn't made any errors or typos. He couldn't expect them to take him seriously if he came across as unprofessional. When he was satisfied, he hit Send, waited until it was gone, then changed the address and did it again. When both emails had flown into cyberspace, he scrubbed them from the computer, sat back, and sipped from his coffee.

He wasn't sure which would appeal to him more—seeing the faces of the media people when they read the emails or seeing Blake Morgan's when he was nailed about the contents. He only wished he could be there in person.

At last he headed back to the hotel, hoping to get some rest. Tomorrow would be a big day. He hoped.

I'm doing this for you, my lovely. Soon the whole world will know.

* * * *

Sam's cell phone woke them in the morning. She blinked the sleep from her eyes and grabbed the phone. The screen showed Avery's name, so she hit the Accept button.

"Morning. What's up?"

Blake had rolled over so he was spooning her, stroking her arm lightly with his fingers and giving her early morning thrills. She was rapidly getting used to sleeping wrapped up in the warmth of his body, looking forward to his tender caresses as well as the sex that was off the charts. Walking away from this was looking less and less likely, but there were things she had to get straight first.

"You'd better be extra alert, Sam," her boss told her. "And I mean vigilant, like our name."

"Why?" She sat up abruptly, holding up the covers in front of her. "What's happened? What's going on?"

"You know how we thought Blake's number one fan had skipped D.C.?"

"Uh-huh." She slid a glance at Blake.

"Apparently he was there, just not in a proactive mode. Probably just to spy on the two of you. It seems he somehow discovered which rooms were registered to you and got in there."

Sam frowned. "How the hell did he do that? They weren't even in our names."

"We're looking into that. Anyway, it seems he went into your rooms, discovered you weren't there. When the maid went in to clean this morning she got quite a shock."

"What happened?" Sam tried to keep her voice as even as possible. Beside her she could feel Blake tense up.

"He tore up everything he could with a knife, slashed the place up pretty good. Then he left sheets of paper with his usual message on it all over the place, just like at Blake's parents' home." She sighed. "Anyway, I'm glad we got you out of there when we did and made the changes in the hotel at Philly."

"If he somehow has the information of our original rooms here in Philly," Sam said, "let's hope he doesn't decide to do a slice and dice there."

"I think he'll be more careful this time," Avery told her. "He'll be expecting some sleight of hand. Be smart, Sam, and be careful. Watch yourselves. I think this guy is really off the rails."

"No kidding."

"What was all that with Avery?" Blake asked when she hung up.

"Shower first, coffee, and then out for breakfast. When we're clean and fed I'll lay it all out for you. Okay?"

She could tell he wasn't happy but he'd apparently decided to pick his battles. Still, his edginess that seemed to grow each day hadn't been helped by the visit to Andrew Foley. Which was why, when he went to take his shower, instead of using the other bathroom as she'd been doing, she followed him.

Was this a bad idea? Was she giving him the sense things were moving faster than she'd intended? Maybe, but there didn't seem to be much she could do about it. With each day her feelings for him grew stronger, along with the intense chemistry that sizzled their nerve endings whenever they made love.

Yes, Sam, made love. You might as well call it what it is, even if it terrifies you. Because you know every sign from Blake is that he's all in.

It had to be the situation, she told herself over and over. Living with danger at every turn tore down walls and amped up feelings. She'd seen it happen with other agents. She just hadn't expected it to happen to her, not when she'd tried to lay down the ground rules in the beginning.

Yeah. Right. Look how well that turned out.

Steam had fogged the glass door but she could see a hazy image of his naked body. She still had no idea what was going to happen with them when this was all over, but she'd made up her mind to enjoy it while she could. Besides, right now he needed something to take the edge off his nerves so he could face the day's schedule.

When she slid the door open he looked at her, startled.

"What—"

"Shh." She touched the tip of a finger to his lips. "I know you're about to jump out of your skin and I have just the prescription for you."

"You don't have to do this."

"I know. But I want to." And the thing was, she really did.

She poured the bodywash into her palm and worked it into a good lather before she began stroking it over the hard wall of his chest. She could practically feel his body vibrating beneath her touch, but she took her time, massaging the tight chest muscles. When she scraped her fingernails lightly over his hard nipples he sucked in a breath and reached for her.

"Uh-uh. This one's for you."

She shook her head and stood on tiptoe to place a light kiss on his wet lips. Then she went back to her task, sliding the slippery bubbles over his skin, down each arm, over his hips. More soap, more lather. When she began to trail her hands over his abdomen he sucked in a breath.

"Watch it." His voice was strained. "That could be a problem."

She grinned. "Not for me."

Before she reached his groin, she eased around him and lathered up his back, rubbing his shoulders then slipping her hands down to his hips again and then to the tight muscles of his butt. When she squeezed the muscular cheeks he groaned, so she did it again. Tempted, she slid one soapy hand into the cleft, just teasing, then easing it back when he again inhaled a sharp breath.

Pressing her body against his, she slipped her hands around to his front, threaded her fingers through the crisp hair on his groin until she reached the hard, swollen thickness of his cock.

"Oh, God!" he groaned, and moved his hips back and forth.

"Put your hands out and brace yourself on the wall," she told him.

"As long as you don't stop."

She stood on tiptoe and nipped his earlobe. "Not a chance."

She slid her fingers up and down on his shaft, feeling the hard steel beneath the soft skin. She pressed her body against his as hard as she could, wanting to feel every muscle, every quiver, soaking up the heat of him.

"Aaahhh." The sound rumbled up from his chest.

Sam rested a hand lightly on his shoulder as she squeezed his shaft and increased the pace of her strokes but just slightly.

"Relax into it," she whispered. "Close your eyes and just feel. Forget about everything else."

She didn't rush it, varying the tempo of her caresses, moving her body with his as he rode her hand. She paused only long enough to squeeze more soap into her palm and work it into a rich lather. Then she picked up the rhythm again.

"More," he groaned. "Faster."

But she was determined to make this last as long as possible, to draw him out of himself so he focused only on one thing—release. So that everything else fell away and disappeared in the intense release of an orgasm. She took her time, never hurrying, until she could tell he'd about reached his limit of control. Then she increased the pace, stroked harder, and squeezed more, until he exploded, pouring himself over her fingers.

She never let up until she'd wrung the last drop from him. Then she caressed him slowly and softly, bringing him down from the intensity of the climax. Finally she turned him around, pressed herself against him, and wound her arms around his neck.

"Better?" She smiled at the expression on his face.

"I don't know." He grinned back at her. "You might have to do it again to make sure."

Her laugh was soft. "I would but there'd be nothing left of you. *Now* I think you're ready to meet the day."

"I should make you promise to do this every morning."

She tensed at the implications of his words, but then forced herself to relax. This wasn't the time or place for a discussion about where they were headed. Or not. Was she hiding behind the past? Maybe. She knew she should be strong enough to face this head on, but her emotions seemed to be the one place where her strength failed her.

God, what a fucking mess she was.

"But then it wouldn't be special, like this was." She reached around and gave his ass a light smack. "Now we have to shower for real and get dressed. Your day is about to kick into high gear."

She might not have done her own need any good, but Sam smiled to herself when she saw the difference in Blake. Maybe he wasn't completely relaxed. Who would be, considering the situation? But the lines around his eyes weren't as tight and he wasn't gripping the mug like a club when he drank his coffee.

"Ready?" She put her own empty mug down and picked up her tote.

"As I'll ever be." He took one more swallow before shrugging into his sport jacket and picking up his messenger bag. "We have a morning flight for Cleveland, right?"

She nodded. "But if you're up for it, I'd like to leave after the signing tonight. Just in case, Avery is going to try and book us last minute on a very late flight. You can sleep in tomorrow."

"I need to get some writing in, too. I'm way behind."

"No problem. You'll have two days and we'll just block off the time."

"Just as long as that asshole doesn't disrupt things." He shook his head. "I'd love to get my hands around his neck."

She laughed softly. "I'll put it on the list."

* * * *

The drive to the television station was accomplished without incident. This time Blake was scheduled for a spot on the noon program, which was news and interviews. He still had the feeling someone was constantly watching him.

"I know telling you to relax won't help," Sam told him. "But we took a different flight, got here two days early and we're staying at a different hotel. I think we're good."

"I never thought I'd say this, but I'll be damn glad when this tour is over."

She reached over and gave his hand a quick squeeze. "At least the signings themselves are successful."

"Thank God for that." He blew out a breath. "That's one thing he hasn't managed to fuck up, although I'm sure that's what he wants."

"When I talked to the manager for tonight's event, she echoed what the others have said. Tons of phone calls, lots of customers asking about it. And a hefty order of presolds for you to sign."

"Yeah, I can't complain about any of that."

Sam turned into the entrance to the television station parking lot. Blake was glad to see that it, like all the others on this tour, was gated and guarded. And the guard had a list of guests to approve. At least the stalker wouldn't be able to get in here, thank the lord.

As soon as they entered the lobby, a tall man who had been leaning on the reception desk came forward with his hand outstretched.

"Roger Buchanan." He shook Blake's hand. "I'm the producer of Noontime News and Views. We're very pleased to have you with us today."

"Thanks so much for inviting me." He introduced Sam to the man.

"Nice to meet you. If you'll just follow me?"

Buchanan led the way through double doors and down a corridor. The room he ushered them into was almost a carbon copy of the other guest lounges they'd seen on the tour.

"We have coffee, tea, ice water, and juice." He pointed to a buffet against the wall. "Also some pastries, so feel free to help yourselves."

"Thanks, but we're good."

Buchanan studied him for a long moment, a look that made Blake fidget. "Is there a problem?"

"What? Oh, no. This show is a little different from some of the others you've done. We ask readers to email us with questions ahead of time and we got a lot more than we expected. You're a very popular man, Mr. Morgan."

"Blake. Please. And questions are fine. Good, even. I'm happy to answer them if I can."

"Good, good. Well, we'll be to get you in just a few minutes."

As soon as Buchanan had left the room, Blake turned to Sam.

"Did he seem a little fidgety to you?"

She nodded. "He did. Do you think there's a problem?"

Blake shrugged. "I have no idea. The more of these I do, the more I realize how much hosts like to blindside their guests. But other than my stalker, my life is an open book."

"And I don't think he knows about the stalker yet. Vigilance has kept it all under wraps."

Blake rubbed his chin. "What about news reports of Grant Kennelly's assault?"

"Avery told me Sheri and the sheriff have tried to keep a lid on that. It still hasn't hit the major news outlets and they're trying to keep it that way."

"Let's hope."

At that moment the door opened and Roger Buchanan entered.

"You're up," he told Blake. "Miss Quenel, if you'd like to watch in the studio, come on ahead."

"Thank you. That would be very nice."

Today was a repeat of the other studio visits. Someone found a director's chair for Sam to sit in. Blake was set up at the news desk, rather than a conversation area.

"We've taken to doing all our interviews like this," Buchanan told Sam.

Then it was show time and he gave her his public smile. Ditto with the producer who walked them out to the lobby. The host introduced herself and welcomed Blake. They discussed his career and the rise to best-seller status of the last three books. The host read emails from several fans, simple questions such as "When is your next book coming out?" "Which was your favorite to write?" and "Do you have a favorite author you like to read?"

Blake was finally allowing himself to relax when the host pulled a sheet of paper out of the pile, skimmed it, and looked across at Blake.

"This one's a little different," she said. "Let me read a line or two if I may?"

Blake tensed, but nodded.

"Mr. Blake, can you tell us what secret you've hidden about your career? What did you do that's so bad you refuse to discuss it? Did you steal someone else's work? The person who wrote this said you'll know what you did."

Blake froze in place, feeling like a deer caught in the headlights. *You know want you did.*

What the hell? What the fucking hell?

"Excuse me." He smiled at the woman seated across from him. "Is someone saying I plagiarized their work? Is that what this is?"

"Mmmm, I think maybe copied from it might be more what they're hinting at." She looked down at the email. "This person is saying your whole career is based on a lie." She looked back up at him. "Do you have any idea why someone would say that?"

Blake was stunned and for a moment unable to move or speak. He bit the inside of his cheek, hard, to get himself under control. He was, after all, on television.

"I'd have to say," he told the woman slowly, "someone should check their facts before floating something like that out there."

"So the answer is no?" she persisted.

"Absolutely. Completely. No and no." He drew in a steadying breath. It would not do to let his anger take over here on television. "All of my work is original and it's my own. I keep all my original notes, even my late-night scribblings."

"That's a good habit to have."

He turned to face directly into the camera, doing his best not to show how hard his heart was hammering. "Whoever sent in that question, ask me anything about my work, my planning, my outlines, anything at all. I think you'll see every book I've written is mine without question. I'm sorry something made you think otherwise. But plagiarism just isn't in my vocabulary. The work and the research? All mine. And thanks to all of you who keep buying my books." He looked back at the host. "If we have time, I'd like to tell you a little more about my latest release."

The host, who apparently had expected a much more volatile reaction from him or else an angry one, was shuffling her papers to give herself time to pull it together. Blake stared directly at her. She'd probably thought she had a bombshell. Too bad to disappoint her, but he'd hang on to his control no matter what.

The rest of the interview was almost an anticlimax. They reviewed the details for the signing tonight, he spoke a little about the book he was signing, and then they were done. He wanted to rip the mic from his clothing and toss it to the floor, but he sat patiently waiting for the studio grip to unhook him.

Samantha came forward at once, taking advantage of the break, and touched his hand.

"We're good." She smiled at him. "Let's just get out of here."

He shook hands with the host and thanked her very much for having him. Did the usual book signing in the guest lounge, then walked out to the lobby with Buchanan.

"Hope you didn't mind that we threw that little curve ball in there." He threw his arm around Blake's shoulders in a fake gesture of camaraderie. "We don't want people to think we're hiding things or burying controversial emails."

"Understood." He eased away from the man's arm and glanced at his watch. "I'd love to hang around and chat but we have another appointment to get to." He looked at Samantha. "Right, Sam?"

She nodded. "And we need to get moving."

More thank-yous and they were out the door. Neither of them said a word until they were in the car and driving out of the lot. Then Blake exploded.

"God fucking damn!" He slammed his fist on the dash. "Fucking, fucking, fucking damn."

Beside him Sam quietly maneuvered through the streets of Philadelphia, clearly waiting for his rage to ease.

"We need to call Avery," she said at last. "She needs to know that he's upping his game. If he's coming out of the shadows like this, we need to be prepared for anything. And I want her to ask Buchanan to forward that email to Vigilance so they can try to track the IP address."

"I don't know which is worse." He ground his teeth. "Having him embarrass me that way, or the fact that someone might actually think I plagiarized my books."

"Blake." She did that quick hand squeeze that always seemed to calm him down. "No one in their right mind thinks that. You've been interviewed so many times. If the books weren't yours, you'd never be able to answer a lot of those questions. But let's think about this a minute. Who do you know that would think that?"

He shrugged. "I have no idea at all. It's never come up. I can't—" His cell rang and he looked at the screen. "It's Henry. I gotta take this. Yeah, Henry, what's up?"

"What's up? What's up? Who is this idiot accusing you of plagiarizing his stuff?"

"Damn, Henry. I just did the show. How did you get this so fast?"

"A friend in Philly watched it for me. What the hell is going on? Why didn't you call me?" He could hear the anger in his agent's voice. "There's no truth in that, is there, by the way?"

"No, Henry." Blake reined in his anger. "Don't you know me better than that?"

"Then who the hell is doing this?" Pause. "Wait. Does this have something to do with your stalker?"

"We think so."

"Okay, so now we might have a reason for what he's doing. He thinks you stole his stuff."

Blake tightened his grip on the cell. "He might think he has a reason, but there is no damn truth in it."

"We have to find this guy and straighten this out."

Blake actually laughed. "Yes, Henry, let's make sure he tells everyone he's lying. We don't want to even worry about whether he's going to kill me, right? Especially since he's almost killed once."

There was a pause. "Okay, I'm sorry. You're right, your safety comes first. Of course." Another pause. "It's just...Christ, Blake. What the hell is going on?"

"Henry, if I knew I'd tell you. I don't even know why he chose this particular stop to give us a hint of his motive. I thought he'd keep us in the dark as long as possible. On edge."

"Are we all set—wait, hold on."

Blake sat holding the phone, wondering where Henry had gone.

"More trouble?" Sam asked.

"Just Henry being Henry. A friend saw the interview and Henry got all freaked out." He raked his fingers through his hair. "You'd think after all this time he wouldn't pay any attention to assholes like this."

"Blake?" Henry's voice sounded in his ear, "you still there?"

"Where else would I be? What's up?"

"You aren't gonna believe this." His heavy sigh carried across the connection "The store manager of tonight's signing saw the interview, too, and got all freaked out. But then, she told me, she started to get the weirdest calls, from people asking if you really stole your material and if you'd answer questions tonight. She says the phone's been ringing off the hook."

"You're kidding." Blake ground his teeth. "So now I'm supposed to get put on display like some criminal that people can harass?"

"Just be your charming self," Henry told him. "You'll wow them, you always do. By the time you finish they won't care if you wrote the damn books or not."

"But—"

"I gotta get back to her. Call me later."

Blake just stared at the phone in his hand.

"What?" Sam asked.

"I'm not sure you'd believe it if I told you."

"You can save it for later. We're at the restaurant where the reporter is waiting." Sam wheeled the car into the parking lot. "Are you good to go?"

He blew out a breath. "Yeah. As good as I'll ever be, I guess."

She turned off the ignition and shifted in her seat to look at him, taking one of his hands in both of hers. "You can do this, Blake. You're a professional. I've watched you in action. The way you handled being blindsided on television? High marks for that, buddy."

"I know I can do it." He lifted her hands to his mouth and placed a soft kiss on her knuckles. "It's just a bitch to do."

"Price of fame," she teased. "Come on. Let's get this over with. I'll call Avery. Then I'll take you back to the hotel."

"He's in the city, Sam. I can feel it. And I know he was in D.C. He just changed up his game plan."

"And we have our plan, too. Now come on. Let's go back to the hotel. I think I have a way to help you chill until tonight."

He squeezed her hands. "I can get down with that plan. Any time."

* * * *

The stalker sat in the lobby of the hotel with his coffee and a tablet. The morning had been exhausting and he was already in a foul mood. The damn interview hadn't come off the way he wanted. Morgan had oiled his way around the question, just as smooth as could be, and turned it into a publicity push. How could he say he never stole anyone's work? The stalker had the proof right here in his laptop. He couldn't wait until the appropriate time to reveal it to everyone. He had just the time picked out, too. The big event that would close out the tour.

But meanwhile he had connected with his prey again. His souped-up software had done a massive search and located another fake company name, so he'd hotfooted it over to where they were staying. Hiding, was more like it. Vigilance no doubt thought they outfoxed him, but he had written software that they'd pay a fortune to have. It was his ace in the hole. He could find anyone anywhere any time.

Now if he could just find their room number he could create a little more mischief. That was the only problem with the program. It could tell you everything except what room numbers had been assigned. He didn't want to take a chance running the program right here, but if he took his laptop someplace else, he might miss them. Watching for them was his only recourse.

Glancing at his watch he saw it was the middle of the afternoon. The man had to be coming back soon to get ready for tonight. As he sat there running scenarios through his mind, a woman entered the lobby and headed for the elevators. Something about her caught his eyes and when he looked, she was walking away from him. His pulse ratcheted up a little. He hadn't seen her face, but the slender body and long braid were very distinctive.

It was her! The bodyguard!

He'd bet every penny she was more than a bodyguard, too. He'd heard all the stories about Blake Morgan and his women. The man just could not keep it in his pants. He had no idea where Morgan was but catching the woman alone might be a bonus. *Dangerous game, buddy!*

Yeah, he knew it, but he couldn't seem to help himself.

With his cap pulled low over his face and his jacket collar turned up, he entered the elevator with her, slouching into a corner. She hadn't even looked at him, just took out her cell phone and busied herself texting. When the car stopped at her floor, he followed her off, but pretended to be looking for a room. She still ignored him, only putting her phone away when she got to her room. A swipe of her key card and she was inside.

But where the hell was Morgan?

Never mind. He'd send a message to him.

He waited a few minutes, just in case Morgan was a little bit behind her, but when no one arrived he knocked on the door. She pulled it open.

"Did you forget your card—oh! I think you must have the wrong room."

"No mistake." He shoved her inside and slammed the door behind him. "I have a message for you to give your boyfriend."

Her eyes widened with fear. "My what? I don't have a boyfriend. You have the wrong person here. Please leave."

She started toward the door but he grabbed her arms. "Don't lie to me. I recognized you."

"I'm telling, you, this is a mistake."

"Didn't Vigilance teach you to lie better than this?"

"Vigilance? What? Who?" She looked thoroughly confused. "Let me show you my wallet. Please. You'll see that you've got the wrong person."

He let her pull away long enough to grab her purse from the dresser and take out her wallet, but he still held on to her arm. She pulled out her wallet and flipped it open, her hands shaking. "See? This is me. Diana Roeden. I'm from Seneca, New York, and I'm here with my husband."

He frowned. "Husband?"

"Yes. And he'll be here any minute. If you just let me go I won't say anything."

"Yeah, right." Five seconds after he walked out of the room she'd be on the phone to the hotel manager and then it would be the cops. Shit.

"Please."

He saw the fright in her eyes and the tears rolling down her face. He'd made a colossal mistake here because his ego got the better of him. But just walking away and leaving her wasn't an option.

"I'm sorry," he said. "Truly."

She opened her mouth to scream but he clapped his hand over it, as he pulled the knife from its sheath and plunged it into her abdomen. Next came the slice across the throat, and in seconds it was all over. He wiped the blade on the bedspread and returned it to the sheath. Then he got the hell out, hoping he made it to the elevator before her husband showed up.

As he rode down to the lobby, he thought how astonishingly, unexpectedly good it felt to kill someone.

Chapter 13

The newspaper interview went better than Sam expected, even though the reporter kept coming back to the accusing email. She really admired the way Blake handled the man, deflecting every negative question with something positive. But she was bothered by a niggling feeling that all was not right with the world. Then when they returned to their hotel, a call from Avery confirmed it.

"This time he's killed someone," her boss said, and gave her the details. "We've used the hotel where we originally had you scheduled several times, so I know the manager. I asked him to let me know if anything unusual happened while you guys were in town."

"And?"

"He freaked when he called me. I don't think he expected what happened. The woman could almost be a double for you. Her husband found the body."

"Jesus," Sam breathed. "Is he okay?"

"What do you think?"

"Yeah." She rubbed her forehead. "Stupid question." Sam swallowed back the bile rising in her throat. "This guy has to be a maniac."

"No shit," Avery snorted. "I'm wondering if I should send one or two more agents to team up with you."

"No." Sam shook her head, even though she knew her boss couldn't see her. "I can handle it. If I can't I'll let you know."

"Just watch your back all the time. And Blake's."

"That's a big ten-four."

"I know it's something bad," Blake said the minute she hung up. "So give. All of it."

When she told him what happened, he turned so white she was afraid he'd pass out.

"That's it." He smacked his fist against the wall. "I'm cancelling the rest of the tour, and don't try to argue with me. I can't put your life in danger like this. Whoever this is, they're batshit crazy."

"We're not cancelling. This is what I get paid to do. I'm well aware what the risks are. We just need to take more precautions."

"More precautions?" He glared at her. "How are we supposed to protect people like this woman and Grant Kennelly? The only way is for me to go home and let him come to me."

"Home? As in Tampa? You'd go home to the place where you have your biggest event of the tour scheduled and just ignore all those fans who have been waiting to see you?"

It took a little more pushing and shoving but she convinced him not to change things. He did, however, agree to pack up their things and take them with when they left the hotel to the signing. To take the very late-night flight Avery had booked them on at the last minute. She wanted to get him the hell out of Philadelphia.

The book signing was insanity. So many people had shown up, and many of them way ahead of time, that the store manager had started giving out numbered tickets. The store was a stand-alone, not in a mall or strip center, and when they drove up they saw a line already curling around a corner of the building.

Blake stared at it. "Holy shit!"

"I agree." Sam turned and parked in the back of the building. "I have an itchy feeling about this. Do exactly as I tell you tonight, and don't give me any arguments, okay?"

"No problem. I just hope they don't attack me."

Sam got out first and rang the bell by the back door. As soon as it opened she motioned to Blake, who hustled into the store, where a woman was waiting to greet him.

"I'm so sorry about all this, Mr. Morgan. It seems the hint of gossip brings out more people than just a good signing."

He gave a short laugh. "Yeah, well, we all know about that."

"We couldn't let everyone in at once. Fire marshal, you know. Would it be possible for you to cut down your presentation and give it twice, so everyone has a chance to hear you?"

"And ask questions, right?"

"Well, yes." She drew her brows together. "Would you be willing to do that?"

He looked at Sam, who nodded. "Sure, if we can keep each one short."

And then they were into it. She stayed at Blake's side the entire time, watching the crowd, taking pictures as she'd done at every other signing. Every nerve in her body was on full alert, especially when people started asking him about the infamous email. She and Blake had rehearsed an answer and he stuck to it, no matter what anyone asked.

"My work is my own. Having someone claim plagiarism is nothing new in this business. But I can assure you, I wrote every single word in my books and none of them were copied."

Sam thought the evening would never end. After each presentation, he was bombarded by questions. But the requests to take pictures with him were incessant, and people were fighting each other for the remaining books.

At last the event was finished. Blake signed the presolds, the manager and the staff thanked him, and then they were back outside. It seemed, however, the evening wasn't quite over yet.

"The fucker was here tonight." Blake motioned to the note beneath the windshield wiper.

"I sent all the pictures back to Vigilance," Sam assured him, "just as I've done after each signing. They're running them through programs to see if any face shows up consistently."

"Don't you think he'd wear a disguise? Facial disguises are easy enough to do."

"Yes, but sometimes it only takes a few characteristics to make a match. Let's see what our guy has to say tonight." She plucked the note from beneath the windshield wiper, smoothed it out, and held it so they could both read it.

It won't be long now. I know what you did and I'll prove it.

Blake shook his head. "I wouldn't think he'd still be around after killing that poor woman."

They climbed into the car and Sam cranked the ignition. "Remember, we don't know who he is yet, and right now, there's nothing to tie him to that killing. He thinks he's home free. But just so you know, Avery's got her people going over everyone on your list again to see if we missed something."

"I have no idea what they'll find." He rubbed his face. "Do you have any idea how it feels to think that someone you know, even tangentially, wants to do this to you?"

"I can only imagine." She pulled expertly on to the Interstate and headed for the airport. "They dusted for fingerprints in the hotel room here, but just like in Arrowhead Bay, they didn't find anything. Avery said everyone's pretty sure the guy wears latex gloves."

"You know it's the same person."

"Yes, but every bit of proof helps for when he's caught." She was quiet for a moment, mentally trying to absorb the facts of the murder. To have some poor woman stabbed to death because someone mistook her for Sam made her sick to her stomach. This maniac's control had slipped and they needed to be prepared for anything.

She didn't draw a full breath until they were on the ground in Cleveland and at the hotel. Avery had arranged for someone to meet them at the terminal with a car so they could avoid the rental desk. The hotel they were at was again different than the one originally planned. She knew the agency was doing everything possible to protect Blake and keep him safe. She just hoped it was enough, and that she could do her part.

Finally they were checked into their rooms. They undressed and fell into bed, too tired for anything except to curl up together. Her last thought as she fell asleep was to wonder what would happen to the two of them when this was over and the stalker was caught. More and more she was falling in love with this complex, intriguing man. He'd all but declared himself where she was concerned. Now she just needed to figure out if she could find the trust that the past had stolen from her.

* * * *

The stalker was ready to spit nails. Nothing was going the way it was supposed to. Morgan didn't act like someone who was afraid or rattled. He'd deflected the whole plagiarism thing on the television spot. Worse than that, instead of turning his fans away from him, it seemed to incite them more and draw them to him more strongly. The scene at the book signing had been nuts. Twice as many people showed up and by the end of the event, all the books had been sold. Damn!

And then, when he'd followed their car to see where they were staying, they'd gone directly to the airport and gotten on a flight he hadn't even expected. He was beside himself with frustration.

Damn it! He wanted people returning his books or boycotting them, not buying them.

He was on a mission here, a mission to set things right. *He* was the one who should be getting all the breaks, so why was he being thwarted every way he turned?

Well, one more stop before Tampa, and he'd arranged a surprise for that next one. He hoped that would put Morgan off balance, and that bitch that was with him as well. He had plans that neither of them could stop, and he'd be sure to get both of them. Yes, she'd be part of the grand finale, too.

He grabbed a beer from the minibar and poured it into a glass, drinking half of it down in three swallows. He needed it to calm his nerves, as enraged as he was about the way things were happening. Or not happening. How could one man be so lucky? By this time, he should be on his last nerve, unable to meet his readers, hiding from the media.

He was just a lucky bastard, was all.

But your time is coming, Blake Morgan. Then everyone will know. And remember.

* * * *

"What?" Sam held the cell phone to her ear, her eyes wide. "I'm sorry, can you repeat that?"

Blake frowned. What was going on? They'd slept in because of their early morning arrival, and her first order of business after room service coffee was to give the store where he was signing in two days their usual courtesy call. But looking at Sam's face, Blake could tell something was not right.

"What's happening?" he mouthed.

"Well, that's definitely wrong. Someone is playing a trick on you. And on us. I promise I'll get this straightened out right away." She hung up and looked at Blake. "You won't believe this." She huffed a breath. "Well, on second thought, maybe you will."

"What's the deal? You look totally blindsided."

"That's because I am. Someone called pretending to be from your publisher and told the store the signing was cancelled."

"What?" For a minute he forgot to breathe. "Are you kidding me?"

"Not even a little. The manager said they got the call yesterday. The person was all apologetic but explained that you were involved in a problem with the rights to your books and so all signings had been cancelled."

Blake had to swallow twice before he could speak again. "I need to call Henry," he told her, "and have him get in touch with my publisher. And the bookstore. Did this woman get a name from the caller?"

Sam nodded. "Craig Wilhousen."

"Shit." He slammed his fist down on the dresser.

"Is that a real person?"

"Yes. He works in the publicity department. Getting the store manager's name would be very easy for my stalker. I'm sure she's listed as the contact person for the event."

"Go ahead and call whoever you need to. I'll contact Avery."

Predictably, Henry blew a cork.

"Blake, you must have some idea who's doing this. A person like this doesn't just pop up out of thin air."

"I swear to you, Henry. I have not got a clue. And believe me, I've tried to figure it out."

"Alright. Let me call the store and do damage control. They'll need to get signs posted that the signing is on. We'll call the radio stations. I'll have our office do a single notice blast with your newsletter sorted by zip code so it goes to everyone in the Cleveland area. We've got two days to fix this wreck. Let me think a minute."

"Will that do it?" Blake wanted to know. He was midway between angry and nauseous. "Is there anything I can do?"

"No." Henry almost shouted the word in his ear. "You take a back seat here and just show up for the signing with a big grin. Oh, and I'm going to call the manager and get the name of a top bakery in the area. We'll pop for refreshments and have them delivered."

"This is a fucking mess, Henry."

"No shit." His sigh was audible across the connection. "Alright. I've got to call the publisher first and check out this Craig Whoever. I'll get back to you as soon as I can. Meanwhile, don't leave your room."

"No problem there."

Sam hung up her call about two seconds later, a weird expression on her face.

"What?" he asked her. "Something's going on. Tell me."

"Sit down, Blake. Come on, let's sit at the little table here."

"I don't want to sit down." He fisted his hands. "I want to hear what Avery had to say."

"Then sit down and I'll tell you."

When he was seated, reluctantly, he glared at her. "Okay. Give."

Sam drew in a deep breath and let it out slowly. "I know you told us this had nothing to do with Annemarie, but—"

"Goddamn right it doesn't," he snapped.

"Will you just manage to be quiet for a minute so I can get this out? Okay. We were running into dead ends everywhere. Even Andrew Foley turned out to be nothing. So Avery had her people go back to the beginning to see what they might have missed, which usually for them is nothing.

But one of the things she decided to do was dig deeper into the key people in your life. Like Annemarie."

"She's dead," he reminded her, his voice cutting. "So you can write her off. This is not the work of a dead person. She wouldn't be a party into something like this, anyway. That's just not who she was."

"You're right," Sam agreed. "But how about someone close to her?"

"Like who?"

Sam took one of his hands in both of hers. "Blake."

"Uh-oh." A tiny knot formed in his stomach. "This can't be good."

"Avery got an updated version of the accident report."

He frowned. "What else was she looking for?"

"Well, someone had to be notified. Someone had to claim the body. She checked and she hadn't been buried at county expense."

"I'm telling you," he protested, "she had no one. She even told me that once. She said the job was everything to her."

"And yet she left with no notice at all," Sam pointed out. "Just disappeared into thin air. What does that tell you?"

He shrugged, but he was getting a sick feeling. "I don't know. What?"

"That she was lying? Or keeping secrets?" She squeezed his hand again.

He closed his fingers around her hand as if drawing strength from her. He had a feeling whatever she had to say wasn't good.

"Annemarie Schaefer's parents were dead. That was the truth. But her mother had been married twice and she had a stepbrother. Gregg Rowley. He lives in a little town in Maine about a mile from where she had her accident. Avery thinks she was on her way to his house when it happened."

"So she was going to see her stepbrother? So what?"

"Avery sent one of her agents up there to interview his neighbors."

Blake scowled. "Why not him? Couldn't you get the truth from him? Besides which, I'm not sure there's anything to get."

"They didn't find him, but they found people to talk to." She made a face. "Although the reports are that they were very reluctant to say anything. I guess they protect their own, no matter what."

He could hardly stand the concern in her eyes. "Can you please just spit it all out? Give it to me straight. What's the deal?"

"It seems Gregg Rowley has been in love with Annemarie since they were teenagers, when her father married his mother. The marriage only lasted a couple of years but they kept in touch with each other. As they grew older, according to friends of his, the love grew into an obsession, at least on his side of the equation."

"I swear she never mentioned him."

"Which is a little strange, since he was the only family she had and the only person she was close to. God only knows what she told him about you, but we're pretty sure he's the one behind all this. That he believes you cheated Annemarie in some fashion and that's why she left you so suddenly and ran home to him. That maybe you're even responsible somehow for her death—"

"Wait just a minute." He slammed his hand on the table. This was enough. "I'm not responsible for anything. I didn't steal anyone's material and I didn't abuse Annemarie's dedication to me. This guy is totally nuts. Certifiable."

Sam nodded. "We all agree on that point. But—"

"But what?"

"We think he sees himself as some sort of avenging angel on her behalf," she explained. "The people who know him in that little town in Maine, the ones willing to speak to us, said he'd been in love with her for years but apparently hadn't told her. One man said Rowley had told him Annemarie was coming home. That she'd called and needed to come be with him."

"She never even mentioned him." Blake shook his head. "I never heard of him until now."

"It's obvious he's heard of you," Sam pointed out, "and what he heard was nothing good. He wants to make you pay."

"But how? For what?" He was totally lost here. "I haven't done a damn thing."

"Everyone Vigilance spoke to, when they finally opened up to them, emphasized how obsessed he was with her. Bragged about her job with you and told them she was on her way to being a famous writer herself."

Blake shook his head. "She had no interest in that. She said how much she loved what she did." But even as he said the words, he wondered if he'd missed something, some clues along the way.

"But you don't know what she might have told him, or hidden from you. Right?"

He rubbed his hands over his face as if trying to wipe away this whole mess. "I guess. It's just hard for me to imagine because she wasn't like that at all."

"They also hinted at the fact Rowley might be a little unhinged. More than one person told our people he was very reclusive and antisocial."

"And nobody knows where he is now?"

"Uh-uh. He claimed her body," Sam went on, "and buried her next to her parents. After that he went off the grid. Completely." She paused. "And get this. His job before this was in cyber engineering. He designed and wrote software for security systems for computer businesses."

"So hacking into my laptop or phone or anything else would be no problem for him." Now he really did feel like throwing up.

"Right. Or into the airline manifests or hotel registration software. Or anything else."

Blake closed his eyes and dropped his head into his hands. This was a nightmare and he could not seem to wake up from it. As he sat there, the cell phone in his pocket chimed. He almost hated to pull it out and look at it, but he placed it in the center of the table.

Unknown caller.

"It's him." He swallowed back the bitter taste surging in his mouth.

"Let's see what he has to say today." Sam hit accept, and a new text filled the screen.

You can't always undo what I've done. I know what you did. In just a few days your career will be over forever.

"Jesus." Blake dropped his head into his hand. "I think I'm about to lose it, Sam."

"No, you're not. You're stronger than this. I know you are. We'll get through this and beat him at his game."

"He's already killed someone," he reminded her. "How many more will he get to before this is over?"

"None, because we're going to take precautions, now that we know what we're dealing with."

"An obsessed maniac," he ground out.

She nodded. "We'll be prepared. Avery's flying two extra Vigilance agents up here for the book signing to help out."

"If he sees them he'll know we're on to him," Blake pointed out.

"They'll never recognize them. I promise you." She grabbed the cell. "Meanwhile, I'm going to deactivate this one and set up a new one." She smiled at him. "We haven't even gone through half of them yet, Blake. We're in good shape."

"We have to keep our guard up between now and the book signing," Blake reminded her.

"You leave that to me and to Vigilance. We've got a lock on it."

* * * *

Gregg Rowley sat in his hotel room doing his best to tamp down his frustration. Again they'd given him the slip, but he was getting used to it. He'd stopped using up his energy in useless rages and unproductive searches. Instead he'd thought to give them a little something to keep them on their toes in Cleveland, but they'd checked in with the store a day earlier than usual and managed to fix things.

Shit!

Not that he expected it to be a big deal. So there was a mix-up in his signing date. People might be angry for a moment but they'd still buy his books and tell everyone how wonderful he was. He'd just wanted yet another opportunity to embarrass the selfish, people-using asshole. Too bad Morgan had managed to shortstop it. When Rowley had gone by the store to check on the situation, expecting big signs that the event was cancelled, he'd been shocked to find out it was still on and that the media would be covering it.

He hadn't wanted to ask too many questions and draw unwanted attention to himself, but damn! This jackass must live under a four-leaf clover. Tomorrow night he'd put on yet another of his disguises and check out how the signing actually turned out. Maybe, just to keep them on their toes, he'd leave yet another note on the windshield of their rental car. Just to make sure they knew he still had eyes on them.

But he was saving most of his energy for Tampa. The thought of what he had planned excited him almost as much as good sex. He had done all his research and had everything planned down to the last detail. He'd leave Cleveland right after the signing—and holy crap! What if Morgan and his bodyguard bitch took a late plane again, too? Good thing he had a number of disguises with him, just in case. He'd been able to make sure he was never seen twice as the same person.

He opened his laptop and stared at the picture of Annemarie that was his wallpaper. With great tenderness, he ran his fingers over the screen, stroking her cheeks and running his fingertip over her lips. The last time he'd touched her she'd been so cold, taken far too soon by death. He had been so thrilled when she called him out of the blue, crying, saying she couldn't take it any longer. She'd spent four years waiting for recognition of her work and it was apparent it would never happen. She wanted to come home to him and asked if he would help her.

He never got the chance. He should have told her not to drive in that horrific storm, but she had been determined to come to him at once. And he had waited so long for her to turn to him, to understand and accept his love, to want to be with him, he'd just agreed to let her drive in the pouring rain.

Now he'd never be able to hold her soft body next to his. To make love to her the way he'd dreamed about for so long. To build a life with her and help her achieve the success she so richly deserved. He'd had so many plans for them now all gone in seconds. The least he could do for her was to carry on her plans and expose Morgan for the fraud and user he was.

He cracked open a beer from the minibar and took a healthy swallow. He wouldn't waste his time chasing after them today. Tomorrow he'd hit the book signing, just because, but then it was off to Tampa and the big event. He could hardly wait.

* * * *

After consulting with both Avery and Henry, Sam and Blake had done what they could to minimize damage from the false cancellation. Blake had personally called the host of the local talk show and asked if they could slot him five or ten minutes the next morning. He didn't remember why he wasn't already booked on it but they were delighted to have him, especially as the rumors of the fake cancellation were circulating in the entertainment community. Then he invited one of the reviewers from the local newspaper to lunch.

"I warn you, I give a fair review," the man had told him.

"Understood. I just want a chance to chat with you."

Henry had overnighted a large envelope of promotional material that included copies of his stock photo. Sam had driven him to the store so he could meet the manager, apologize again, and sign the pictures and posters that the store could use in future promotions.

By that time the two agents from Vigilance—Mike Pérez and Justin DeLuca—had arrived and the four had dinner together. Blake liked the two men immediately. Like Sam, they were friendly but always alert, casual but aware of everything around them. In jeans and sweaters, they could have been any two guys having dinner. By nine o'clock Blake was ready to call it a night. The day had exhausted him emotionally and he needed down time to get himself ready for the next day.

"I'd invite you to join us for a drink, Sam," Mike said as they finished dinner, "but I know you want eyes on your client at all times."

Blake looked at him through narrowed eyes, trying to decide if the man was being sarcastic, funny, or snotty. He finally decided they were just acknowledging the situation any of them would be in—stick with the client at all times. When they reached their rooms, he excused himself to take a shower. He wasn't sure if what he was feeling was the emotional grime from tension or not but he stood under the hot water for a long time.

When he finished, he toweled himself off and climbed into the bed he and Sam were sharing, stark naked.

He heard sounds from the other bedroom so he lay there, waiting, not sure if she'd be in the mood for anything more than just spooning their bodies together. When this tour was over he was going to get Sam alone somewhere and lay everything on the table. This thing between them, in his mind, had substance to it. Strength. Emotion. He was sure he felt the same thing from Sam. Getting her to admit it was the next step.

Sure there were a lot of challenges in his life—his writing and touring schedule, her assignments for Vigilance which could last anywhere from weeks to months. He'd come to realize, though, that he could handle anything as long as he had Sam with him. But then came the big question: What did she really feel for him, now, all these years later?

He was still batting it all around in his mind when Sam crawled into bed with him, also naked. He didn't say a word, didn't ask, just rolled so he could pull her body to his and take her mouth in a scorching, hungry kiss. Her lips were so soft and her mouth, when he slid his tongue into it, tasted faintly of her toothpaste. Threading his fingers through the soft strands of her hair, he fed on her, licking every inch of her inner surface, sweeping his tongue across hers before easing it back and coasting it over her lips.

She gave as good as she got, holding his head in place while she scraped her tongue over his teeth. When he turned her head to give himself a better angle, she moved with him and eased right into a kiss that asked everything of her.

Without another word, he eased her on to her back and began sprinkling kisses down the column of her neck, across the graceful line of her shoulder, pausing to place a hot kiss on the beating pulse in the hollow of her throat. She arched up to him, a silent offering, and he moved his mouth in a slow sweep across the top of each of her breasts, so plump and delicious. Taking one hard nipple into his mouth he sucked on it, grazing it lightly with his teeth before soothing it with his tongue. She scraped her fingernails down his back as a soft, low moan whispered from her mouth.

Her nipples were like sweet berries, so ripe and pebbled and so sensitive that each slide of his teeth and pull of his lips elicited another of those delectable moans. He moved his mouth down the gentle curve of her stomach, probing the indentation of her navel with the tip of his tongue. She tried to push her body up to his, making those same erotic little sounds. They were almost as hot as the touch of her skin and the feel of her beneath his hands and his mouth.

He took his time, letting himself taste every bit of her skin that he could reach, and by the time he reached her sex she was thrusting at him and trying to open her legs, to urge him to put some part of him inside her body.

But Blake was in no hurry. She was better than any tranquilizer, better than any fine aged brandy or cognac, and he wasn't going to be rush. Finally shifting his body so he was between her legs, he placed a string up kisses up the inside of one thigh and down the other, just barely brushing his lips over her skin and following that with a string of gentle tiny nips.

On and on it went, always circling the heated place she wanted him, always rousing her a little more and a little more. By the time he reached the lips of her sex, rubbing his tongue along the damp, slick flesh and tracing the line of her slit with his tongue, she was writhing beneath him, moaning softly, begging.

"Please," she hissed.

His laugh rumbled against her arching body. "Please what?"

"Please use your mouth on me," she pleaded. "Your hands. Anything."

"Like this?" He took the swollen bud of her clit in his teeth, tugging it just a little.

"Yes!"

"Or like this?" He licked the length of her slit before tracing the line of her opening with the tip of his tongue.

"Yes! Yes!" She was writhing, twisting back and forth now.

"How about this?" Opening her lips like petals with his thumbs, he thrust his tongue deep inside her hot, wet, delicious flesh.

"Yes!" she screamed, and came so suddenly and so hard he had to hold her tightly in place.

He worked her with his mouth, probing with his tongue, thrusting it in and out as her hot flesh spasmed around it. Her fingers gripped the hair on his head and hung on as if she were clutching a lifeline. He kept up his rhythm until the last of the spasms had subsided and she lay limp on the bed, still slightly out of breath.

"God! What are you doing to me?"

He chuckled. "Hopefully making you happy."

She lay there a moment, the beat of the pulse at the hollow of her throat slowly subsiding. Then, without warning, she pushed herself to an upright position, and pushed him to his back.

"What's going on?" he asked.

"My turn," she told him. "Or yours, depending on how you look at it.

She straddled him, the wet heat of her core imprinting itself on his thighs. As she leaned forward took his cock in her hands and ran her tongue over the sensitive head. His body jerked.

"Jesus, Sam."

"Not good?" She stared down at him.

"Too good," he gasped. "I want to be inside you when I come."

"Not yet. I haven't had my fun yet. Turnabout's fair play."

With that she proceeded to drive him crazy, her soft tongue licking the length of him, her lips closing around him, her graceful fingers stroking him. There was no pattern to it, so he had no chance to prepare himself. He didn't know which drove him crazier, her mouth of her hands or both of them together. He had to grit his teeth to maintain some measure of control. As much as he wanted to come in her mouth, tonight he wanted to be inside her hot, tight channel, her walls gripping him like a fist.

While he still had the strength to do it he lifted her from his body and settled her on her back. Rolling to his side, he reached in the drawer of the nightstand where he had hopefully stashed some condoms, grabbed one, and rolled it on. But when he went to position himself, Sam pushed him and reversed their positions.

"My turn," she repeated.

Adjusting her position, she closed her fingers around his cock and guided it to her opening. He barely felt the tip of it enter her when she took a deep breath, threaded her fingers with his and lowered herself on his rock-hard shaft.

Jesus!

He sucked in a breath and tried to hold himself still, hanging on to the edge of the ledge as he was. And then Sam began to move, slowly at first then faster and then faster still. The moved as one, so perfectly in sync that Blake was awed. If an orgasm could be said to be perfection, this was it. Fingers threaded, her thighs bracketing his legs, she rode him as if it had all be choreographed.

He didn't want it to end, wanted it to go on forever. But they were both reaching the point of no return.

"Look at me," he ordered. "Look right into my eyes."

Gazes locked, they climbed up and up that sensuous slope, breathing harder, clenching their muscles, her walls so tight around him they were like a wet fist. And then...they were there, coming together, so hard he knew nothing but the explosive force that gripped his body and the contractions that shook them over and over and over again. Sam fell forward, resting on his body, her head tucked into his neck.

He had no idea how much time had passed before she finally eased herself to a sitting position and very carefully lifted herself from his body. Tonight, she was the one who disposed of the condom, who climbed back into bed and curled herself in the curve of his body. Neither of them said a word, but he knew something had shifted and changed between them.

The big question was: Could they move forward from here? Together? By now he knew he was pretty much all in, but what about Sam? What did she feel?

He fell asleep with the questions spinning in his mind.

Chapter 14

Blake wasn't sure if he was glad to be back in Tampa or not. They'd all had a discussion with Avery about where he'd stay—Tampa or Arrowhead Bay. Blake finally said he wanted to sleep in his own bed. That Gregg Rowley could find him either place and he wanted his creature comforts. Mike Pérez rented a car at the airport and drove Blake and Sam to Blake's condo before checking in at a hotel five minutes away. One of the benefits, Blake pointed out, of living practically downtown.

The first night back Blake fell into bed, Sam curled up next to him, and passed out more than slept. The stress of the whole situation was killing him and was very draining. Never in the four years he'd known Annemarie Schaefer—and he'd thought they were pretty close—had he ever thought she considered he was stealing her work. And exactly what work was that? Nor had she ever seemed to be emotionally unstable.

Maybe it was this Gregg Rowley guy who was reading things into it because he superimposed his own feelings for Annemarie onto the situation. Certainly someone who was a stalker wasn't the most emotionally stable person in the world.

He and Henry and the publisher had set up the tour with high hopes, and truly it had accomplished the goals they'd set out. Except for the stalker who also turned out to be a murderer. And factoring out what happened at the last two stops, the publicity had been great. On top of that, he sold nearly all the books at each signing. In fact, Henry had texted him at one point that he needed to come to New York to sign stock because some stores had requested books with his signature.

Only one incident had marred the final stop before Tampa. Halfway through his presentation a man had pushed to the front of the crowd and begun shouting at him. Peppering him with questions. Asking him how it felt to steal someone else's work and claim it as their own.

Mike and Justin had eased him out of line with only a minimum of fuss. The man was no match for the two strong agents who hustled him to the back of the store. The man had never returned, thanks to the agents. They'd taken him out the back door and into the waiting arms of a local cop Justin had called, without disrupting the rest of the signing. But Blake had finished the event with his stomach tied in knots. When it was over he learned the man was a frustrated author convinced plagiarism was the only key to success. If he could generate enough noise at the signing he'd get some publicity, too. Blake still felt ill when he thought of it.

"People have weird minds," Blake told the agents.

Mike nodded. "Believe me, you don't know the half of it."

Now they were all gathered at the Royal Event Center to make plans. Blake looked at the number of people sitting around the table in the manager's conference room and for the first time felt a tiny thread of real fear. Gregg Rowley was no longer just some nut job, but a stalker who easily killed, and it was his—Blake's—life they were all here discussing how to protect. In addition to himself, Sam, Avery, Mike Pérez, and Justin DeLuca, Avery had brought two more Vigilance agents. Four deputies from the sheriff's office, who would provide even more protection, had joined them and Detective Chuck Fornell, who was handling the Grant Kennelly beating, had driven up, also. They all had diagrams of the building so they knew what areas to cover. Avery was running the show, and everyone knew they'd be taking their orders from her. Blake refilled his coffee mug from a carafe set on a small table and sat quietly next to Henry, who had flown in to protect one of his lucrative commodities.

"Justin and Mike will take point," she told everyone. "Blake, they'll pick you and Sam up when it's time for you to get here. I don't want the two of you driving here in a car that's been sitting in the garage for hours. There's no telling what this guy might have done to it."

"I'd think he'd want to wait until Blake was here before doing anything," Henry broke in. "He's leading up to some big statement. That would fizzle if he harmed them before they even got here."

Avery nodded. "Agreed, but at this point we're taking no chances." She handed out a photo to everyone. "Sam took pictures at every one of the signings and I had my guys run the shots through facial recognition to see if there were any repeaters. But now that we're pretty sure who this is, we have a clear picture of him. Study it, memorize it, and keep in mind he is a master of disguise. Okay, let's look at this event from the moment Blake arrives."

They plotted a path from the parking lot through a back entrance, along a corridor into the event center. Blake had the weirdest out of body feeling as he listened to them discuss how they were going to keep him from being killed.

"Sam will be in charge of Blake," Avery told them. "Wherever he goes, she goes. It will be up to the rest of you to cover all the rest of the bases. Chase and Reuben"—she looked at the two agents she'd brought with her—"you'll be here and here." She pointed to spots on the map of the room. "Refreshments are being served and they'll be set up along this back wall here. And here"—she pointed again—"is where the table will be for the book signing."

"I can handle that part of it," Henry broke in. "I'll make sure no one messes with the books after they're brought in or tries to rearrange anything." He looked around the table. "Should I have a gun?"

Blake burst out laughing. "Henry, they don't expect you to be the Lone Ranger. They'll be watching out for your ass, too."

Henry shrugged. "Just asking."

Avery went on to mark where the others would be stationed, including one of the officers and Justin, who would mingle with the crowd looking for anything out of the ordinary.

"We'll be setting up the metal detector like you asked," one of the deputies told her. "We've got a good portable one we use for events around the county that we can process people through very quickly."

"Will it detect anything but metal?" Avery asked.

"No, but we've all done this enough that we can smell out trouble. We may ruffle a few feathers if we pull some people aside for further checking, though."

"Better ruffled than dead," she told him.

Blake was stunned when she pointed to Mike as a trained sharpshooter.

"Do you think we'll need one?" he asked.

"You never know, and I don't want to be caught with my pants down because we weren't prepared."

"We'll have media here," Henry told her. "I can't very well refuse them and we need all the favorable press we can get."

Blake stared at his agent. "You think I'm a pariah, Henry?"

"Oh, no. No, no, no. But the media is going to rehash that email and we need them to see what an honest, upright, intelligent, talented, resourceful author you are."

Blake actually burst out laughing. "Could I get a T-shirt with that on it?"

"Not funny," Henry said. "This is your life here, personal and professional."

"We'll handle it, Henry," Avery promised. "Just make sure they all have proper identification and have been vetted."

"No problem."

"Okay, back to the diagram."

By the time Avery was finished, everyone had his or her assignments and Blake was pretty sure Gregg Rowley would have a hard time getting to him.

Blake shook hands with the deputies and with Chase and Reuben. Avery passed out timetables and also a list with everyone's cell phone numbers listed. Then she turned to Blake and Sam.

"Chase and Reuben will be here in the morning when the staff begins their setup. They'll check the catering staff and keep an eye on everything they do. Never can tell what someone might smuggle in."

"Jesus!" Blake raked his fingers through his hair. "This really is like something from a book. Or a movie. Maybe we should just cancel the whole thing."

"Absolutely not," Henry snapped. "This is your big night, Blake. We're not going to let some nut job shut it down." He turned to Avery. "That's what we have Vigilance for, right?"

She nodded. "It is. Blake, if you cancel tomorrow night you are just going to make him angrier because you've taken away his stage. He'll just create another opportunity where many people could be hurt."

He felt sick to his stomach. He was damned if he did and damned if he didn't.

"Fine. But let's make triple sure all bases are covered."

Avery nodded. "Of course. Alright, everyone. Let's do a walk-through so everyone knows their places." She lifted the duffel she'd carried in with her and placed by her chair. "I have comms for everyone and I want to test them out."

If they can't protect me, no one can.

The thought flashed through Blake's mind as he watched the team walk through their setup, test their comm gear, and go through their list of what ifs. At least he was confidant Rowley couldn't smuggle a gun in, pull it out, and shoot him. Of course, that didn't mean he couldn't try something else.

Sam will make sure that doesn't happen.

And he knew she would, whatever she had to do. This morning, standing in his shower, he'd thought about fate bringing them together after all these years. So many unrelated events that combined to make this happen. Okay, they'd scratched an itch that had been there all this time and it was good. Great. The sex was actually beyond great. And they got along well. So many days together in a tense situation and they'd never had even a hint of a blowup.

Maybe they were due one. He knew no relationship moved forward without some kind of conflict. If there wasn't any, it meant there was no real deep emotion to the relationship. And he believed in his heart of hearts that he and Sam had something special, but did she? What about her career, where she could be gone on dangerous jobs for days at a time? Or his, when he locked himself away writing, or was busy out on tour?

By the time he'd finished giving himself a headache, he'd decided that right now he just needed to concentrate on his final appearance and getting out of it alive. After that they could see where things went between them. If they both wanted it, that was.

"Looks like some pretty deep thoughts there." Sam nudged him with her elbow.

"What? Oh, just thinking about tomorrow night. And today's media events."

Henry had previously scheduled a television spot for him as well as an interview with a reporter from *The Tampa Times*. But with the rumors circulating since that email, he'd decided that a small press conference was in order, hoping to kill the rumors once and for all. Or at least put them in perspective.

"You'll do great," she assured him. "You always do."

He gave her a lopsided grin. "From your lips."

"Let's hope."

By four that afternoon everyone had memorized the layout of the event center, where each of them was supposed to be, and who had what responsibilities. The small media conference had been held in a private room at the hotel where Henry was staying, with reporters from the various weeklies and even a couple of television stations in addition to the one where he did his interview.

Blake had been tense through everything, especially when the inevitable subject of the email came up, but Henry had helped out there and he'd gotten through it. By the time he fell into bed that night, all he wanted was for everything to be over. And wasn't it just too damn bad that with his third book in a row to hit the best-seller lists he didn't know if he'd even enjoy the final event which was supposed to be the best one yet.

The following day dawned sunny and warm, something Sam said was a good omen.

"I'll take anything," he told her.

They'd slept curled into each other last night, sex the furthest thing from either of their minds. The one thing swirling in Blake's mind, however, as he drifted off, was how well they fit together and how natural it was for them to sleep like this. Something he did not want to let go of. When tonight was over, he and Sam were going to have a talk, one where he laid his heart on the table for her. Told her how important she was to him. How he didn't want her to walk away when this was over. He'd do whatever it took for her to believe every word he said. Believe *him*.

She hadn't said much but he could tell by the way she behaved, and by the level of their intimacy, that her walls were coming down brick by brick. He'd find out whatever was keeping her from being all in, slay her dragons, and move ahead with their future.

This morning they had breakfast in the little coffee shop down the street from his town house. Henry insisted on taking them to lunch the day of the event, although Blake could hardly swallow a bite.

Things were scheduled to start at seven thirty.

"The caterers will be there at six to set up and the bookstore at six forty-five," Henry told them. "They won't need all that time but people will arrive early and I want everything ready when they walk in. The deputies brought their portable scanner and got it set up so they can start processing people through it when the first person arrives."

Blake barked a sort of laugh. "Never thought I'd be signing books where people had to go through a metal detector and be searched for weapons."

"You can put it in your next book," Henry joked.

"I'll take you directly to the bride's room when we get there," Sam told him.

He lifted an eyebrow. "Bride's room? Is someone getting married?"

She laughed. "Frequently. It's the room where the bride and her attendants go to get ready. We figured there might be some good mojo to help out."

And then the evening arrived. At seven o'clock, Justin and Mike arrived to drive them to the event center. Mike told them he and the other Vigilance agents had met with the four deputies working with them at six o'clock to do a walk-through of everything and supervise the setting up.

"We've got it covered," Mike assured him.

Blake just wanted to get this over with. He'd be "on" for his readers, despite the bad case of nerves he was battling.

"I haven't felt this edgy since I did my first signing," he told Henry, who arrived shortly after Sam and Blake.

"You'll be fine," the agent assured him. "We've got this taken care of."

* * * *

Gregg Rowley popped two aspirin in his mouth and washed them down with the last of his water. Putting everything together for tonight had taken some work, especially considering the materials he was using. But one thing about being a techno-nut, you could find anything on the Internet, no matter what it was, and arrange how to receive it.

Lucky stroke for him that refreshments were being served tonight. Well, pastries and coffee. Hacking into the event center's computer he'd learned the name of the caterer and when setup was scheduled. And lucky for him, when he checked out who the caterer had scheduled to work and searched for pictures, he found someone who looked enough like him that Gregg could easily pass for him.

Getting into the man's home had been child's play. Knocking him out and tying him up so he could steal the man's clothing and badge was just as easy. If he kept his head down no one would look too closely or ask him the wrong questions.

And that was just the way it worked out. He'd called the caterer and said he'd have to meet the van at the event center. Small family problem. When he got there, the other three workers had already set up the tables inside the hall and were carrying things inside.

"You missed all the heavy work, you slacker," one of the girls said.

"Sorry," he mumbled. "Family problem."

He picked up two large boxes of pastry and moved quickly to carry them inside before she could ask him any questions.

The most nerve wracking was the security check by one of the Vigilance agents. Those guys were tough to fool and had eyes everywhere. He managed to work it so he was alone when they came to check him out, releasing a pent-up breath when they cleared him. Then a quick trip to his car parked next to the van, an adjustment to his clothing, and he was all set.

He'd seen the men walking around with their secret agent microphones and earbuds. Their jackets that concealed whatever weapons they carried. And Morgan's bitch bodyguard glued to his side. No matter. He'd be outsmarting them all.

This is for you, Annemarie. My only love. Tonight they'll all know who the real star is.

He looked at his watch. Seven fifteen. Show time!

* * * *

By seven twenty the hall in the center they were using was packed. The reporters had shown up, which surprised Blake since he'd already given his interviews. But Henry had told him to expect it.

"If there's anything going on with your stalker, they don't want to miss it."

"Swell." He grimaced. "I'm glad I could provide news fodder for them."

Sam took his hand in hers and squeezed it. "You'll be fine. You've been a trooper through all of this. Whatever happens, we've got it covered and tonight it will all be over."

Ignoring the fact that Henry was in the room with them, he cupped her jaw, tilted her face up to his, and gave her a warm, thorough kiss.

"For luck," he said.

"Okay." She grinned. "For luck."

As Sam walked him into the event room, he noticed the pastries and coffee and the larger than usual setup of books were all in place. Reporters hung out along the back wall. And every single chair was filled."

"They had to pull out more from wherever they keep them," Sam whispered. "Is this the biggest crowd you've ever had?"

He nodded. "By far."

"Evan, our sharpshooter, is at the back wall." She nodded her head in his direction. "Everyone else is in their place. I'll be on stage with you, in the wings, on one side. Mike will be on the other. You ready?"

"As I'll ever be."

The manager of the bookstore that was hosting tonight came forward and introduced herself.

"We're just delighted you chose to end your tour here," she gushed. "Everyone's so excited about it, and about the big crowd. Thank you so much."

He swallowed a laugh, wondering if he should point out to her he remembered when they didn't even want to carry his books.

She mounted the steps to the stage ahead of him and headed for the podium. She'd be the one introducing him. Two taps of the microphone to make sure it was working and they were set.

"Good evening, everyone. I want to thank you all for coming out for this very special book signing. We're thrilled to host Blake Morgan, who lives here in Tampa, and thank him for choosing to make this his last stop on his current tour. He's going to tell you a bit about his writing career and then about his latest release, the third in a row to hit the top of the best-seller lists. Please help me welcome him." She turned toward him, smiling.

Blake walked out to the center of the stage, carrying the folder with his notes. He shook hands again with the woman, thanked her, then thanked everyone for coming tonight. His throat, as usual, was dry as dust and he reached to the shelf beneath for the water he'd requested. Nothing there. He bent down and looked, but the shelf was empty.

He looked over at Sam, who was frowning.

"Sorry, everyone." He smiled at the audience. "I still get stage fright and my throat closes up." A soft laugh ran through the crowd. "If someone can get me some water we'll be good to go."

A man in the uniform of the caterer hurried up to the stairs carrying a bottle.

"Sorry. It was my job and I goofed."

"No problem. Thanks."

The man handed the water to Blake but as soon as he did he yanked off the waiter's vest to reveal another vest beneath it. The crowd gasped as one.

* * * *

Suicide vest!

The minute she saw it, Sam knew exactly what it was. It was smaller than the ones she'd seen, made to fit beneath the uniform vest he wore, but no less deadly. It was apparent Rowley had no plans to take out everyone, just Blake.

No! She couldn't let it happen. She loved him, and could not lose him.

The word itself terrified her, but she'd worry about that later. Right now she had business to take care of.

With one hand, Rowley tore off the wig and fake moustache he was wearing. He lifted the other hand and Sam saw the suicide switch he had his thumb on. The switch was depressed. The moment he released his thumb, the vest would blow. That's why it was called a dead man's switch. The goal was to get a cop to shoot him, and when he fell the thumb relaxed and the explosives blew sky high.

Which was why no one was rushing the stage. She just hoped her key man was ready for the signal.

Shit!

"Situation, situation," she murmured into her lip mic. "How copy."

"Five by five," came the answer from everyone.

"I have to figure out how to get that switch away from him without blowing up him, Blake, and me. Wait for my signals. Evan, you know the code word."

"Copy that."

Everyone acknowledged and she slowly inched her way out to the stage.

"You all came to see the big novelist Blake Morgan tonight, right?" Rowley shouted. "Well, I'm here to tell you he's a big fraud. He stole every

word he wrote from the love of my life, Annemarie Schaefer." When he
didn't get the reaction he apparently wanted from the audience frozen in
its seat, he raised his voice. "Did you hear me? She worked for him for
four years, slaved away as his assistant, did his research, and then wrote
his books for him. I have the proof."

Sam spared a look for Blake, who might have been ready to wet his
pants but outwardly was very calm.

"Is that what she told you?" he asked in a mild voice.

"Damn straight. She had all those folders on her laptop with all the
work she did for you. She told me about them. About how you couldn't
put it all together so she had to do it for you. About how she gave you the
plots when you couldn't create one."

Blake nodded. "She was a very big help to me, Gregg. You're right."

"Oh. You know my name? Did she tell you?"

"Yes. She spoke very well of you."

Keep lying, Blake. You're doing great.

Sam slid forward a few more inches.

"I wrote to your publisher. Mailed the letter today. Told him they needed
to recall all those books and put her name on them." He was sobbing
now. "She died trying to get away from you. Running to me. It's your
fault she's dead, so you need to die, too, but not before everyone knows
exactly what you did."

Sam noticed that Blake had turned so he was facing her more, which
meant Rowley now had his back to her.

Keep him focused, Blake. Just a little further. A little further.

And then she was there. She leapt forward and grabbed the hand with
the switch, pressing her thumb over his.

"Umbrella!" she yelled into the mic.

Evan's shot split the air barely a second later, hitting Rowley in the
forehead, and he fell, with Sam on top of him and her thumb still on the switch.

Then everyone moved. Justin hurried onto the stage to grab Blake, who
protested he wasn't going anywhere until Sam was safe. Someone got up
to the microphone and urged everyone to be calm, and to help themselves
to refreshments until they could get the program started again.

Sam had to stifle the hysterical urge to giggle. Yes, coffee and pastries
while she was lying here on a dead body hoping she didn't get blown
to kingdom come.

"We called the bomb squad the minute we saw his vest, Sam." Avery's
voice came through her ear bud. "They'll be here any second."

"Thanks."

Someone pulled the curtain on the stage to hide the gruesome sight.

"I thought this was supposed to be my show."

She turned her head to see Blake crouching beside her, a worried look on his face but his lips forced into a grin.

"I decided I wanted to see what all the fuss was about being a star."

He took her free hand and wrapped one of his around it, holding tightly.

"I think my heart stopped beating twice. Was this your way of upstaging me?"

"Yeah." Again she swallowed a hysterical giggle. Lying on a dead body wasn't her idea of a pleasant way to pass the time. "I figured there was no way you could top this."

Finally the bomb squad was there, moving Blake aside while they did their thing. Sam felt as if a year had passed before the leader told her she was good to go and someone lifted her from Rowley's body. Blake, waiting right next to her, hauled her into his arms, crushing her to him as if he'd never let her go. And for a moment she thought how great it would be if that happened.

But just for a moment.

"Let's move over here," he urged, tugging her away from the body.

"You okay, Sam?" Avery's voice sounded in her ear bud.

"I'm good." Good? She was alive. That was good enough.

"We've got the crowd corralled and we're feeding them pastries and coffee. The bookstore manager gets a lot of credit for not losing her shit and for making all that happen. Henry, too." She paused. "Blake okay?"

Sam looked up at him. "He seems to be. He'll probably fall apart when we get back to his condo but right now he's a real trooper."

"I can help down there," Blake told her.

She frowned. "How? You planning to be a waiter?"

"Always the smart-mouth. No, I figured if I started the book signing now, it would take people's minds away from what happened. Besides, they can bombard me with questions and get their picture taken with the author who almost got blown up."

Her eyes widened. "You know, that's a damn good idea. You up for it?"

"I'll make it work. Let's tell Henry to set it up."

In the end that's what they did. The media, of course, salivated over the story they had to report and begged a few minutes to question Blake before he sat down at the signing table. She gave Henry points for pulling it all together and Blake for managing to appear relaxed and focused only on his readers. He answered questions, chatted with people. Signed books until she was sure his hand would fall off.

That meant hardly anyone paid attention when the wagon came to cart Rowley's body away. The deputies stayed on to help the Vigilance agents with crowd control, but all things considered, Sam thought, the rest of the evening went off okay.

For herself she'd never been so damn glad to see an evening end.

Chapter 15

Noted Author Victim of Stalker
Bestselling Author Victim of Bomb Plot
Plagiarism Debunked as Bestselling Author Faces
Off with Stalker

Blake closed out the screen and fixed another cup of coffee for himself. The acid reflux reaction told him he'd been drinking too much coffee for his own good.

Better than alcohol, he told himself.

It had been his drug of choice as he got through the aftermath of the scene at the event hall. In all his life, he was sure he'd never forget the sight of Sam lying on Gregg Rowley's dead body, blood pooling beneath his head, her finger holding his thumb on the dead man's switch. He was sure his heart had stopped beating altogether and he'd trembled so much he was afraid he'd fall down. When he crouched beside her and took her hand in his, he never wanted to let it go.

Which was part of what brought him on today's journey.

With the danger gone, Sam's assignment was over. She had stayed with him the next day while he did all the public relations things provoked by the dramatics of the previous evening. Gone with him to drive Henry to the airport. They'd come home, had a light dinner, and then indulged in some of the most intense sex he'd ever enjoyed. He knew, however, it was only that way because of who he was with.

He fell asleep determined to talk to her the next morning about where they could go from here, because he sure didn't want to walk away from her again. He loved her and he was pretty damn sure she loved him. If he'd ever had any doubts about his own feelings, they were gone. He wanted a future with her and he sensed she felt the same, if he could just get past whatever was holding her back.

But in the morning when he awoke, having slept the sleep of the dead, she was gone, as were all her things. He looked around for a note, a message of any kind. Checked his phone for a text because he'd shut it off when they went to bed.

Nothing. Nothing at all.

At first he was angry. No, raging mad. How the hell could she just walk away like this without a backward glance? Hadn't what they'd found meant anything to her at all? They weren't those teenagers anymore. He thought he'd proven to her that this was real and deep and lasting. Now he wanted to find a way to for them to build a life together.

But how could he move forward when she had walked out of his life? With each passing day the need for her grew more intense until sometimes he actually ached with it. He stopped himself from calling her for the first couple of days, thinking to give her some time and space to wrestle with whatever problem was plaguing her. He also didn't think haring off to Arrowhead Bay while he was still so worked up would get him anywhere.

He was grateful that he had enough to keep him busy so he didn't sit around feeling sorry for himself and driving himself crazy. The story of Gregg Rowley, Annemarie Schaefer, and the suicide vest turned out to be a nine days' wonder. Henry was fielding calls from bloggers, magazine feature writers, reporters, television shows, anyone with media access and the ability to use it.

"Your sales are literally going through the roof," Henry told him a week after the event. "Your publisher is doing a very happy dance, let me tell you."

"Is this the same publisher who sent me Annemarie Schaefer without knowing she was a basket case?" He swallowed back his bitterness.

"That was your editor, and no, he had no idea." Henry's sigh carried across the connection. "He feels very badly about it, Blake. He really does."

Blake sighed. "I guess I can't berate him too badly. I didn't see it, either. And how the hell did I not?"

"Blake." Henry's cleared his throat. "We discussed this. She gave no signs at all of what was going on with her mentally and emotionally. I met her several times and I didn't sniff anything wrong. And hell, I'm suspicious of everyone."

"I just keep thinking I should have sensed something wrong. But damn, Henry, she acted so normal. She was incredibly efficient and kept me from losing my shit more times than I can count." He rubbed his jaw. "Maybe I should have tried harder when she packed up so suddenly, forced her to tell me what was wrong, I mean, damn. I think I'm so smart and I had a head case falling apart right under my eyes."

"Okay, I think that's enough wearing the hair shirt. She was a disturbed young lady who somehow convinced herself that helping with your research and spellchecking your manuscripts meant she was writing the books. We need to move on."

"The media isn't letting it go," he pointed out. "Look at this list of suggested interviews you sent me. They'll be talking about it next year."

"Or until the next hot topic comes around. Which leads me back to that list. Come to New York. We'll do a big signing here, some interviews, maybe host an event for readers. Good stuff."

"I don't—"

"Blake." Henry's voice was sharp now. "You worked your ass off to get where you are. Through no fault of your own you're riding a big wave of media attention and sales. Tomorrow it could all disappear. Let's catch this while we can."

Blake swallowed another sigh. "Yeah, yeah, okay. Let's set some dates."

So he'd gone to New York for ten days. *A change would help*, he told himself. He could put some space between himself and Sam while she worked things out in her head. Henry had set a good schedule for him, including a book signing at one of the major stores where it took more than three hours for him to sign for all the people who stood in line to see him. His editor fell all over him with apologies and the publisher took him to the Hamptons for a weekend where he rubbed elbows with people to whom his earnings were pocket change.

By the end of the trip he was burned out on it all, and didn't care if he ever talked to anyone about it ever again. In fact, he hoped he wouldn't. Three days into the trip he tried to call Sam. He couldn't stand it anymore. He wanted to ask her what the hell was going on and could he please see her, but all he got was a message telling him it was no longer a working number. He remembered she told him Avery gave the agents fresh phones for each assignment, which meant she was probably off somewhere guarding someone's body. Or something.

Dozens of times he brought up Avery's number on his cell, his thumb hovering over it to call her and ask when Sam would be back. But just as many times he swiped the screen and shoved the phone in his pocket.

Finally, two days after his return from New York, his curiosity, if nothing else, got the better of him and he called Vigilance.

"I've been reading all about you," Avery greeted him. "You're our resident celebrity."

"Yeah, well, I could do with a little more publicity and a little less notoriety."

"So how are you doing, Blake? Really."

He thought for a moment. "Okay, I guess. Still stunned by the whole thing. What happened hurt a lot of people. One person was badly injured, another killed just because she looked like someone else. I'll always feel responsible for that."

"You're not," she said quickly. "There isn't a thing you could have done. I know you've probably had a lot of people telling you that, so I'll add my voice. Gregg Rowley was a very disturbed man. You had no control over what he did. I know you'll never forget any of it, but you need to move away from it."

"Yeah. Everyone tells me the same thing. I'm working on my next book, so that should help." He uttered a rough laugh. "And it's not about a deranged man who wants to blow up an author, no matter what people tell me."

"I ran into your folks the other day," she told him. "I think they'd like you to come down and visit them."

He laughed. "No kidding. My mother calls every other day telling me she wants to see me with her own eyes. They came up to Tampa just before I left for New York and right after I came back. I told her I haven't changed."

"You're right, but I think they'll be a long time getting over what happened."

"Especially with what happened to Grant Kennelly," he agreed. "Something else I feel responsible for."

"Maybe you should talk to someone, Blake," she suggested.

"You mean like a shrink?"

"It wouldn't hurt."

He had no plans to do that but he didn't want to argue with her.

"I'll think about it." He paused, trying to think how to frame his next words. "How's Sam?"

"She's good. Very good. Off on an assignment but I'm sure you tried to call her and figured that out."

"Yeah. So where's this one?"

Avery chuckled. "Now you know I can't tell you that. But she's able to travel and the client loves her."

Loves? Was it a man? Did he feel about her like Blake had? Like he *did?*

"That's nice." Another pause. "When does her assignment end?"

Now it was Avery's turn to pause. "I don't know if I should tell you, Blake."

"Why? What's the problem?"

"Sam didn't say a word to me after her gig with you was over. She just came back to the office and said she was up for immediate assignment if I had one. I didn't think it was my place to ask her what was wrong. I'd hoped you guys could at least part friends.

"Yeah. Friends."

"I'm not getting in your business, but she's a grown woman, Blake. She has her own issues to deal with. If she wants to see you, she'll get in touch with you."

Issues. Right. Thanks for nothing.

"Okay. Well, if you talk to her tell her I said hello."

What about seeing where this goes and taking it from there? What about after the gig was over?

Okay, so they'd never really discussed it again, but still…

But still what, dipshit? She never promised you a rose garden. Get over it.

And wouldn't he love to be able to do that. But she'd walked out of his life before he could tell her in plain English how he felt. Tell her he wanted a life with her. That he loved her, for God's sake. He didn't want to face the fact he might have lost that chance.

I love her, damn it.

Then find her and tell her. Make her listen.

He'd do that, he told himself, just as soon as she got back from her assignment. Otherwise he might be haunting Vigilance for information.

For the next couple of weeks, he buried himself in the new book, deliberately shutting everything else from his mind. It was something he'd learned to do when he was working on his first book and he'd become very good at it. Now he really needed that discipline because no matter how hard he tried, he couldn't get Sam out of his mind. He wondered how her job was going and if she ever gave a thought to him.

After two weeks of locking himself in his condo and writing like a fiend, he finally decided he needed a change of scene. His parents had been after him to come down to see them again, even though he'd been with them more in the last couple of months than he had in the last couple of years. Just that morning his father had called again and insisted he take a break right now. Come spend a few days with them.

His problem was it was still hard for him to look across the yard at the Kennellys' house. Grant was recovering well, but Blake would never get over feeling he was somehow at fault.

"I know you still feel guilty about Grant," his father told him, as if reading his mind even from a distance. "It was not your fault, Blake. You did nothing to cause this."

Maybe if enough people told him he'd believe it.

"Your mother says she'll cook all your favorites for you," he added.

Blake decided his father might be right. Maybe his mother's cooking and some time over a beer with his dad would help him deal better with what happened to Grant. He couldn't go on avoiding it forever. Maybe he could air his head out. *And maybe you're fooling yourself,* he thought. *Maybe you think being there will somehow bring you closer to Sam.*

"Okay," he gave in. "I guess you're right."

He disconnected the call, packed up, and headed south. All the way down the Interstate he kept telling himself not to expect anything. Sam was still out on her newest assignment. He thought of all the reasons he should just forget this. She'd taken off before they could sit down together and put a name to their feelings, but maybe that was her way of telling him it wouldn't work. It hurt his heart to think she might be right yet. He ached for her, needed her in a way he'd never needed anyone or anything else. So here he was, a lovesick fool, heading off to Arrowhead Bay hoping to at least catch a glimpse of her.

He took the exit for Arrowhead Bay and turned off the Interstate onto the two-lane road that led into town. He drove slowly through the downtown area. Even though it was a weekday, they were in snowbird season so every day could be busy. He scanned the sidewalks as he rolled down the street, then mentally smacked himself when a horn honked behind him. He wasn't going to see her walking on the sidewalk or clocking out of one of the stores. She probably wasn't even here.

Sighing, he headed for his parents' home.

"We're so glad you decided to come down for a few days." His mother hugged him, always insisting he was never too old for one of her hugs. "Your dad's already out on the back patio. He grabbed two beers and headed out there as soon as he saw you pull into the driveway."

Blake wasn't sure he'd be able to sit out there, with the Kennellys' house straight across and filling his vision.

"It's tough," his father said, reading his mind. "But we move forward because that's all we can ever do."

Blake dropped into a chair, opened the beer and took a big swallow.

"I'm trying, Dad. Every day."

"I thought maybe we'd go sailing tomorrow, if you like. I haven't had the boat out for a couple of weeks. If you can spare the time, that is."

"I'd like that." Maybe it would clear his head.

But when they got to the marina the next morning, his father handed him the keys to the boat and the basket his mother had packed.

"You go ahead. I'll catch up with you in a minute."

He frowned but just nodded and headed down the dock to where the boat was berthed. The boat was low enough in the water that he could hoist himself aboard, basket and all. He went to open the door to the small cabin to put the basket inside when a figure came around from the other side of the boat, shocking the hell out of him.

"Hello, Blake."

He nearly dropped the basket at the sight of Samantha in a soft T-shirt with some kind of sparkles on it and cutoff denim shorts. For a moment he wondered if he was seeing things. But he blinked and she was still there.

"It's me." Her voice was hesitant, a tone he wasn't used to hearing from her.

"But you—but I—my dad—"

"Did me a favor. I was afraid if I called you myself you wouldn't answer, seeing as how I ran off in the night like a scalded cat."

He set the basket down and drew in a full breath, releasing it slowly.

"You did that," he agreed.

"I kept up with the media reports on the whole stalker/suicide bomb thing. You were sure all over everywhere."

"No shit. I think I'd rather get my publicity some other way from now on."

She took a step closer, and he had to restrain himself from hauling her into his arms. He had to know what the deal was first. Did she just want a friends-with-benefits thing once in a while or what? Because he was definitely not on board with that.

"How long have you been back from your last deal?"

"A little over a week." She lifted her hands and dropped them. "It was pretty intense and then I needed some time to sort out what was in my head."

Don't badger her with questions. Let her say what she has to say.

She took his hand and tugged him toward the seats in the bow. "Sit with me, please?"

"This is a pretty elaborate way to give me the brushoff, if that's what this is," he told her.

"Just let me talk, okay?" She tugged him down to the seat beside her.

"Okay."

"I know we said we'd talk about us when everything was wrapped up, but I wasn't ready for that yet. I don't know if you can understand, but I had a lot of baggage to sort through first. So I did what I always have. I ran."

"How did that work out for you?" He forced himself to be calm despite the turmoil raging inside him.

"Pretty good, actually. It wasn't just about what happened on that date so long ago, and afterwards. You told me why you did what you did. I told you how I felt. And you pointed out this was a chance for us to see what might have been. We connected so well on so many levels it almost seemed possible to me that this was meant to be. But then the stalker upped his game and that got in the way of everything."

"Yes, it did," he agreed.

"First, before I could talk to you about us, I had to figure out if I was even capable of sustaining a relationship, no matter how good this was."

"And how did that go?"

She stared out across the water. "I'll tell you this. Soul searching is not for the faint of heart." She sighed. "I owe you an explanation. All these years I kept telling myself how silly it was to hold on to that one night as if it was the most special in my life. Except it was. Very special. And anyone who says people can't fall in love on a first date and when they're that young is crazy. Because that's what happened. I fell in love. With you."

"Sam, I—"

She held up a hand. "Not until I finish." She blew out a breath. "I kept trying to find that feeling with other men but somehow it just never worked. Or maybe I just made bad choices. I always seemed to pick men who couldn't commit for more than fifteen minutes."

She looked down at her hands, and Blake had to dig his fingers into his palms to make himself sit quietly and wait.

"I was about done with the Air Force, ready to move on to the next stage of my life, wondering if I'd ever find anyone I could trust and love. And then I met a guy on my last assignment, another Raven. In a way, he reminded me of you. I guess I thought, okay, if I can't have Blake I'll take second best. I actually believed it was working until the night I overheard him talking to a couple of his friends about how hot it was to screw another Raven. How he hoped it would last at least until his assignment was rotated again, and that I wouldn't turn out to be a clingy female after all."

"Jesus, Sam." He said the words softly, trying not to show how shocked he was. Or ashamed because that might have been him if he hadn't grown up.

"So by the time I left the service, came home, and then went to work for Vigilance, I had decided relationships just weren't for me. I must be lacking in something to have this keep happening." She turned to look at him again. "Then you came back into my life. After all the things you said and after the way you made me feel I asked myself, can this really happen? I was just so afraid to trust it. Can you understand?"

He nodded, restraining himself from reaching out to haul her into his arms.

"I do. And I tried to give you space. But Sam, I'm not any of those guys. And I'm for sure not that insensitive teenage asshole anymore. I'm old enough to know what I want, and what I want is you. Not just for now but forever. Is there any way I can make you understand that?"

Her lips curved in a hint of a smile. "I think I got the message. At least enough that I want to try for us to be together. I love you, Blake. That isn't going away. I know you love me and I'll just have to trust that this is going to work. Just be ready to catch me if I fall off that ledge again, okay?"

"I'll always be there for whatever you need." He tried to put everything he felt into his voice.

"I also talked to a couple of the agents who are married or in a permanent relationship, and they told me how they make it work." She studied his face. "My situation isn't easy, Blake. It requires a lot of give-and-take on both sides. I can be gone for weeks on an assignment. Maybe out of the country. But then usually I get time off between. Avery is good about that. She doesn't want her agents to burn out."

"I'm not so easy to take either, Sam. When I'm in the middle of a book I can lock myself up for hours, days, only showing my face to eat and shower. The person I spend my life with has to be able to handle that. Has to be strong enough." He gave her a hard look. "Like you."

"Running away from you didn't do me much good, because you were still everywhere I turned. In my head. In my dreams. And it wasn't any teenage crush."

He'd told himself to wait, to hear what else she had to say but he'd run out of patience.

"Here's the deal, Sam. I love you and I'm *in* love with you. I'm all in here. I want a life with you. If two people love each other enough, the rest of it is just mechanics. So just say it straight out, right here, right now. What do you want?"

She took in a deep breath and let it out slowly. He ground his teeth while he waited for her answer.

"I love you, too, Blake." She lifted her gaze and looked directly into his eyes. "I guess I had to run away from you to be able to admit it to myself. And I want to spend my life with you. I want us to figure out a way to make it work."

He was done waiting. What he saw in her eyes convinced him of her feelings even more than her words. He reached for her and hauled her into his lap. His mouth devoured hers, his tongue probing. She still tasted like seven kinds of sin. Her soft breasts pressed against his chest. He wanted her more than his next breath, and he wanted her forever.

"Marry me." He tilted her face up so he could see what was in her eyes. "Marry me, Sam. We're smart. We'll figure a way to make it work."

"Yes." She relaxed against him. "Yes. I'll marry you, Blake."

Yes!

He wanted to do a fist pump, maybe a little victory dance, but he had one important question to ask.

"One thing, though. What's Avery going to say?"

She laughed. "Are you kidding? She's the one who helped me set this up."

That was the last barrier as far as he was concerned.

"Then I think we'd better seal this deal right here and now."

Sam looked around at the people moving up and down the dock and in the nearby boats.

"With an audience?" she teased.

"Hell, no. Not for the things I want to do with you."

He swept her up in his arms, carried her into the small cabin, and shut the door, shutting out the world. And starting the first day of their life together.

Meet the Author

Desiree Holt is the *USA Today* bestselling author of the Game On! and Vigilance series, as well as many other books and series in the romantic suspense, paranormal, and erotic romance genres.

She has been featured on *CBS Sunday Morning* and in *The Village Voice*, *The Daily Beast*, *USA Today*, *The* (London) *Daily Mail*, *The New Delhi Times*, *The Huffington Post*, and numerous other national and international publications.

Readers can find her on Facebook and Twitter,
and visit her at www.desireeholt.com as well as www.desiremeonly.com.

Hide and Seek

In case you missed it, keep reading for an excerpt
from book one in the Vigilance series

Anything can happen when you let your guard down . . .

After receiving a violent threat on the heels of her father's disappearance
from the town of Arrowhead Bay, Devon Cole fears for her life—until
Vigilance, a local private security agency, steps in to shield her from
danger. Although she isn't usually quick to surrender her freedom, she
has no problem stripping her defenses for her new sexy bodyguard . . .

Tortured by the painful memory of lost love, Logan Malik is determined not
to fall for a client again. So when he's tasked with watching over Devon day
and night, he's focused on doing his job. Day is no problem, but as tensions
rise at night, nothing can protect them from giving in to unbridled passion . . .

A Lyrical e-book on sale now.

Learn more about Desiree at
http://www.kensingtonbooks.com/author.aspx/31606

Prologue

Graham Cole clutched his cell phone, barely restraining himself from throwing it against the wall. Where the hell was Vince? Everything was falling apart and they needed to get the hell out of Dodge.

How had they even gotten to this point?

A drug cartel. He was laundering money for a drug cartel.

It had all started so slowly.

"We think if you changed these suppliers, you'd help your bottom line."

"If you switched distributors for these products, you'd be in a lot better shape."

"These people are the cause of all that red ink. Get rid of them."

When Graham had discovered the true source of the funds he'd used to save his business, and wanted to pull out, Vince had convinced him it was too dangerous. Vince had been right. No one ever walked away from a cartel.

Still, he'd been determined to see if there was a way out of the choke hold. Somehow—he had no idea how—word had gotten through to Cruz Moreno, head of the vicious Moreno cartel, that Graham wanted out. He was told to take his money and shut up.

"They could go after Devon, too," Vince had told him.

God! On top of everything else he'd made both Vince and Devon targets of these miserable assholes.

In the end the only answer he'd come up with was to disappear. Maybe without him there, they'd leave Vince and Devon alone. Giving up the lifestyle he'd worked so hard to build wasn't even a factor. If he stayed, things would be a lot worse. If he was arrested, Moreno could use a threat to Devon to keep him from testifying. If he was gone, he was no longer a threat and she'd be safe.

He hoped.

El Jefe had laid it out plain and simple. *"We own you, compadre. Never forget that. And don't screw me over."*

So he'd made his plans, quietly and under the radar.

He leaned back in his chair, rubbing his chest, feeling the acid burn of indigestion. He hoped to hell he wasn't having a heart attack.

As always, the television in his office was on so he could skim the day's headlines, keeping an eye on the financial reports for anything that might affect the conglomerate. Old habits die hard. Now, a running news story caught his attention.

"That's all the information we have at the moment. Repeating, Vincent Pellegrino, vice president of corporate finance for Cole International, has been found dead in his car on Interstate 75. It appears he swerved for some reason, crashed through a barrier on a curve, and went over the side. Authorities are calling it a one-car accident but they are still investigating. We'll bring you more information as it becomes available."

Vince dead?

Jesus Christ on a crutch.

Beads of sweat formed all over his body. He rewound the story twice but the details never changed. What the hell had happened? Had Moreno somehow found out what he was planning and killed Vince as a warning? For the first time in a long time, he knew real fear. What had once seemed like the answer to a prayer now felt like an octopus wrapping its tentacles around him, choking the life out of him. They could be coming for him any minute. Who knew that when he attempted to repay the money, he was inviting a possible death sentence?

Now he needed to get the fuck out of here before Moreno's men showed up at his doorstep. But he was damn sure taking all the evidence with him. He might need a bargaining chip.

He checked the desktop computer one more time for the feed from the security cameras. Nothing. He'd triple-checked before getting ready that the alarm system was still on. Also good to go.

Satisfied he was still safe, he unplugged the external hard drive from his desktop computer and stuck it in his briefcase along with the laptop and the portfolio. Then he opened the tower, removed the internal hard drive, and shoved it into his briefcase, too. When he got to sea, he'd deep-six the internal one along with the laptop. Even if he wiped it, a good technician could restore everything, and who knows what would lead them to him. As long as he had the external he was all set. He was almost ready now, heading for the one person he could trust, to a place where he could set himself up with a new computer and figure out how to best use this stuff as leverage.

He sent a quick text to a prearranged burner phone, then took a moment to restore his phone to factory settings. His briefcase was locked, so he stuck the phone in his pocket. He was planning to toss it anyway. As soon as he was away from the harbor he'd chuck it overboard. Anyone trying to find him with a GPS locator would have a hell of a hard time doing it. Let them stick that up their collective ass. He'd be long gone by then.

If he had one regret, it was for Devon, the daughter he was leaving behind, and the damage he'd done to their relationship. He considered leaving a note for her or sending her a text, but he didn't want anything that could connect her to this. Too dangerous. Still, it saddened him greatly that he'd probably never see her again. He hadn't been the best father in the world the past couple of years. Once he got to his new location, he'd keep track of her through the Internet, Googling her name, and checking the newspapers as well.

He thought again of Vince's so-called accident, and nausea bubbled. But right now he needed to get the fuck out of here. Blotting the sweat on his forehead with the sleeve of his shirt, he unlocked a drawer in his desk and pulled out a slim portfolio. Then he grabbed his Glock 9mm from another drawer and stuck it in his pocket. He didn't have much time, needed to move right now.

He lifted the briefcase and headed for the garage. A sound caught his attention as he opened the inside door. It sounded like it came from the kitchen and his stomach knotted. No, no, no. Impossible. There was no one here. He was imagining things. He'd given the housekeeper and groundskeeper the week off. The alarm should let him know if someone was trying to break in.

I'm imagining things. That's what happens when you put yourself in a dangerous position, screwing over dangerous people.

He needed to calm down or he'd stroke out before he even got out of here.

Then he heard it again. A squeak, as if someone walked on the highly polished hardwood floors. He held his breath, straining to hear. Was that yet another one? His heart pounded so hard he thought it would beat itself out of his chest, his fear so strong he smelled it.

He hadn't seen anything on the security cameras, but why hadn't the alarm sounded? No, he was imagining things. It was his state of mind. Edging up to the door, he peeked out into the hallway, looking one way, then the other. At this time of day, the house was filled with sunlight. Surely he'd see anyone if there was someone to see.

I'm driving myself nuts. I need get the hell out of here. I'm running out of time.

Letting his breath out, he turned once more toward the garage door, stopping when again he thought he heard another sound. He grabbed his gun and started to turn around, but a hard, muscular arm locked itself around his neck. A hand yanked the gun from his grip as if it were nothing more than a feather duster and pressed it into the small of his back.

Fuck! Double fuck.

His legs had turned so rubbery he wasn't sure he could stand if the man released his hold. If only Vince hadn't cried wolf so many times before, Graham would have paid more careful attention to his warnings. If only he'd left earlier. If only he'd been more careful. If only a lot of things.

"Going someplace?" A guttural voice ground out the words in his ear, hot breath singeing his skin.

Real fear crept through him, paralyzing him. He hadn't made it. His escape was so close but exactly what he feared had happened. His timing sucked. Was this it? Was this how it was all going to end for him?

"H-How did you get in?" What had happened to his high-priced alarm system?

"You're not quite as safe as you think you are, asshole. A strong radio frequency can knock out even the best alarms."

"You're choking me." Graham could hardly get the words out as the stranger pressed harder on his windpipe and dragged him along the floor. He was sweating so badly now he could smell it on his body. How would he ever get out of this? He'd been so close, so very close.

"We're going to take a little trip, you and I," the man went on, "along with whatever is in that briefcase. Mr. Moreno says you're unhappy, *amigo.* He wants to meet with you and make sure you understand nothing is to change. Your friend, Vincenzo, tried to run, too. Unfortunately in his haste he met an untimely demise before he could give us all the information we want."

Vince. Goddamn.

"Let's move." The man urged him forward, still exerting the pressure on his neck and nudging him with the gun.

He couldn't let Moreno's thug get him past the front door. Graham dragged his feet and looked around wildly for something, anything, any option to get him out of this. Whatever it was, he'd have only a few seconds to make it happen. Then, in the hallway, he spotted something that gave him a faint ray of hope, if he could get hold of it.

"I—I can't breathe." He made his voice as faint as possible, and sagged against the man behind him.

"Too bad."

"If you deliver a dead body," Graham gasped, "Moreno won't be very happy with you."

He could have sworn the man growled, but he finally loosened his hold. Knowing he'd have scant seconds to do anything, Graham yanked on the man's arm and ducked beneath it. In one desperate movement he spun around, grabbed a bronze statue from the hall table, and hit the man over the head. For an endless moment nothing happened, and he was afraid he'd misjudged. Then the man toppled to the floor, nearly taking Graham with him.

He had no idea if he'd killed the man or merely knocked him out, but he didn't stop to find out. If the man was dead, in a few days his housekeeper would find the body, somewhat rancid by then. If it was the latter, he was short on time to get the fuck out of here.

He picked up the gun and the briefcase that he'd dropped and raced for the garage. He was sweating profusely and shaking so much he bumped into the car, the briefcase slamming into the fender. He yanked his keys from his pocket, hoping he was steady enough to drive. He jumped into the most innocuous of his vehicles, a gray Mercedes, and hauled ass down the driveway to the road.

When he made the turn onto the highway, he spotted a black utility vehicle parked near the trees with a man in the front seat.

Fuck!

The driver, spotting Graham's car, pulled out onto the road just as his partner, wobbling slightly, came racing down the driveway.

I should have hit him harder.

Lucky for Graham the few seconds the driver stopped so his partner could jump in gave him a miniscule lead, but not much. Graham punched the accelerator and hauled ass down Seacliff Road. He had a small window of opportunity to get the fuck out of here, and he wasn't wasting any of it. That SUV would be on his tail any minute.

Faster! Faster!

He glanced at the speedometer and saw he was doing a hundred. He hoped he didn't wreck the car and kill himself just when he was nearly out of here. He was so focused on reaching the marina that it wasn't until he touched his pocket that he realized his cell phone wasn't there. Fuck again! What the hell had happened to it? If the wrong person found it and managed to restore it, his ass would be grass. Of course, first they'd have to find him. Right?

Breathe, he told himself. *Just breathe. Almost there.*

All the way to the harbor he kept checking the rearview and side-view mirrors. The road twisted and turned around the shoreline so at times his view of the rear disappeared. There. Was that a black SUV? No. No, it was a pickup and it turned off into a strip center before it caught up to him. He was definitely going to vomit first chance he had.

Jesus, Graham, don't lose it now.

Or any more than he already had. He just had to get to the boat before they caught up with him. Then he'd be safe. He always kept the smaller of his two boats provisioned and ready for anything, as part of his emergency plan. Just in case. He also made sure he had all the equipment on board he'd need.

Don't think about it. Don't think about it. Too late now.

He rounded a curve in the road and there was the marina up ahead. He could see *Princess Devon* now, its twin hulls bobbing in the water at its berth. Almost there. Still no SUV in his rearview mirror, but it could appear around the curve at any moment if those two guys had gotten their shit together.

At last he was parked and headed down the pier where the boats were docked. All he needed was another few minutes. A few more steps…

Chapter 1

"Your father is missing."

Devon Cole tightened her grip on her cell phone and tried to make sense of what Sheridan March had just told her, as fear swept through her. Maybe she hadn't heard right.

"What do you mean, missing?"

"The Coast Guard found the *Princess Devon* drifting five miles offshore early this morning," the Arrowhead Bay chief of police explained. "But there's no sign of him anywhere. And no clue to anything in the house. We went through every inch of it. The alarm was fried, probably needs to be replaced, but otherwise the place was clean as a whistle."

Devon clutched the phone. "Was there anything on the boat? Something he might have had with him that could give us a clue?"

"Nada."

"Where's the boat now? Would the Coast Guard hold on to it?"

"In its slip at the Bayside Marina. After the Guard went over every inch of it, they had one of the men on the cutter bring it back in and berth it. I have the keys."

Devon swallowed to ease the tightness in her throat. "When was the last time anyone saw him?"

"Sunday," Sheri told her. "As soon as I got the word from the Coast Guard we began checking with his friends. The last time anyone saw him was when Cash Breeland had lunch with him at the Driftwood."

"That's the same day I talked to him." She rubbed her hand nervously on her jeans. "He didn't say a word about going anywhere. Did the Moorlands say anything about seeing him?"

Ginny and Hank Moorland owned both the Driftwood Restaurant and Bayside Marina.

"Hank was in Miami for a couple of days, but Ginny was there. She said she never laid eyes on him."

"And Gary at Bayside? Did he see anything?"

Sheri made a rude noise. "I talked to him myself but he's usually so off in his own world a marching band could have taken off and he'd never notice. I swear I don't know why Hank doesn't can his ass. Besides, it was a Sunday, so the marina was jammed with people arriving and leaving and some just working on their boats. He did say a couple of guys were asking about him, but he thought they were just friends."

"Did you talk to anyone who has a boat in a slip near his?"

"The ones we could find."

"God." Devon tamped back the rising fear. "I can't believe this could happen. He's an avid sailor and very, very safety conscious."

Her father had been sailing for as long as she remembered. When he still lived in Tampa he was out on the water every Saturday, sailing down the coast, sometimes with business associates but more often with her mother. That was how he'd discovered Arrowhead Bay. But he almost never went out during the week. Saturdays were his days on the water. And, after her mother passed away, sometimes on Sundays. It was something both her parents had enjoyed, and Devon often thought it was a way for him to recapture her presence.

"I know," Sheri agreed. "Everyone knows that about him."

"And the other boat?" Devon asked. "The *Lady Hannah*?"

"Still here. There's not even a sign anyone was on it." She paused. "We know he's an excellent sailor. The Coast Guard thought maybe he'd fallen overboard, but—"

"I guess that's possible, except he was a nut about water safety. He'd be careful."

"That's what I told them," Sheri agreed.

"The Coast Guard started searching immediately, right?"

"Yes, but it's a big ocean. They brought in another cutter to search as well as one of their Dolphin helicopters. I promise you it's a full-out search and rescue operation. And there's another thing."

"What?" What else could there be?

"I don't know if you caught it, but there was a story on the national news yesterday that Vincent Pellegrino, one of your father's vice presidents, was killed in a one-car accident."

Ice chilled her blood. "Are you saying the two things could be related? That my father didn't just fall overboard?"

"I'm saying we have to look at all possibilities. This is too much of a coincidence to ignore."

"Did you call his office? Ask his admin if he'd decided to take an unannounced vacation?"

"I did, but she knew nothing. And they are all in a turmoil over Pellegrino's death."

"But who would want to kill him?" Nausea bubbled up in her throat. "Either of them?"

"We don't know, and that may not be it at all. I'll just have to connect all the dots."

"Holy crap, Sheri."

"One other thing. His house was meticulously clean, as if someone had gone through and sanitized it. But—this is weird—his computer was on his desk but the internal hard drive has been removed."

"What? What the hell?"

"My thoughts exactly."

"What about the external hard drive? It should be right next to it."

"Nada," Sheri told her. "Gone, gone, gone."

Even as she tried to dial back the sick feeling creeping through her, Devon was already dragging her suitcase out and pulling things out of her drawers and closet. She ran through her mind all the projects she had in process, which could be put on hold, who she needed to try to renegotiate deadlines with.

"I'm coming down there right now. I can't just sit here and wait around. I'll finish packing as soon as we hang up and be on the road right away."

"Good. I think you need to be here. Corporate is sending some people down here and I know they'll want to talk to you, too. Call me or come see me as soon as you get here." Sheri paused. "We're all over it, Devon. I just wish we had more to go on."

"I know. It's just…" Just that she'd already lost one parent and didn't know if she could deal with losing another. "I think I'll go to the house first and take a look around."

"Sounds good. I'll wait to hear from you."

The minute she hung up from Sheri's call, she packed the suitcase and threw it and her computer stuff into her car. Less than thirty minutes later she was headed south from Tampa on Interstate 75. She alternated between the threat of tears and full-blown panic as the conversation replayed like a looping tape in her head as she ate up the miles.

While she drove, she kept trying to reach her father. She had both the cell phone and the house phone on speed dial, but she got nothing. Where the hell was he? She'd been on the road for about an hour when her cell rang. The readout showed Sheri's name so she pushed the remote button to answer.

"Have you found him?" she asked, forgoing any kind of greeting.

"I wish. No, I just wanted to give you a heads-up."

Now what?

"What's going on?"

"We've got a couple of reporters sniffing around here, asking about your father's disappearance."

"How did they find out so fast?" Devon asked.

"A million ways. This is the age of the Internet. Maybe they were after your father to ask him about the death of his executive. I wouldn't put it past them to rent a boat and go check on the search."

"Damn, damn, damn." Devon pounded a fist against the steering wheel.

"You said it," Sheri agreed. "Anyway, I'll bet anything the first story will hit the newspaper tomorrow and they're looking for more details."

"Oh my God. Sheri, I can't talk to them now."

"Don't worry. I'll keep them off your back. But it's possible if they give it a big play, someone seeing it might remember something."

"You're right," Devon agreed. "I'm just not good with stuff like that and right now my mind's in too much of a whirl to even speak coherently. I'll probably say the wrong thing and make the situation worse."

"I understand. We can't shut them out, and but I will do my best to keep them off your back for as long as I can."

"Thanks." Devon blew out a breath.

"If they catch you, the best thing is to tell them no comment. I'm sure they'll hit the Cole International offices in Tampa. Just let the people there make any statements."

"Sounds good to me."

"Don't forget. Call me or come by as soon as you get here."

"I will."

She disconnected the call and stuck the phone in the console.

Great. Just great. Reporters, looking for juicy scandal about the disappearance of a business giant.

Oh, Dad, how could you do this to me?

The fact was, she'd been worried about him for the past several months. Her mother's death five years ago had thrown him for a loop. Piled on top of that were problems with Cole International. He didn't discuss them with her but there was a hint here and there, and he was constantly on edge. Then, suddenly things seemed to be better.

She'd missed him when he moved to Arrowhead Bay, but she understood him wanting a change. The house was filled with too many memories of her mother. Plus her father said he was tired of city living.

On the trips to the little town while he was still living in Tampa, he met people. Made friends. The times she sailed down there with him she'd gotten to know people, too, and fallen in love with the small, sleepy Southern town. He was as happy as she'd seen him since her mother died.

She'd met Sheri March at one of the many festivals the town held and they'd connected at once, becoming good friends. Through Sheri she'd met a lot of other people, including the chief's sister, Avery, who ran a private security agency. With friends to hang with and her father almost himself again she'd begun to look forward to visiting him. He loved hearing about the growth of her graphics design business and praised her for what she accomplished.

Then he'd stopped asking her about it except on rare occasions.

She tried to pinpoint just when that had all started. *Almost two years ago*, she thought. The tenor of the visits had changed. *He* had changed, becoming more tense, edgier, sometimes even withdrawn. When she asked about it, he just brushed it off. She missed their tight relationship. They had always been close, so it bothered her more than she let on.

He was abruptly more preoccupied with the business than ever, even obsessed with its financial situation. It never made sense to her because Cole International was worth millions. Whenever she asked him what was wrong, he assured her everything was fine. Just some pesky business details, he told her, that were taking a little more of his attention.

She'd continued to make sporadic visits, hoping to recapture the tight sense of family they'd had. After all, it was just the two of them now. But no matter how hard she tried, she'd felt them drifting apart more and more. There was a wall of some kind around the man she just could not breach.

When she noticed the change in him, she tried to question Cash Breeland about it. Cash was the president of the locally owned Arrowhead Bay Bank. Devon didn't know him all that well, but he and her father had become friends even before the big move. In fact, it was Cash who had introduced her father to friends of his and drawn him into their social circle. But Cash just downplayed her questions.

"I know your daddy's been preoccupied some," he drawled when she asked him to meet her for coffee. "He's just working through some knotty business problems. With all this overseas competition, some of his units aren't performin' the way they should. He'll pull out of it as soon as there's an uptick in trade."

But he hadn't and now he was gone.

Missing.

The word gave birth to a lot of speculation and none of it good.

She spotted the highway signs for Arrowhead Bay and gave herself a mental shake. She needed to clear the garbage out of her head until she could find out for sure what was going on.

She took the farthest exit for the town, the one that took her to the road where her father's house was. He had built at the far end of town in the area known as Seacliff. More land, larger homes. He liked space, he'd told her. Cole International board members and executives routinely visited him there. And from his side patio he had a magnificent view of Arrowhead Bay and the harbor.

His house was the next to last one on Seacliff Road, and in minutes the familiar gateposts came into view. She gave silent thanks that there were no reporters around. They must have taken Sheri literally. She pulled up in the driveway and shoved the car into park, then stared at the house for a long moment. Automatically she reached into the half-empty bag of red licorice bites on her console and popped a couple in her mouth.

Sitting there now, chewing on the candy, she remembered the last time she'd seen him, a little more than a month ago. Their brief conversation played out in her head.

"You're leaving already?" He had looked up from his desk when she stopped in the doorway to the den.

"You're busy and I have work back in Tampa to take care of."

"I thought you brought your laptop with you."

"I did, but I think I'd be more comfortable at home."

For a fleeting moment, a pained expression crossed his face, one almost of sorrow.

"We should spend more time together."

She'd nearly snorted at that. They'd always been so close, especially after her mother died, but he'd withdrawn from her.

Still, he was her father and she loved him.

Was it possible this was voluntary? Had her father chosen to disappear so completely? No. *Too outrageous*, she thought. He was the epitome of the corporate icon. A mover and shaker. Winner of awards. Profiled in magazines. Business school graduates used him as their aspirational model. What on earth could make a man like that choose to vanish as if he'd never existed?

Even with his changes in personality and behavior, she could say this was 100 percent unlike him. What if he'd been grabbed by someone? But who? It could be a competitor, a disgruntled employee, someone on the bad end of a business deal. She knew very little about his business dealings. Would there be a ransom request? Would they contact her or his corporation? How would she get the money if the call came to her? How—

No. Sheri hadn't said anything about a kidnapping.

Another thought stabbed at her, one that chilled her. Had someone killed him and dumped the body overboard? But who? And why?

She would ask Sheri those questions as soon as she spoke to her again. Meanwhile, back to square one. If neither of those things turned out to be a reality, why had Graham Cole disappeared? What was going on with him?

Stop!

God, she was driving herself crazy.

She felt an unexpected rush of tears and a tightening of her throat. Despite the state of their relationship, he was her father. She still loved him and his disappearance frightened her.

Enough, missy. Get your ass into the house.

But the moment she climbed out of her car, a sudden chill raced down her spine and an ominous feeling gripped her. She stood there, gathering herself. Could a house be menacing?

Ridiculous. Stupid.

She wasn't the type of woman given to feelings like that. She was down to earth and practical. *Some might even say hardheaded*, she thought with a tiny smile.

Okay. I'm here. I should go inside and see if I can find anything the police might have missed. Or that would give me some kind of clue as to what had happened, something that would mean something only to me.

Go on. Don't be a chicken.

It was just bricks and stucco. What did she think was inside? A body? Not likely. The police had already searched the house. When she was sure she had herself under control, she hiked up the steps to the front door, for the moment leaving all her stuff in the car. As she slid the key for the front lock into place she wondered if it still worked. When the key turned and the lock clicked open, she breathed a sigh of relief.

Automatically, she reached for the alarm panel in the front hall, then remembered Sheri said it wasn't functioning. That a whole new one would need to be installed. How very weird. It was always on.

At least the air-conditioning had been left on, a blessedly cool change from the furnace that was Florida heat in the summer. Jingling the key ring, she walked through the house, looking around, although she had no idea what she expected to find.

The house was open and airy, with a wall of windows the length of one side that looked out to the lawn and beyond that to the bay itself. Her father had hired a decorator and given her free rein. The result was a tastefully decorated home that was open and welcoming.

As she walked from room to room, the same eerie feeling that gripped her when she'd stood in front of the house swept over her again. As if something very bad happened here. The chill racing over her skin had nothing to do with the artificially cooled air. She sensed a presence of evil in the air, and kept looking over her shoulder, as if expecting someone to pop out of a closet.

Stupid, stupid, stupid. I've been watching too much television.

She wandered into his den, seeking any kind of clue. Framed photos of herself and her mother and the three of them sat on the credenza but the desk was uncharacteristically bare. There was nothing on it, not an open book, a stack of papers, nothing. No sign of any activity, yet this was the room where he spent much of his time. How strange. Except...

Damn. Sheri was right. The computer was on his desk but the hard drive was gone. She checked all the drawers, although she was sure the police had already done this. No hard drive, internal or external, and no laptop. She'd forgotten to ask about that. Would he have taken all that with him? What did he plan to do with all his information if he'd decided to disappear? Could he run his business if no one knew where he was?

Again that icy feeling raced over her skin, the kind you got when people told ghost stories in the dark. As if strangers had been here, and not the ones investigating Graham Cole's disappearance. Could evil leave a sense of its presence?

Evil? Really?

Dramatic much, Devon?

She just couldn't shake the feeling something was off.

If only she'd forced the issue, made him talk to her. Fixed whatever barriers had been thrown up between them. Maybe she'd have a clue as to what was going on.

For a moment she considered the B and B in town, but why spend money she didn't have to? A house couldn't harm you, right?

A loud noise from the kitchen made her pulse leap and her heart thump. She grabbed a golf club leaning against the wall, tiptoed down the hall, and peered into the room. Nothing. No one. Should she step inside? What if someone was hiding in the alcove? With the alarm system not working anyone could come into the house.

Then the noise repeated, and she blew out a breath when she realized what it was. The icemaker in the refrigerator was disgorging cubes into the container.

Devon sat down at the breakfast bar, hands still shaking, and tried to steady herself. Maybe staying here wasn't such a good idea at all. Was she crazy to think someone had left an imprint here and it wasn't her father?

There's nothing here. Give your imagination a rest.

The landline on the kitchen wall rang, startling her. Who would be calling? Most of her father's calls had come in on his cell phone. Automatically she reached for it.

"Hello?"

Dead silence.

She waited, then, "Hello? Is someone there?"

Still silence. Why did the words *dead silence* come to mind? Then she heard it, the faint sound of someone breathing.

"If someone is there, speak up, or else I'm hanging up this phone."

When there was still no answer, she replaced the receiver, irritated. And troubled. She wanted to believe it was kids making prank calls, but with her father's disappearance it took on a more ominous feeling.

Right, Devon. Make this into some big deal. A lousy phone call. Probably just some wrong number and they were too embarrassed to say anything.

Maybe. She was not someone given to flights of fancy or premonitions. If anything, she was solidly grounded and practical to a fault. Only nothing had felt right to her since she walked in the front door, and the phone call had just added to the feeling of unease. She had a sudden need to get out of there, be with noise and crowds. Her stuff could wait until later. Right now she needed to be with people. A lot of people.

She had just headed out of the kitchen when the phone rang again. With a mixture of impatience and dread she picked up the receiver.

"Hello?"

Silence again.

"Listen. Whoever you are, either talk to me or I'm hanging up. If you call again, I won't be here."

She slammed the receiver back in the cradle. That did it for her. She needed to get out of here and find Sheri right away.

Her stomach chose that moment to grumble, reminding her she also needed food. She'd left Tampa two hours ago with only a large Starbucks in her stomach, and said stomach was now sending her signals. She remembered the housekeeper kept the fridge and the freezer stocked with basics so she could just fix herself something if she wanted to. But the eerie feeling wouldn't let go.

Sheri had said to call or come by as soon as she got into town, and right now seemed like a very good time to do that. Going straight to the police station seemed the best thing to do. She'd feel better seeing Sheri, anyway. Maybe she could help Devon put her feelings in perspective. The police had gone over the house thoroughly. Surely if something was out of whack, they'd have found it and told her. Something besides the jacked alarm system.

I'm just letting my mind play tricks on me. That has to be it.

Okay. That was it. She was getting out of here for a while. She'd head right for the police station and try to find out where things stood. She should have gone there right away. And she wanted to know what the latest was with the Coast Guard. The whole thing was still so unreal to her.

She walked through the house to the garage, still carrying the golf club and peeking around doors and walls. And feeling like an idiot. She found the extra remotes for the garage door and grabbed one, then hurried back through the house and out the front door. Without understanding why, she checked three times to make sure the front door was locked. She also looked carefully around as she got into her car, as if expecting to see someone peeking at her from behind the garage or one of the many massive trees that dotted the place.

Damn. If reporters might be hanging around, she'd better get that alarm fixed in a hurry. Anyone could get onto the property if they wanted to.

She wasn't easily frightened, but the whole situation spooked her. Maybe she *should* stay in town at the B and B until she figured out if she was needed for anything. Still, she'd be damned if she'd let anyone chase her out of her father's house.

Seacliff Road was sparsely populated, the homes built much farther apart than those in town. There was only one house on the road past her father's and after that was a dead end. The lack of traffic made her nervous, as did the thick growth of trees that lined the side opposite the houses. Probably no one was lying in wait for her—where had *that* thought come from?—but she'd feel a lot better being part of a crowd. She kept looking in her rearview mirror.

"Just in case," she whispered.

But in case of what? Besides, who even knew she was in town? She was letting the entire situation spook her. What she needed to do was get into town and talk to Sheri face-to-face. Once she got a better read on the situation, she'd settle down. At least she hoped she would.

Just as she came to a slight curve in the road she glanced in the rearview mirror and her heart nearly stopped beating. A black SUV that seemed to have come out of nowhere rode her bumper. Oh, God! Doing her best not to panic, she gripped the wheel and pressed down harder on the accelerator, but no matter how fast she went the car kept pace with her.

She navigated the next turn, hoping she could pick up a little speed and put distance between her and whoever this was. But then she felt a jolt as the SUV hit her rear bumper, just enough to scare her. Her engine was built for economy, not speed, and no matter how hard she pressed the accelerator she couldn't seem to outrun the vehicle riding her back end. Praying for someone to show up and help was useless. This was a thinly populated road where half the residents were snowbirds. Getting help right now was in the region of impossibilities.

In the next moment the other vehicle bumped her again, much harder, causing her car to lurch to the side. Suddenly she was losing control, no matter how she wrestled with the wheel, and she veered off the road. She came to a stop in the deep ditch that ran alongside the road. The SUV bumped her once more before it pulled up and stopped in front of her at an angle, blocking her even if she could move.

What the hell?

The first thing that popped into her mind was Vincent Pellegrino's so-called one-car accident. Was this what happened to him? She was equal parts scared and pissed off. Scared because it was obvious whoever this was meant her no good. Pissed off because her day just kept going downhill and she was sick of it. She grabbed her cell phone, but dropped it because her hand was shaking. By then a man had climbed out of the SUV and was instantly at her side of the car. Another man appeared at the passenger side, boxing her in.

The one next to her knocked on her window, startling her so she dropped her cell phone again. She reached down to get it but the man on the driver's side banged on her window once more.

"Open the window," he barked in a harsh voice.

She shook her head, double-checked to make sure the doors were locked, and reached down again for her phone. The next thing she knew something hit the passenger window, hard. The window cracked and shattered into what looked like a million pebble-sized chunks that flew across the seat. Startled, she let out a little scream and pushed back as hard as she could against the seat.

The man on the driver's side knocked on her window again.

"If you don't want me to break this one, roll it down," he growled.

Devon shook her head. She knew she should probably be cowering in fright, except that wasn't her style, even in a dangerous situation. Surely someone would come along on this road, right?

She closed her eyes for a moment and when she opened them, the man on her side knocked on the window again and held up an iron bar.

"I'm not going to kill you, bitch." His voice was a low monotone, slightly accented. "Not yet. This was just to get your attention. Next time it could be your legs. Tell me where he is and I'll leave you alone."

"Please. I—"

"Do you hear me? Where has he gone? When you talk to him, tell him we'll be happy to have you as our guest until he shows his face. We know where to find you."

Devon slid her gaze from one to the other. The two men looked as if they'd kill her before breakfast and still eat a hearty meal. She opened her mouth but no words came out. She pushed back against her seat again as the man on the right started to reach through the broken window to unlock the door.

At that moment a four-door pickup zipped around the curve behind them and slowed, the driver obviously spotting the tableau on the side of the road. The truck passed both of their vehicles, then pulled over across the road and stopped. Was this backup for the two men already bent on terrorizing her or could fickle fate be sending her a savior?

Printed in the United States
by Baker & Taylor Publisher Services